LIFE
on the
LEVEL

ON THE VERGE: BOOK THREE

ZORAIDA CÓRDOVA

DIVERSIONBOOKS

Also by Zoraida Córdova

On the Verge Series
Luck on the Line
Love on the Ledge

Diversion Books
A Division of Diversion Publishing Corp.
443 Park Avenue South, Suite 1008
New York, New York 10016
www.DiversionBooks.com

Copyright © 2016 by Zoraida Córdova
All rights reserved, including the right to reproduce this book or portions thereof in any form whatsoever.
Cover Designed by Najla Qamber Designs

This is a work of fiction. Names, characters, places and incidents either are the product of the author's imagination or are used fictitiously. Any resemblance to actual persons, living or dead, events or locales is entirely coincidental.

For more information, email info@diversionbooks.com

First Diversion Books edition February 2016.
Print ISBN: 978-1-62681-666-4
eBook ISBN: 978-1-62681-581-0

To Laura Duane,
for totally getting me.

CHAPTER 1

ZERO DAYS SOBER

"I hope the sky's not the only big thing in Montana," I whisper in his ear.

His full lips smile against mine.

"You're a handful, aren't you?" His voice is like the whiskey, burning right through me.

I pull away from him to get a good look at his face again. The dim blue light of Grizzly Country Bar frames his sharp cheekbones and strong jawline. He has dark eyes and darker hair that coils around the tips of my fingers. I've finally met a guy that makes my heart skip a beat.

I've been in town for a little less than two days, on the road to salvation. Actually, on the road to Sun Valley, Montana. Tomorrow, my life changes forever. Tonight, I'll allow myself one last hurrah, and his name is—well, actually, I don't know his name. But from the moment I set foot in the bar and saw him hunched over his beer, looking like he was just as lost as I was, I knew it had to be him—and only him.

I went right up to him, grabbed his beer, and took a swig from it. It was still frothy and cold. His midnight-black eyes went wide and a little angry. Then he looked me up and down, and his eyes softened. Unlike other guys, he didn't linger at my long, suntanned legs. He looked straight into my eyes, and I didn't look away for a minute.

"Hey, Trouble," he said, an irresistible grin spreading across his beautiful face.

The rest of his body is solid, and even sitting down, he

looks tall. I bet he's one of those guys who rides around on horses, rounding up cows and stuff. Men aren't built like this in New York. Salt of the earth and all that.

"Hey, kind stranger," I said. "Can I buy you a drink, since I stole yours?"

He looked taken aback by the offer. Some guys don't like aggressive girls, and even more girls don't like aggressive girls. But what did I care? If he was into me, great. If he wasn't, then it wasn't meant to be. He looked a little nervous. He asked me my name, and I pretended the music was too loud. I loved watching him turn toward me. I asked if he wanted to sit in the corner booth for more privacy.

My heart skipped when he hesitated—just because a guy is smoking hot doesn't mean he's a manwhore. I put on my best mischievous smile, thrilled when he decided to follow.

And now we're here.

I was surprised at how easily he talked about himself. I didn't want to care. But I found myself smiling while he spoke. He was born and raised in Montana, and went to the U of M right here in town. He's going to tell me what he does for a living, but the waitress comes over and drops off our next round. He wants to know too much. Asks too many questions. In turn, I'm super vague.

I'm from out east, I say, and he guesses New York because of the way I asked for water. *I'm an only child, and an orphan.* What do you know? So is he. Then we're kind of quiet, and I feel something tight in my heart. He smiles so easily and reaches for my hand. I tell him, *I'm just passing through. No, I don't go to school. No, I don't have friends in town.*

He watches me like he's trying to unravel a mystery, and I watch him because I want him to kiss me first. When he doesn't, I kiss him. I press my lips to the corner of his mouth, and he watches me for a long while. It feels too intimate, but what do I know of intimacy? My skin flushes when he reaches for my long blonde curls. He brushes them over my shoulder. I see him trying to make up his mind. I see him convincing himself that this anonymous hookup is right.

"You look nervous." I rest my back against the leather of our cozy little booth.

He chuckles. "I'm not used to putting on a show."

A few locals nudge each other in the ribs. Waitresses eye us in their perfunctory ponytails and maroon tank tops two sizes too small, to get that perky and pushed up look. Or I should say, they eye me. It's like I've taken something precious from them and kept it for myself.

My best friend Sky always reminds me that I don't like to share. That goes for my fries and my men.

"Only when you're sharking some dudes at pool?" I ask.

He cocks his head to the side and takes a sip of his beer. It's local, and there's a picture of a moose on it. It matches the moose head on the wall, among other mounted wild animals. This is the closest to nature I've been in a long time. Unless you count the squirrels that try to hijack my food in Central Park.

"I know what you're doing," he tells me, pulling my legs across his lap. "You're trying to make me guess your name."

It's a funny thing—I don't remember his name. I don't know his birthday. I can't figure out if his sign matches mine in any sort of astrological way. I don't know where he got those cheekbones, that creamy skin, those callouses on his hands, or the scar right under his bottom lip shaped like a crescent moon. I don't know any of these things, but I sure do love looking at him.

Sure, it's not the first time I've been with a guy whose name I'm not too sure on. At least, I'm planning on being with this guy. At least, I know I want to. At least, until morning.

Morning. Tomorrow. Focus.

Think of the now. But isn't the now what gets me into trouble in the first place?

"It's not a guessing game," I say, knocking back the rest of my whiskey. The warm, harsh liquid strikes a match down in my belly. I can feel my head spin, my skin get all tingly. "It's not a guessing game, because I just don't want to tell you."

I start to call for the waitress to get us another round, but he catches my wrist in his hand. "I think you've had about enough whiskey to sink a battleship."

"No sinking," I tell him, wrapping my arm around his neck.

Someone whistles in our direction, or maybe I just feel exposed in a way I'm not used to feeling. If I were in a bar in New York, no one would pay attention to us the way people are paying attention now. That's the downside of strolling through a new town. Not that I intend to stay past the sentence of my self-induced exile.

"You know what I think?" I hold his chin in my hand. "I think we should take this show on the road."

His eyes are so dark I can see myself in them. So dark, it's like looking at the night sky. "You're killing me."

"Oh my god, are you a virgin?"

His lips turn in the sweetest pout. "I could be. I don't even know your name."

"Most guys would have told me to shut up and then packed me up in their cars."

He frowns. I decide I don't like it when he frowns. It makes me feel like I've done something wrong, and I've had enough of that to last me a lifetime.

"I'm not most guys, sweetheart."

"No petnames," I tell him.

I can see the struggle in his face. His dark eyes trace my body. My neck, my face, my legs. He lingers on my legs. It might be the early end of August in Montana, but the heat clings to the mountains, and I cling to my denim shorts. His struggle is real, and I can feel it bulging against my thigh.

I bet he's the type that thinks of himself as a stand-up guy. He probably goes to church, but in places like this that's pretty much a given. I bet he drives a pick up truck the color of Red Delicious apples. His hands are covered in rough skin and hard callouses, and by the way his leg muscles want to rip right through his jeans, I'd say he's either a farm hand or maybe one of those rodeo guys. But nice. He personally thinks of himself as a nice guy.

Nice guys finish last, because I always come first.

I know I have a tough road ahead of me. I never thought

that at twenty-four this is where I'd end up. In some bar off a highway flanked by mountains and valleys. I never thought I'd have hurt the people I love most in my life. I never thought I'd be strong enough to make a change. And I am going to make a change. I swear it. I just... I just need one last *thing*. One last moment to solidify that this is the end. This is the beginning of a whole new River Thomas.

This is my last hurrah, and he is gorgeous.

"Come on, cowboy," I say, because I've decided he has to be a cowboy.

The waitress throws a check on our table. I reach for my purse to pay for my drinks, my crumpled bills threatening to spill over.

"What'd you do, rob a bank?" he asks, closing my purse before I can dig through it. "Put that away."

When he reaches for the wallet in his back pocket, it's solidified in my mind that this guy, Mr. Montana Cowboy, is a *nice guy*.

He pays and leaves a nice tip, takes my hand, and leads me through the bar. A series of hoots and hollers follow us until we walk across the parking lot. When we get to his car I give myself ten gold stars because, lo and behold, it's a shiny pickup truck with wheels the size of boulders. He opens the door for me and helps me climb up. He tries to ask me about myself.

What am I doing here, really? Am I a runaway bride? What's my favorite color? What's my favorite song? Where am I going?

I want to tell him that I don't even know anymore, but that seems like a bit of a downer, and I want to stay up.

So I get closer to him on the cool leather seat. He drapes his arm around me and tells me something about the mountain we're passing. He says something about the school and how he played football before he graduated, but wasn't very good. This explains the leg muscles, and chest muscles, and all the muscles.

"I was hoping you were a rodeo star," I tell him.

"I'll tell you if you tell me something about yourself," he says, parking in front of a small house. It's weird that people out here have entire houses to themselves. Makes my little rental in the Lower East Side look like a closet. Probably because it is. "It's only fair."

"Life isn't fair, cowboy."

I follow him through the entrance, kicking off my boots. Things fall on the floor when we bump into a table: mail and keys and loose change. But we don't look down. We don't pick anything up. We walk with our mouths pressed together. He lifts me up and carries me into a room.

Maybe there are pictures on the wall. Maybe there's a dog running for cover. Maybe the sheets are blue.

Maybe I'm more nervous than I realized.

My hands fumble with his buttons. Why would anyone wear jeans with so many buttons? That's why God invented the zipper.

There's the pop of his buttons snapping, the squeak of mattress springs bouncing. His torso is a thing of beauty. Every muscle ripples as he takes his shirt off over his head. He climbs on top of me. I trace my fingers down his hard abs, and I smirk a little because I was right.

The sky's not the only big thing in Montana.

"It does little for my confidence that you're laughing right now," he says.

"I'm not laughing *at* you," I say, reaching for his shaft. "Just remembering something good."

He shuts his eyes and lets out a slow hiss as I slide my hand up and down. He presses his hands on either side of me. He bends his head down so our noses touch.

"Tell me your name," he whispers. Then nearly whimpers, "Please."

No names. It'll make tomorrow so much harder. Instead, I shut him up with a kiss. The weight of him takes my breath away. He holds me by the shoulders and works my lips slowly, hungrily, as if we've done this a thousand times before. I wrap my legs around him, feeling him pulse against my belly. He grunts and pulls himself away.

"Damn," he says.

"Damn yourself." I turn over onto my side and watch his

spectacular ass as he walks across the room to the dresser. He looks over his shoulder. That devilish smile makes my heart race.

He puts on a condom, and returns to me in a mad dash. He buries his face between the curve of my neck and my shoulder, pressing his whole body against me. I dig my fingers into his dark curls and tug until he hisses. There's the headboard, and I can only think that it's a good thing there's not just a wall separating us from his neighbors.

"You're so beautiful," he tells me.

I try to laugh it off. I don't need him to tell me any of that. Guys think its flattery, like it's something I don't know, like I'm the kind of girl that needs to hear it all the time. But he repeats it. He holds my face in his hands, smoothing my long blonde curls back and over the pillow. I gasp when he presses into me, when he closes his lips around mine, when I'm so wound up I think I'll just snap in half.

My other best friend, Leti, likes to tell me that I'm a terrible judge of character.

She's only half right.

Because this guy between my legs smiles like a nice guy, but he fucks like a wild man.

CHAPTER 2

I call a cab—Uber hasn't made it to Sun Valley, Montana. The woman on the other line seems confused by my pick-up and drop off locations. I bet they don't normally get requests to get dropped off at a bar this early in the morning.

"Fifteen," she tells me.

I wait, hoping my cowboy won't wake up in those fifteen minutes.

Instead, I walk around his apartment, carrying my clothes with me. There's a box of cold pizza in the fridge. I take a slice, and my first thought is that this is the second best slice of pizza outside of New York. My second thought is that I must be that hungry.

I bet if I open the pantry I'll find trail mix, beef jerky, and health shakes. I give myself a dramatic five-second count, like I'm on a game show and Vanna White is revealing what's behind door #2. I grin. Granola bars, chocolate protein mix, and dried jerky. There's also some dog food, and cans of assorted soups.

A strange sense of pride comes over me. Granted, this isn't the kind of thing I should be doing. I'm in this lonely, quiet, mountain town for one reason and one reason only. When I decide if that reason is a good idea or not, I'll shout it to the world.

Right now, I'm still trying to figure out if I made the right decision. I've never lived anywhere outside of New York, so this road trip has been a long one. I stopped a few times. Once in Nashville to hear real live, country music, once in Kansas City to eat a steak bigger than my head, once in Colorado to smoke a joint in the middle of the street, and then in Missoula.

My road to recovery has been paved with debauchery.

LIFE ON THE LEVEL

Somewhere between Ohio and Salt Lake City I started to forget why I was running in the first place. That's the only good thing about being on the road—it helps you forget, because you just keep moving. That, and the rushing sound of a car zooming down a highway, the windows open, going so fast it feels like you might break the sound barrier.

I throw out the soggy pizza crust in the garbage can. The springs of the mattress move, and my heart does a little jig. I hurry up and get dressed, realizing that I don't have my underwear. My thong might just have to be a casualty in the War of Love.

Then I step outside, slowly, so the screen door doesn't make noise. I walk up the street a bit, standing in the middle of the road. There isn't a neighbor in sight. Having grown up in a sixteen-floor building knowing all the old ladies on my floor, this is just odd. Good fences make good neighbors, and in New York, thick walls make even better neighbors. But there isn't the need for all that out here.

As the car pulls up, I hear the door behind me. A dog barks.

I wave at the taxi. (I hope it's a taxi, and not some random car that happened to drive by.) I hop into the backseat just as my shirtless cowboy stumbles out of his house.

"Go, go!" I shout at the driver.

He hits the gas, and as my cowboy steps onto his lawn, we're well on our way.

I don't look back.

. . .

The cab driver gives me an odd look. He's my age, but still has acne. His lower lip hangs a bit, and I can see the yellow and black stains that tell me he chews tobacco, and probably has since he was a teen.

"E'rything all right?" he asks. It's an accent I've never heard. I'd say southern, except we're not in the south.

The question itself throws me a bit. I'm not used to getting driven around. Unlike Sky, I got my license when I was seventeen, but I'd been stealing my dad's ride since way before that. Still, the times I take a taxi, I'm not used to the drivers trying to engage with me.

"Everything's copasetic," I say. "He didn't kidnap me or anything."

There's a smile, like he's not sure if I'm joking.

"You're not from around here."

"How can you tell?"

He shrugs, and makes a turn onto a highway. My stomach churns. Partly from everything I drank last night, and partly because I don't remember if Cowboy drove on a highway. Suddenly, all the stories I read about girls getting kidnapped by taxi drivers in backwoods towns in the middle of Nowhere, USA start sounding a screeching warning in my mind.

"Seattle?" the cabdriver asks.

"New York," I say, indignant for no reason.

He cocks an eyebrow and presses his lips together in that nod people do when they're impressed.

When we turn back onto a street with more shops, I start to worry less. He's probably not a kidnapper. I'm going to be reunited with my car. I'm going to continue with my plan. Tabula rasa. Clean slate and all that. It's the first time I've done this. First time I've committed to it, at least. It's usually just one of those things I keep threatening to do to please the people who love me.

This time, I'm doing it for me.

"So, what do people do around here for fun?" Not that I'll be partaking in that fun. The next ninety days I've already volunteered away. It's not a done deal, but a girl can dream.

"First time in Zoo Town, then."

"Zoo what?"

He chuckles, and glances at me through the rearview mirror. "That's what we call Missoula."

"Ahh. So what do people do for fun in Zoo Town?"

"Depends. What do you like?"

I roll down the window and fish out the cigarettes in my backpack. The car already has the stale smell of smokes. When

I light it, he doesn't say anything, and I take that as permission that I can.

"You know," I say. "Fun. Card games, good food, surly bartenders."

Why are you doing this, River? Sometimes my inner voice sounds like Sky, all disappointed and stressed out.

"You've already been to Grizzly Bar. Not bad, 'cept the college crowd makes half the places in town shitty. Grizzly for greasy food. The Iron Horse turns into a bar after dinner. The Golden Rose is the last bar in the city where you can smoke indoors. Red's if you're a football fan, and if you're in town for a while, you'd better be."

"Casinos?" I ask.

Stop it, River.

"A few near the mall," he says. "But it's not Atlantic City or anything."

I take a deep drag and blow it out slowly, pushing the gray smoke as I make eye contact with him in the rearview mirror.

"Hmmm," I say.

"The Golden Rose has a backdoor that never closes. Three grand buy-in. They make you check your cellphone at the door."

I smile, but don't say anything. Sometimes it just helps to know things. I know where I can go if I need a fix. But I won't need it, because this time it's different.

I finish my cigarette just as we reach the bar. My car is parked in the lot beside three others.

"Lucky they don't tow on Sunday mornings," he says. "That'll be twenty bucks."

I give him thirty and tell him to keep the change. He doesn't leave right away, and I gather it's because he wants to ask me a question. His window's rolled down and he's hanging his arm from it. If I turn around, I bet he's licking the spot on his bottom teeth that's started to turn black.

I don't look back. I take a deep breath and get in my front seat. The taxi drives off before I do.

As I drive, the town starts to wake up. Downtown Missoula is a colorful little town. Bigger than a town, but not big enough to be a city. It seems like the kind of place that's small enough that you could bump into people you know while out to dinner, but big enough that you might find a way to get lost in the lush mountain valley. It's not the same kind of lost as New York, but then again, I don't think I could find that anywhere.

I pull on to a street where morning joggers make their way to Mount Sentinel, where a giant white letter M is a beacon for the city.

Dogs are getting walked. Church pews are getting filled. A pretty blonde girl sets up the daily specials board outside a coffee shop. A guy with a backpack is all ready to be the first customer. I feel like I'm halfway between Pleasantville and the most charming place I'll ever visit. Even though I've never called anything charming in my whole life. Not out loud anyway.

I set up the GPS on my phone, and let the polite robotic lady voice guide me up a hill and forty-eight miles south. After how far I've traveled, that's just a stone throw, and a sign that Sun Valley is easy enough to miss if you're not looking. On the main street there's a bar, a diner, a gas station, and then that's it. Everything there is to see is on the main strip. I turn on my right signal light as I spot the other sign I'm looking for. It's hard to get lost when the road is this straight. An unpaved road lined with trees and tall grass leads to a ranch.

The sign at the entrance is nondescript and unassuming— it's just a symbol of a pine tree with a sun logo. It means something to the people looking for it.

I drum my fingers on the steering wheel. I flick on my turn signal even though I'm the only car on the road. My wheels crunch against the gravel path that leads up to the main building, a giant log cabin mansion.

Because of course it's a log cabin.

There's someone standing at the front. A woman with brown hair and brown eyes, dressed in jeans and a plaid shirt. She doesn't smile, but doesn't look angry either. She holds a clipboard, and motions for someone to come out and help her.

I park in front of her, and lower my window.

My heart is hammering a thousand times per minute. I look

over my shoulder, down the path I just came from. It's not too late. I can turn around. I can hit the gas and get back on the highway. I've had a pretty good time so far. Just driving. Just me. Just the road and the quiet and the safety of knowing that I'm in control.

Except I'm not in control.

I squeeze the steering wheel, and try to unstick the breath lodged in my lungs. I'm not in control, and that's the reason I got on that road, and looked for that quiet, and went on the run.

That's the reason I needed one last night to say goodbye to everything that made me who I am now. I close my eyes for a second and think of him—his dark hair and his perfect mouth. A tiny shiver runs through my body. That's enough. I push the thought of him away and concentrate on my future.

"Good morning," the woman standing out front says, looking up from her clipboard.

"Hi, I'm River Thomas."

"Oh! We weren't expecting you 'til tonight."

"Is it okay?"

"Of course! Just park over in the lot, and I'll meet you back here. I'm Helen. Welcome to Horse Creek Recovery Center."

I can't help but laugh to myself. That's a pretty fancy way of saying, "Welcome to rehab."

CHAPTER 3

My daddy liked to say I have the perfect face for poker. He didn't believe in tells, but he knew other people believe in them. He said when people are looking for tells they're easier to fool. Said I have a face that could fool a man into betting his whole fortune. Just like my mother.

He'd know, because he lost everything to her.

Everything except me.

"This is the lobby," Helen says, needlessly pointing out what I can figure out for myself.

Maybe she thinks I'm so out of it I can't tell what I'm looking at. Someone else is already checking in, being given the grand tour by a middle-aged African American guy with a nice smile. The patient looks disoriented, clutching a backpack to his chest. He doesn't look any older than me.

Horse Creek Recovery Center doesn't look like a typical rehab place. I've never been forced to attend before, but I was at one back when my dad took a bad turn. I was in high school and he was on a month-long losing streak, heading straight into the grave. If his bookie hadn't been his best friend, I don't know what my dad would've done. Maybe killed himself before his cancer got the chance to do it. It sounds terrible, but I'll call a spade a spade, and that was my daddy.

Dad's rehab center was all white with blinding lights that made you feel like you were walking through a dream of Limbo. The patients walked around like ghosts of themselves, haunted eyes and open mouths moaning for another hit.

This place is nothing like that. Everyone wears normal clothes. Some people even look happy. We pass a room painted bright blue where groups are gathered around tables covered

LIFE ON THE LEVEL

in board games. There's a tiny theater with old couches, and popcorn kernels littered on the floor. A girl with raccoon eyes is watching a romantic comedy while a guy snores at the other end of the room. It doesn't seem to bother her. What does seem to bother her is me standing at the door.

"Do you mind?" she mutters, sinking into her seat.

Helen purses her lips, but doesn't comment further.

"As you can see, there are many things you can do here at HCRC. There are daily group meetings, and weekly individual sessions with an assigned counselor. Besides that, we like to keep active. Equine therapy is our specialty, though we do offer outdoor excursions like hiking and weeklong camping trips. During the winter there's skiing and ice fishing."

"You're not afraid someone's going to get lost in the wilderness?" I joke.

She laughs. I decide I like her laugh. It's not fake or motherly. She's more like a friend who has lots of responsibility and is in charge. She doesn't wear a ring, and her clothes are comfortable, but professional. I bet she's single, perhaps divorced once and trying to focus on her career this time around.

I lick my canine as I study her some more. She's got deep laugh lines, but this is the first time I've heard her laugh since I arrived. She holds her pen the way longtime smokers hold their cigarettes. I spot the start of a tattoo on her forearm, but the long sleeves of her shirt cover it. A name, perhaps. Her ex-husband, or maybe her mother. No, definitely her ex.

"Today you'll start off easy," she says. "Explore the grounds; talk to the others. Dinner is at six thirty, and once the kitchen's closed for the night, there isn't any going back for seconds. Do you have any food restrictions?"

I shake my head.

"Is there a—commissary? I don't know the right word."

There's that laugh again. "Goodness, River. You're not in prison. I hope you're here because you *don't* want to go to prison."

I can feel my cheeks turn red. "It's my first time trying."

"It's very brave of you. And no, you're allowed to have your own money. Meals are included in your fees, but things like cigarettes and junk food you can get at the concession stand."

I nod, digging my hands so far into my pockets I'm afraid I'll rip the seams. Helen places a hand on my shoulder and pats me like I'm a child in need of comforting. Everyone here is in some need of comforting. That's why they're here in the first place. Too much taking comfort in bad things. Too much instant gratification.

"Look," she says. "We don't get many people who admit themselves. Most of the time it's a parent or family member, or the rare good friend. Too often it's the law giving someone an ultimatum. You're here of your own free will, and that takes a whole lot of courage."

I don't say anything. I guess the right thing to say is "thank you." But I don't think that I'm brave at all. Bravery would have been doing this sooner, or sticking around to right my wrongs. Brave is not something I am.

"Now," she says, leading me down another corridor decked in more Montana taxidermy and freshly waxed pine floors. "We'll go get the rest of your things and finish check-in, and then I'll show you to your room."

• • •

"Is this necessary?" I mutter, crossing my arms over my chest.

The ranch's hand, Taylor Patrick, inspects my car. He chews gum as he looks me up and down. His eyes linger on my legs a little bit too long.

"It's standard," Helen tells me from the other side of the car. "Everyone submits themselves to inspection. You're coming into a facility where people are trying to recover. We have to make sure nothing gets in. Now, is there any alcohol or contraband in your possession or vehicle?"

I gnaw on the inside of my lip. I'm liking Helen a little bit less at the moment. I duck to tie my shoe, just as two cars pull into the driveway. They go around back to park, which means they're employees. I sigh, deflating like a balloon. *Fresh start, River*, I tell myself.

"We're not going to arrest you," Helen reassures me. "We

want you to have a clean slate."

"There's a flask under the passenger seat and a makeup bag with my prescription drugs. All legit."

I wasn't going to bring it in with me. It's just a backup, you know. It's not like I was going to share.

Helen takes the bottle of Xanax and Vicodin, along with my flask, the one with an R engraved at the center. It's full of Tullamore Dew, my daddy's favorite whiskey. She puts it all in a large white ziplock bag.

"That's it," I say.

But that's not it. I have a baggie of percs in the lining of the bra I'm wearing. I can feel sweat beads protrude on my forehead, but I blame the noonday sun.

I follow Helen and Taylor past the front desk and into the main office. Taylor sets down my bags and Helen puts on latex gloves. They unzip it and go through the contents. I swallow. My mouth is dry.

Taylor laughs. "Guess it's true. People do wear a lot of black in New York City."

I give him a pained smile.

They search my wallet. I've got a hundred in change, a photo of my dad from when he was in the Navy, and another of my girls and me from the beach this past summer. I'm annoyed that I have to tug it out of Taylor's hand, like he's trying to be cute.

They take my nail clippers, eyelash curler, and my self-defense keychain that looks like a golden cat, leaving my clothes, books, and overpriced hair products. They ask for my cell phone, but let me send all the texts I need to first.

Sky: I know you're busy getting tan with your sexy roofer. I can't decide if this place is a cult or not. I've been stripped down and had everything confiscated like a criminal. I'll have access to e-mail (I hope). Love, Me. E-mail: aroundtheriverbend4@gmail.com

Leti: I had the best sex of my life last night. And I didn't even know his name. BOOM. Commencing ninety-day lock down: aroundtheriverbend4@gmail.com

Lucky: Thanks again for hooking me up with that bar in Missoula.

Pepe: I'm sorry again. I'm at the rehab center. It's weird. Love you.

Dad: I miss you.

I get a sender error back from that last one and I swallow the lump in my throat. I want to laugh. Hi, I'm River Thomas, and sometimes I text my dead father, who was also a gambling addict, among other things. That should be my opening statement at group tomorrow.

As Helen moves to pry my phone out of my hands, a new text comes in.

"Just one more, please."

"What is it with this generation and texting?" she mutters.

The text sends a shiver down my spine. It's a New York number. 917. *Heard u skipped town. U don't think I'll find u?*

I press the power button, then slide it off.

"No one turns these on, right?" I ask.

"It's all locked up until you check out. Is everything okay?"

I look around the office. There are tons of little cages where they lock up patients' belongings. The phone in the lobby rings its shrill ring. Taylor walks by, helping an old man with his bags as he's leaving the building.

"River," Helen asks, sounding out my name in that way that doctors have, like they're trying to call you back to earth, like they're trying to get you to focus on the sound of their voice and not on the spinning thoughts in your head. "River. Something upset you."

"It's just—" I shake my head. I cough a laugh. "It's just what you said. My generation and all that. It's all the contact I have with my friends. It's hard letting go."

I feel like she can see through my lie. "There's a computer room. One of our patients is working on her young adult novel. You'll have access to basic e-mail and there's a mailroom for the ancient art of letter writing. There are these artifacts we have called pens and pencils."

"You're funny," I say.

"Don't sound so surprised. Just because we're in the middle of nowhere doesn't mean I don't know a thing or two about life.

You name it, and I've probably done it. Twice."

"Good to know. Well, now that you know my bra size," I say, "can you show me to my room? I'm beat."

As we head up the polished wooden steps, she says, "We're not trying to invade your privacy. We have an open-door policy. Removing possibly harmful things so that everyone here is safe."

"Objects themselves aren't harmful," I say. "People are the ones who are harmful, doc."

She stops at a door marked 3A. Three was my dad's lucky number. Mine is four.

"The left wing is where all the female patients stay, the right wing is for male patients, and when staff spends the night it's downstairs. You stay out of the men's wing, and they stay out of yours. All of you stay out of staff quarters."

"The staff stays here, too? Don't they go nuts?"

Helen laughs dryly. "Not any more than when they started. Because we're so rural, it's easier for some of them than driving four hours each way. But they're free to come and go as they please."

"I take it we don't have the same liberty?"

"Not unless you want to pack up and go for good. We have lots of group excursions. You'll have plenty of opportunities to get out with the others. I doubt you'll feel claustrophobic in Big Sky country."

I gnaw on the inside of my cheek. I'm already starting to feel claustrophobic. "Anything else?"

"There is to be no sexual conduct between patients and patients, or patients and staff members. It would result in immediate expulsion, and incompletion of your trial. Here's our introductory pamphlet with a list of further rules. Your counselor will go over them again at your session tomorrow.

"Tonight's dinner is turkey meatloaf, and quinoa chili if you're a vegetarian."

"I'm just really tired." Suddenly all of my traveling and sleepless nights hit me like a sledgehammer.

She appraises me, the same way I was looking at her before. I change my mind. She isn't divorced. I bet it was a love affair gone wrong. Perhaps he was already married and wouldn't leave his wife.

"I hope we can help you find what you're looking for here, River."

When she's gone, I want to lock myself into my room, except there isn't a lock. Right, for our safety. The windows don't lock either, but I'm on the second story. No chance of a hasty escape unless I want to break my neck.

I don't know why I'm checking every inch of the room or what I'm hoping to find. Paranoia? My past hiding under the bed? Preparing to run away before I've even started? I remind myself to breathe.

I go to the bathroom. My hands are shaking. I look at myself in the mirror. The light is so bright, I look almost translucent. A whole summer tan gone to waste. My blue eyes are clear, and there are bags under my eyes.

I think of the last text I got. That was *him*. I don't have to bet; I already know the text was from Kiernan, the guy whose face I scarred. The guy I called my boyfriend after my daddy died. After I threw myself into a downward spiral.

I grab onto the bathroom sink for support. Remind myself I'm here to get better. The other benefit of Sun Valley, Montana is that it's so far there's no way he can find me. No matter what he thinks.

I let the water run and fill a paper cup. I fish the little bag from my bra. Six pills. That's all I have left. They help me sleep and quiet the busy thoughts in my head. But the whole point is to be clean. Though they're technically prescribed, they're not exactly prescribed to me.

Don't do this, River, I tell myself.

If I take one, just to help me forget my problems for a little bit, it means that I've failed before I ever really started.

I take a deep breath, turn the baggie upside down, and watch the pills swirl down the drain. Then I grab my wallet, reaching for my cellphone out of habit. It's like a digital ghost limb. I guess it'll be good to unplug for a while.

I go in search of the next best thing to drugs: chocolate.

CHAPTER 4

The first time my daddy went to rehab was just before I was born. He said it was his first attempt at getting clean. It didn't work so well, because after Mom left he fell right back into the same old habits—gambling, booze, and women that wanted me to call them "Mom."

It wasn't that he didn't want to have me. Out of my two parents, he was the one that stayed to raise his six-year-old daughter. He was the one that didn't run away when things got hard.

I lie in my bed, staring at the purple ceiling. I was expecting white walls, but I think white walls would have made me go insane. The purple feels like a deliberate choice. I wonder what color the guys' rooms are. I wonder if they're the same lavender, or if they have the same distressed blue bedsheets. I doubt my dad's rehab centers were this nice. This warm. I almost feel like I'm cheating. This isn't even hard.

Granted, it's my first day, and I've been awake all of half an hour. I reach for my phone, then remember it's in a nice little locker with the rest of my belongings. What am I supposed to do without being connected to something?

I go brush the fuzzy morning breath off my teeth. After tossing and turning for eight hours, I'm rocking the biggest dark circles. I wonder how long I'd have to sleep before I felt bright-faced and fresh. Ten? A solid hundred years, like Rip Van Winkle?

I grab one of the books I brought with me, though I remember passing by a library no one was using, and head down for breakfast.

I can't help but feel like I'm repeating my freshman year

of high school. Everyone stares at me. Some surreptitiously from behind upside down newspapers, some not even trying to be discreet.

An older woman tells me to put some clothes on. I look down at my denim shorts, frayed at the bottom like a cat got a good playtime with them, and a black tank top with a (surprise) black cardigan over that. I roll my eyes, yawning loudly as I pass her. Nothing can bother me. I am made of steel. I am made of stone.

I grab a croissant, packets of butter, and a mug. My heart drops. There's a large container for coffee. One.

"You okay?" a small girl with brown pigtails asks me. She's got a red, red nose, like she has a cold, and dark, beady little eyes.

"Where's the coffee?"

When she smiles, her whole face moves to the left. For some reason it makes me think of my mother telling me, "Fix your face, River, or it'll get stuck like that."

"Sorry," the girl says. "We only have decaf. This must be your first time."

My cheeks go red. Right, caffeine. Mood-altering drug of addicts everywhere. How could I possibly not know that?

"I used to drink about a gallon a day," she tells me. "My heart used to race like a hummingbird's."

"Is that why you're here?" I say, trying to be friendly. Then I wish I hadn't. Is that not a thing I'm supposed to ask? Sky or Leti wouldn't have this problem. They're actually good at talking to people. It's not that I'm bad at talking to people (only yeah, I kind of am); it's that I have a general distrust of anyone outside of my close circle of friends.

I've been told it's a shitty way to live. Even Sky and Leti have friends outside of me. But that's just not who I am. How are you supposed to let someone into your personal space and tell them all about who you are, and how are they supposed to accept the mess that you are? The mess that I am?

Shit, River. It's only coffee.

"No," she tells me. "I'm Julie. I think you're in my friend Hutch's group. He always gets the new people."

"How come?"

She reaches over me and fills her mug with the decaf coffee. It smells good at least.

"How am I supposed to know?"

"Right," I say. "Well, I'll see you."

I take my croissant and non-mood-enhancing-coffee drink and head outside. Long picnic tables are filled with patients and smokers. I keep my head down and walk sluggishly. You know what would help me feel better?

Coffee.

There's a brilliant tree with bright green leaves on a bit of a hill. It's so fucking serene I could put it on a postcard. I lay out my picnic, dig out a cigarette, and start observing.

Maybe I was wrong in coming here. Am I like these people? I know I thought everyone looked happy, but that Julie looked like a child actor after all the drugs. Others scurry around like zombies. A handful look put together. Maybe the people that are happy are at the end of their trial. I can't be like those zombies, can I be? I mean really, what's wrong with me?

I drink, but so does everyone.

I don't do drugs all the time, but if the moment is right, sure, I'll do a bump or take a hit. Sometimes I'll take molly if I'm in the right club. But I don't need it to *live*.

I get anxious a lot, so a guy from one of my old poker games, who's a doctor, prescribes me anything I want. But I can live without it.

Look at me, living without it!

That just leaves gambling.

I knew how to count cards before I got to junior high school. It's easy to get caught nowadays. Everyone thinks they're in that Matt Damon movie and shit, and messes it up for the rest of us.

Still, I can quit if I want to. I did it a little less than a year ago when my daddy died. He didn't make me promise him or anything. He wasn't the kind of person to regret things on his deathbed. He just held my hand and told me I was the best bet he'd ever made. Then he was gone, and I decided to quit.

Quitting everything all at once was a test. I needed to prove to myself that I could do it. I went six months without sitting at a table. Hector, my dad's old bookie and my unofficial godfather, even called to check up on me. I quit my job and lived off my last big win.

Then, I don't know what happened. I met a bad guy, and went for one more game. None of my friends know about Kiernan, and I hope they'll never have to. My relationship with him wasn't my proudest moment.

I drink my decaf coffee, now cold, and shiver in the morning breeze. There's a middle-aged woman talking to herself at a table. She scratches at the inside of her arm. Heroin.

There's a group of kids my age who talk like they're in Bryant Park, having a regular day. One guy, with hair parted to the side and dimples that bring all the girls to the yard, sits at the head of the picnic table. I can't hear what he's saying, but I bet he's someone who likes to hear himself speak. He's probably at the end of his time here. I decide I don't like him.

Leaves fall all around me. I look up to see a girl hanging from a branch directly over my head.

"Took you long enough to notice me." She's got leaves in her hands and slowly releases them.

"I wasn't aware I was supposed to be on the look out for human possums," I say. I bite my tongue. Okay, I'm going to make it a point to stop, breathe, and think about my words before I say something sarcastic or mean.

She swings her body up, grabs hold of the branch, then jumps down beside me.

"You're the Yankee right?"

I resist the urge to roll my eyes.

"Montana's in the north you know. Also, it's not 1846."

"The Civil War started in 1861."

"Thanks for the history lesson."

"I'm in room 3D. Across the hall from you. Name's Maddie. Let me guess—heroin and booze. Maybe with a dash of prostitution."

"Fuck you," I snap.

And fuck thinking before I speak.

She laughs. "Oh, relax. It's a game. We all do it. Isn't that what you're doing? Trying to figure out the level of fucked up everyone is here?"

She's got me there. Still, I'd like to think I don't look like a doped up hooker.

"Do me," she says, standing with her hands at her hips like a department store mannequin.

Dirty Chucks, leggings ruined with bleach, and a Seattle Seahawks jersey. Her hair is stringy and can't make up its mind between blonde and brown. She's not traditionally pretty, but she's got confidence to bottle and sell.

"Meth," I say.

"As if," she scoffs.

I shrug. Be nice, I remind myself. You don't have any friends. You don't have to make friends, but ninety days is a long time if you make enemies.

"Fine," she says, grumbling. "I was kidding about you. I just hate when you leggy bleach blondes show up here. It distracts all the boys from the rest of us."

"First of all," I say between long sips of decaf, "I happen to be a natural blonde, sorry to disappoint. Second, what boys? I thought dating was against the rules."

She cocks an eyebrow and smirks with her full mouth. "Who said anything about dating? Besides, it's only against the rules if you get caught."

Somehow I don't think that's how it works, but I just shrug and keep my thoughts to myself.

"So, Maddie from 3D. How long have you been here?"

"'Bout a month. My dad wanted me to get away from my boyfriend. If he wanted that he should've sent me somewhere far away, like New York or Vermont. Not somewhere Billy could drive to in six hours."

"Six hours? I could fly to Florida in six hours."

"Well aren't you fucking fancy. Miss Empire State can fly wherever she feels like."

"That's not what I meant." I shove the rock-hard croissant

into my mouth to give myself some thinking time. "Anyway, it doesn't matter what I can or can't do. I've got eighty-nine days left."

"What counselor did they give you?"

Maddie seems a lot friendlier after I give her one of my cigarettes.

"I don't remember. Anyone to avoid?"

"Well, Helen's a drag. She likes to talk about your past and what led you here. Ransom's cool. He used to play professional football, then killed his best friend while driving drunk. Went off the map for, like, fifteen years, then became a counselor. He's also our sports activity guy. Likes to think we can work out our problems by sweating. But, that's not my kind of sweating."

"Okay."

"Then there's Hutch."

"Sounds like furniture."

"God, wait 'til you see him. Everyone wants him. I don't even care about half the things he talks about. I just want to look at him, you know? He's just got one of those faces, like that's what they used to model Hercules after. Oooh baby! We have a pool going to see if he has a girlfriend."

"He won't say?"

She shakes her head. "I think he's just doing it to play hard to get."

I laugh. "How big is the pool?"

"I put in a carton of cigarettes."

I bet I could win that pool, even if I haven't seen what Hutch looks like.

"You want in?"

Yes. My heart skips a beat. "Nah, I'm good."

"There's a few temp counselors that come in and out, but those are the three regulars. Don't sessions start at ten?"

"What time is it?"

"Ten fifteen."

I jump to my feet and dust grass and dirt off my ass. "Thanks," I mutter drily. She knew what time it was. Then for my own benefit, I add, "*Bitch*," under my breath.

Right. Just like high school, but with fewer drugs.

I race past the woman talking to herself, and the table holding hands and praying. I slosh cold coffee all over the front of my shirt. There's nothing I can do about the leaves in my hair or the crumbs that decide to cling to my face.

I find the room Helen pointed to. The door is open and it says "Chris Hutcherson" on the plaque. The glass is that wavy kind that lets you see blurry shapes from the other side.

There are two people in the room. I can make out two male voices talking. I don't hear my name. For some reason, my heart races.

"That stuff never happens to me," one guy says.

"Me neither…" the other guy says. "It was—I can't even describe it."

I clear the last croissant crumbs from my mouth, then open the door.

"Sorry I'm late," I say, barging in.

I freeze, and let go of the doorknob. The door slams behind me. I think I can actually feel my heart falling right out of my ass.

It's him. It's him. It's him.

If I close my eyes, I can picture him kissing me. If I close my eyes, I can still remember what he feels like. The only thing I wouldn't be able to remember is his name.

Hutcherson.

"Look who turned up," says the second guy, who looks like a blur to me. He laughs good-naturedly, then waves goodbye. "See you on the court."

When the other counselor leaves, and it's just us, I feel like the room is getting smaller. Does he remember me? I mean, we were pretty drunk. Though, I remember him. How could I forget?

He clears his throat and whispers my name. "River."

Damn. Damn. Damn. I love the way my name sounds when he says it. I bite my lower lip, holding onto my coffee cup for dear life. I start to back up, but the door is closed.

This silence drags. I can stretch it between my fingers like a rubber band. I know I need to say something but I've lost my words. Words, you elusive, beautiful things.

Isn't this funny?
How fucking small is this town?
Hey, did you find my underwear?

He doesn't seem to be doing much better. He places his fists on his desk and pushes himself forward. He has this thinking face. He downs his glass of water in several gulps. The silence gets so long I can wrap it around myself like a cocoon.

He chuckles!

He fucking chuckles. Then blows a long breath from those lips. Those full lips I admired so much.

He sits. His seat creaks and groans with his weight. Busies his fingers with papers. My file. That's what I've been reduced to. He pours another glass of water, this one for me. His smile makes my heart flutter, and I wish I could reach into my chest and make it stop.

"Why are you smiling?" I ask. My voice has gone up an octave or two.

"Because," he says, like that's a real answer. Like it makes this less weird. Like I didn't *run out* on him yesterday morning. "Because, I finally know your name."

CHAPTER 5

"I have to go," I say.

I start to turn the doorknob. He practically jumps over his desk.

"Wait."

"What?" I snap.

He shuts the door, then takes several steps away, drawing a line between our personal spaces.

"River, please, just hear me out."

"Stop saying my name!" Why am I angry? Why is he *here*?

"I don't know what else to call you."

Flashback: him, grabbing my face with his strong hands. *You are so beautiful.*

I brush my hair out of my face, wishing I could do something about the heat on my skin. "I don't know. This is—this is not okay."

He looks at me for a bit. Now that I'm getting over the shock of our reunion, I can get a better look at him with a sober brain. If beer goggles make uggos more attractive, then imagine what it's done to someone like him. In my mind, I take into account that I lost the bet with myself. He's not a cowboy. He's a counselor.

He's *my* counselor.

He messes up his hair, making him look all the more adorably rumpled.

"I'm just as shocked as you, River."

"I'm just going to go." I feel like a trapped mouse. "This is just too weird. I can't be here."

He nods, then after another painful pause goes, "You're right."

33

"Okay." I dump my coffee in the trashcan and turn around.

He starts to reach for me. I can feel his fingers graze my elbow. He thinks better of it. Then his touch is gone.

"I shouldn't be your counselor. That doesn't mean you should leave. You came here to get help. I should've seen it when we met."

"Why?" I ask angrily. "Because I was a drunken mess throwing herself at you? You didn't seem to mind."

"That's not fair."

"Welcome to this funny little thing called life."

"I should've seen it because you looked so sad. I could see myself—I mean, I should've seen there was more to you. I don't mean it in a bad way. I mean that part of me didn't want to ask because I just needed—"

"Needed what?"

He shoves his hands into his pockets.

Don't look at his jeans.

"I just needed to have you. I don't do things like that normally."

"And I do? Because I'm some raging slut." Well, I *do* do things like that normally. They just never blow up so spectacularly in my face.

"Stop deflecting."

"Don't Psych 101 me."

He smirks.

"And stop smirking."

He licks his lips, and that just makes everything so much worse. He crosses his arms over his chest, leans against his desk. What a lucky fucking desk.

"Don't leave because of me, please. I'll stay out of your way. I can be professional, even if what happened between us isn't a testament to that."

I'm suddenly cold. I rub the goose bumps from my arms.

"This is like the let's-be-friends speech," I say.

He pushes his tongue against his cheek, and I can tell he wants to say something inappropriate. Maybe flirty.

"Not used to that?"

I shrug. "Won't people ask questions about me switching counselors? Word on the street is people are clamoring to be yours. I mean—your patients."

He smiles, and when he smiles I realize we can never be friends. Not if he keeps looking at me that way.

"Are the gossip mills getting to you already?"

"Something like that."

"Just—be careful who you share things with here. Sometimes information is more valuable than money or cigarettes."

"I don't want to get kicked out. And I don't want either of us to get in trouble. Besides, we didn't do anything wrong. We are two consenting adults. We met before I checked in, and we're not pursuing anything."

"Right."

"Exactly."

"I know."

"Me too."

He sighs. "I'll speak to Helen this afternoon. Tell her you'd be better suited to someone else."

"Okay." Part of me, the part that's committed to doing this, is congratulating herself. This is so grown up. This is mature and reasonable. I don't really need to be here, do I?

The other part—the girl who lost the bet on the man who was supposed to be a rough-and-tumble cowboy—is itching for another shot. God, I wish I had that flask right about now.

"This is the best thing to do," he says.

"For you or for me?"

"For both, I hope."

"Are you sure this is okay?"

"You're the first patient to get transferred out of my sessions." He walks around his desk and sits again. "Don't worry, I can take a hint."

"What do you mean?"

"You walked out on me, remember?"

I nod, and let myself out. I walk away from him for the second time in two days.

CHAPTER 6

Dear Sky Lopez,

I hope you're having a blast on your not-a-honeymoon honeymoon. Guess what I did? In typical River fashion, I shat where I plan on eating for the next three months. The beautiful sexy guy I wrote about before? He's my counselor. WHY ME? Seriously? Out of every guy in that bar, why did it have to be him?

He isn't terrible really. He's the responsible type. Even tried to convince me that I should stay. I shouldn't stay, should I? He promises it won't be weird, but every time I look at him, I think about him naked!

I'm going to find another rehab center and abstain from having sex with anyone in the city limits. Though, with my luck, I could go to rehab on the moon, and something would go wrong.

Also, wouldn't that be cool? Rehab on the moon...

Ugh, you're probably having sex right now. I hate you.

Love,
Riv

• • •

I leave the computer room after googling rehab centers in Idaho. It's not the moon, but it's alien enough to me.

Someone knocks on my door. My heart jumps a little. He wouldn't come looking for me, would he? Just in case it is him, I fluff my curls in the mirror. There's nothing I can do about my dark circles. I shake my head at how absurdly I'm behaving. Helen's words about getting kicked out of the program are clear as a bell.

When I open the door, Maddie's standing outside. She's

wearing a bathrobe that goes down to her knees, yoga pants, and an unfortunate pair of Crocs.

"Group time!" she says, the way anyone else would say "Happy hour!"

She cranes her neck to get a look at my room.

It seems weird to me, so I stand in her way. "What are you doing?"

"Just looking. Can't I just look, Empire State?"

"You're weird," I say, shutting the door behind me. The doors don't lock, which is something that bugs the hell out of me, but I don't have time to think about it now. So I step out into the hall and start walking ahead of her.

"Wait up," she says, trotting alongside me. "I saw you come out of Hutch's office yesterday. Isn't he the hottest hottie that ever hottied?"

I keep looking straight ahead, even though the sound of his name makes me feel strange. The pit of my belly tightens, and a pleasant warmth spreads through me. *No, no, no.* Stop it this minute.

"Yeah," I say, sounding almost robotic. I want to convince her. I want to convince myself. "But I don't think he's the right match for me."

"What are you talking about? He's everyone's match. Literally everyone wants to be with Hutch. You're weird, Empire State."

I shrug, taking the flight of steps two floors down to the group meeting room. There are chairs lined up in a circle. A few people are already sitting. There's a man chewing his nails down to bloody stumps. I recognize some of these people from breakfast.

"You can sit next to me," Maddie says. "At least you'll know someone. It sucks when you go somewhere new and you don't know anyone."

I want to tell Maddie that I don't particularly "know" her either, but today's not the day to turn away new friends.

Having never been to a group session like this, I have no idea what I'm supposed to do. I can't seem to get comfortable on the big wooden chairs. I even consider sitting on the floor for a little bit.

"Don't be nervous," Maddie tells me. She slouches low into her seat. "You don't have to share if you don't want to. I mean, you should when you're ready, but no one expects you to say anything your first time."

"How do you know it's her first time?" an old woman asks. "She could've been bouncing back and forth from rehabs since she was sixteen. She's got the look."

I stare at her. Part of me was raised to respect my elders. Part of me was raised to not take shit from no one.

"What did you say to me?"

"Don't pay her no mind," a young, thirty-something guy says. I recognize him as the guy with the dimples from yesterday. "She's meaner than Satan. That's why no one likes her."

"Do you really have to use the S-word?" a younger guy says.

"Calm your tits, Jesus Boy," the mean old lady says.

"Debbie," Hutch says, walking into the room. "What did we talk about during our last session? Don't call Pete 'Jesus Boy.'"

Hutch's voice is firm, but soothing at the same time. I know he's talking to Debbie, the old lady meaner than Satan, but he glances in my direction. How many girls have hung onto that glance?

Shit. Shit. Shit. Shit.

My body reacts the same way it did when Maddie said his name, with the spreading warmth and the stomach pangs. I sit a little straighter, and instead look at Debbie. She crosses her arms over her chest.

"All right," she says. "I'm sorry I called you Jesus Boy. And I'm sorry what I said about you," she says, setting blue eyes on me.

"See?" Hutch asks. "It hasn't killed you to be nice."

"We'll see if I'm awake in the morning."

A light chuckle, followed by deafening silence.

"Gather 'round, everyone." Hutch sets a stack of papers on the floor. He takes the seat directly across from me.

"Are the lights always so bright?" I whisper to Maddie.

LIFE ON THE LEVEL

I've started sweating.

"We have a new addition to our family," Hutch says, taking a drink from his water bottle. The skylight filters directly over us. Dust particles float in beams all around the room. It looks like we're under the spotlight of the heavens.

In this light, Hutch looks unreal. I've never met a guy who looks like this before. His body is perfection. He smiles willingly, like he's giving you a gift. He's got an air of calm around him. It takes me a second to recognize it as confidence, but not overconfidence. And something else. Something that maybe I'll find here, too—self-acceptance.

"River?"

"Hmm?" Right, I've been so busy staring at him that I missed what he said.

Maddie snorts under her hand. Debbie sucks her teeth.

Pete gives me an encouraging smile. "Hutch asked you to introduce yourself," he volunteers.

"I didn't realize *you* were leading group," Maddie says.

Someone mutters, "Meow."

Hutch holds a hand up, and everyone quiets. It's interesting how much command he has over them. It's even more interesting how they listen.

"River?" Hutch repeats my name.

I clear my throat to give my brain time to catch up to the rest of me.

"Hi," I say. I've never been shy, but I've also never been in rehab, and I guess there's a first time for everything. Sometimes all your first times are going to come at once, and you're never going to be prepared.

"I'm River." Someone (Debbie) scoffs at my name.

There's a chorus of, "Hello, River."

I focus on Hutch's smile. I tell myself that smile isn't just for me. It's a smile that he gives to all the patients, perhaps all the people he comes across. Still, it feels like it's just for me.

"Born and raised in New York. I'm an only child. My favorite food is coffee and cold pizza. Um—I don't really know what I'm supposed to say."

"Whatever you feel comfortable telling us," Hutch says.

I'm River, and I slept with my counselor.

I'm River, and I don't think I belong here.

I'm River, and I want to go home.

Home. My daddy's dead, and I broke my lease. Right now, I don't even know where home is.

I shake my head. "That's it."

"Aw, come on, Empire State," Maddie whines. "You can do better than that. You don't strike me as the wallflower type."

I can't help but look at Hutch for his reaction. He keeps his cool. Licks his lips and looks at the ground before letting his eyes sweep across my face for a second. I turn and look at the door. If I make a mad dash, will someone come after me? Maybe Hutch himself? How long would I have to run before something stopped me?

"Maddie," Hutch says. "Let her speak."

She's right; I'm not the shy type. I'm also not the type to spill my life story to a circle of former addicts with more issues than I'll ever have.

"You've known me for less than twenty-four hours," I say. "How would you know what type I am?"

Maddie opens her mouth to snap back, but Hutch stands.

"That's right, River. We don't know you. How many of you walked in here and considered walking right back out because you didn't think this was the right place for you? Raise your hands."

Maddie raises her hand. Five more hands go up. Not Debbie's. I raise my hand.

"You don't think you belong here?" Hutch asks me. He looks me dead in the eye, and suddenly I want to run faster and further than I ever have before.

"I've been thinking about it, and I still don't know." And that's the most honest I can be with myself right now.

"Let me ask all of you," Hutch says, calmly walking a few paces around the circle. "What made you decide to stay here?"

Everyone fidgets. Maddie gives me a dirty look, then examines the dirt under her nails as if it's more interesting than anything Hutch has to say.

"Pete," Hutch says, pointing at the young guy.

Pete sits with his shoulders back. He's got incredible posture. He's also the only one of us wearing clothes that couldn't pass for pajamas.

"The first time I came here was after the accident that took my best friend's leg." For all of their bickering and snide comments, everyone perks up to listen. They nod their heads sympathetically, and wait for his words.

"I was court mandated to serve twenty-eight days of rehab, and I did it. I didn't touch a drop of alcohol. I even stopped baking so I wouldn't have access to vanilla extract." He looks down at his hands, crossing them on his lap. "Afterward, I went back to church, even though everyone would be talking about the terrible thing I'd done. My family assured me that I was part of a community. I took it one day at a time. I even let myself attend Henry's twenty-seventh birthday party. I was fine, until I wasn't.

"Everywhere I went I could hear people whispering about me. How dare I show my face? Henry would never play football because of me. Henry would never have the same life because of me. I was damned to go to Hell. I was the worst kind of person. After a while they stopped whispering and just said the words to my face.

"The morning after I woke up on Henry's parents' front lawn, I couldn't remember how I got there or even where I got my first drink. I just remember this crowd of people standing around me and pointing." Pete stops talking for few moments. He starts to twist his fingers in his own hands. "I was covered in my own filth. I—I—I knew I wasn't strong enough. So I found a new place. I came here. I thought about turning back. I thought about moving away, finding a fresh start. But then, what if I did the same thing in a new town? What was to stop me from ruining someone else's life? What was to stop me from falling all over again?"

"So the thing that makes you stay is fear of repeating your past mistakes?" Hutch asks.

"The thing that makes me stay is *knowing* I'll repeat my past mistakes. I think that's God's plan for me."

"You don't know that," I tell him. "I mean, I'd like to think that we have control over our choices."

"If you believed that," he tells me, "then you wouldn't be in this circle."

That's a kick to the gut. How many times have I lost control? Sometimes I'd wake up and with no memory of what I'd done. Even if I was with friends, I'd take one look at their faces, and swallow the regret on my tongue. Sometimes I'd be alone and naked, my floor covered in poker chips and wads of cash, the pain in my skull drowning out the ache in my heart. How many times have I told myself it's the last time?

"Come on, guys," Hutch says. "Don't leave me standing here talking to myself. I can do that on my own time."

A Hispanic girl raises her hand. "I'm tired of hurting people. That's what made me turn around and stay."

There's a collective agreement of nods and yeses.

"When I was kid," Hutch says, settling back into his chair, "I lived for the days my dad had custody of us. I must've been about seven, and I had made the football team. Back then I fancied myself the next John Elway, and there was nothing I wanted more than to throw the ball around with my dad. All he had to do was show up twice a month.

"My brother was older by three years, but still, he had more sense than I did and realized that I could sit on that front step for hours and hours, but no one was coming.

"I can't pretend to tell you all that I know what you're going through. I don't know addiction, and I can't preach to you about the effects of addiction. I can't tell you anything that others haven't said a hundred times already.

"But what I can tell you is that I wish that my father had been as brave as all of you. I wish he'd had the courage to say, 'I'm tired of hurting my boys.' That right there is what makes all of you different. No one can make that decision but you. I'm here to listen and offer a hand when you need it."

I feel a swell in my chest after his story. I knew we were

both orphans, but I had no clue we were abandoned around the same time by one of our parents. This is a much different way to get to know someone after sleeping with them.

I imagine Hutch as a little boy. Did he have the same warm dark eyes? Did he have this same smile when he sat there waiting for his father to remember him? I know that when it was me, when I was the one waiting for my mother to come back home, I didn't.

For the next half hour, the pressure is off me. Everyone takes turns talking about things that are bothering them. Maddie talks about how much she misses her boyfriend. Though, this time his name is Brian.

Debbie says she'd do anything for just one last hit. She says she dreams about it. She can't even remember what it feels like. She just wants to remember. Others want to forget.

The whole time, Hutch listens. He's their friend when he needs to be. He's a stern voice when it's called for. He engages everyone and encourages everyone to participate in the conversation.

Everyone except for me.

I guess I shouldn't be too disappointed. I'm the one who left him high and dry. I'm the one who wanted to leave the moment I saw him.

"You're the one who walked out on me, remember?" he asked.

That's right. I am the one who walked out. But now I wonder, like so many of the other things that led me here, was that a mistake too?

CHAPTER 7

My dad used to say, "I might not always be right, but I'm never wrong."

I've managed to adapt that as a personal motto when it comes to arguments. Sky says I'm a simply a stubborn ass. As I linger after the session, not really coming or going, I can admit that yes, I'm a stubborn ass.

First step is admitting it, right?

Hutch is currently being torn between conversations. On one hand there's Maddie, talking about whatever Maddie talks about. Then there are two more girls vying for his attention, asking if he's staying for lunch.

He keeps his distance from all of them. His body language is pretty clear from here. Arms around his body, so there is no touching. He nods politely to what they say, but doesn't leave room for flirting. When Maddie reaches for the beautifully chiseled mass of his bicep, he casually takes a step back. Properly dissuaded from the hot counselor, the girls retreat.

Hutch notices me lingering. He looks around the empty room. One of the doors is propped open. He scratches the back of his head. He shuffles some papers, and it makes me miss my deck of cards.

"What's on your mind, River?"

"Hutch, do you always say people's names before talking to them?"

"Well, River, I like to think it helps people feel connected when you say their names."

I laugh. "I'm sorry about earlier. I think I just freaked. It felt like too much. This place, and... you know. I'm still not sure I belong here."

"Because you're not like the rest of the people you listened to today?"

"Among other things. Don't get all shrinky on me right now, please."

He laughs. "I don't even know what to say to that. But all right. Tell me. What's on your mind?"

You, naked on top of me. You, kissing me like you would die if you didn't. You. Just you.

"I like the way you speak to people. I like that you make everyone feel comfortable. It's important for me. I know I didn't share the way others did."

"Take your time."

"I don't think I know how."

"That's okay, too."

I shake my head. I want to grab him by the shoulders and shake him. "Why are you so… *so*?"

"So what?"

I run my hands through my curls, tangling them even more than they already are. "I don't know. Nice? Understanding? What's wrong with you? There has to be some deep dark secret that you're not telling anyone. No one is that perfect all the time."

He stares at me, lips slightly apart. The corners pull up on one side, revealing that dimple. I want to dive into that dimple and swim laps.

"You think I'm perfect?"

I flush with heat. "Shut up, like you don't know everyone here wants you."

"River…" I watch his broad chest rise and fall. I have his torso—all of him, really—etched into my memory. He looks up at the ceiling, like he'll find his answers in the wooden boards and the skylight.

"Hutch…"

"I'm far from perfect. Maybe it's easy to think of me as perfect because I'm not a patient. Trust me, I've got my own skeletons."

"Real ones?"

He barks a laugh. "I guess you'll never know."

"That's the thing, actually." I don't remember the last time I was this nervous talking to a guy. One time my dad's friend likened me to a bull rider, grabbing life by the horns, but my daddy said no, I wasn't the rider—I'm the bull, and the world is my china shop. But now my tongue is leaded, and I can't decide where to stick my hands because my sweats don't have pockets. Clothes should always have pockets. "I kind of—wanted to keep you as my counselor."

"I'm sorry," he says. "I already spoke to Helen, and she thinks you'd make a great addition to Steven's group."

"Damn, that was quick. You didn't waste a second."

"River," he whispers my name. He holds out his hands helplessly. He takes a step towards me. I reach out and place my hands in his. My hands graze his palms. These are the same palms that pinned me down in his bed. That caressed my face while he kissed me. Now, they're pulling away from me. I look over my shoulder. Day one and I already feel reckless.

"I thought we agreed it was necessary," he says. "It wouldn't be right. Anything else would distract you from what you came here to achieve. I'll get in the way of your recovery."

"Relax," I say, "I'm not doing it because of what you might think."

He frowns. "You don't know what I think, River."

"I think I do, Hutch. I'm not some dewy-eyed schoolgirl. I'm not looking for round two if that's what you're getting at. I thought you might understand me better, but I guess I was wrong."

Someone walks past the door and swings it wide open. Patrick Taylor, or was it Taylor Patrick? Either way, my daddy always told me to be wary of a man with two first names. Since his name was Clark Thomas, he knew firsthand.

"Oh hey, Hutch." he says. "Sorry, I thought group was over." He wheels a mop and bucket into the room.

"We're finished here," Hutch says, and his jaw ripples as he bites down on his words. "Room's all yours, Taylor." His tone is friendly, cool, and even. But his eyes say differently. Whatever he was going to say before Taylor walked in is going to have to stay unsaid.

Perhaps it's for the best. I have to be careful about letting my impulses drag me into any more poor decisions.

I wait for Hutch to leave the room first, busying myself with exploring the photographs on the wall, each one of a different mountain range or lake or forest animal. There's one that quickly becomes my favorite. A man in a cowboy hat, facing an open valley with the greenest hills and bluest sky I've ever seen. It's soothing, and staring at it helps me forget about my tense conversations with Hutch.

Almost.

Was he in that much of hurry to unburden himself of me that he got Helen to approve the request so quickly? Or maybe they just have fewer people to keep track of, because the facility is so small. I'm probably overthinking it. After all, I was the one who didn't want him. Now, all of a sudden, I've changed my mind. I'm allowed to change my mind, right?

The wet smack of the mop on the tiles snaps me from my reverie.

"It looks even better in real life," Taylor tells me.

When I turn around, he's standing right behind me. "I bet."

"You'll be hiking this weekend. Don't suppose you do a lot of hiking in New York City."

"Have you ever been to New York?" I ask, a twinge of irritation crossing my face.

He holds onto the mop, setting his chin on top of his hands. "Nope. Got everything I need right here."

"Then you wouldn't know how much hiking I do."

"You're a firecracker, ain't you?"

I purse my lips. I can't tell if he's teasing me, hitting on me, or making fun of me. Probably all of the above.

"Relax, girly." He resumes mopping again. "Otherwise, it's going to be the longest three months of your life."

. . .

River Thomas!

I'm sorry I missed your e-mail. Hayden and I are on our way to Costa Rica. He's trying to convince me to swing between the trees. I'm thinking hell no, but he's very persuasive, if you get my drift.

I'm glad you're liking Montana? I can't tell. Your dryness doesn't translate via e-mail. Hutch sounds delicious and amazing. Too bad you've got a forbidden love thing going on. Don't leave. You promised you'd try. It'll be weird, but things happen for a reason. I know you think that's just hippie nonsense, but it's true! You are beautiful and smart and loyal and you deserve to find your happiness. If Horse Creek is the place to start, then take that start.

I miss you.

Don't be a stranger. Even if I can't respond right away, I'm reading your every word.

Love,
Sky

CHAPTER 8

FIVE DAYS SOBER

The first couple of days were cyclical. My new counselor is a middle aged African-American man named Steven Ransom, who's originally from Detroit. He played football all throughout college and even went pro for a few years. He went bankrupt after spending all his money on hookers and blow, and was in a terrible accident that killed his best friend.

"You're such a stereotype," I told him.

He laughed good-naturally and shrugged. "The stereotype would have been if I didn't clean myself up. Will you do the same?"

That shut me right up.

As much as I was pissed about Hutch, I think it was for the best. Steven is a cool dude. He doesn't talk the way Hutch does. Hutch is someone young, who comes off as relatable. Ransom is older and has a calmer vibe. He talks to me more like a father, and before I start getting all Freudian, I think I prefer that to a friend right now.

I walk around the facility every morning with my cup of decaf in one hand and a cigarette in the other. The place is huge. It's like two Manhattan avenues long and three wide. People here talk in miles and acres, and I speak in cab fares and minutes.

I haven't joined a group for meal times. I like to sit by myself and watch everyone else. Sometimes Maddie, when she's feeling peppy (her mood swings are out of control), will stroll over and act like we're best friends. She tells me about her boyfriend, Harry this time, and about how she dreams about his ten-inch dick. I don't know what's more unbelievable: that she has a third boyfriend named Harry, or that Harry has a ten-inch dick.

In the afternoons there are voluntary sports activities. Everything works as a points system. It's like an ongoing contest that no one really wins. Helen says it's supposed to be a way to motivate people to participate and be active. I think it's a way to treat us like we're in kindergarten, begging our teachers for stars. Pete argues that it's borderline harmful for gambling addicts.

"No," I tell him. "Not everyone gambles to win. Some people gamble because sometimes it's the only thing that makes sense."

Besides, I'm not the most competitive person I know. My arm muscles aren't totally impressive. One time Sky made me go to hot yoga with her. I nearly died.

I begrudgingly promise Ransom that I'll try jogging on my own. His eyes always linger on my cigarette, and I shout, "You can't take away all my vices!"

Dinners, I spend in my room.

I don't know why I'm being so antisocial. Maybe it's that everyone here is so damn nice. Even Debbie says hello to me when she sees me, even if her hello sounds more like a habit than an actual need to be polite. There's always laughter passed around. I can hear it from my window when I leave it open. After dinner, there's a bonfire with marshmallows. Pete can play guitar, and everyone lets him as long as he plays anything, anything but Kumbaya.

Kumba-fucking-ya.

If I told my past self that I would be here, I wouldn't have believed me. It's like these people live in a world where nothing else exists. Don't they realize they're all addicts? Don't they realize they're all some level of fucked up?

Sometimes I wake up in the middle of the night and rummage through my room for a deck of cards. I can't gamble on solitaire with myself, but I like to break the cards. I like the way the deck cracks under my hands as I shuffle them in and out of place. I miss that sound. *Crack, shuffle; crack, shuffle.*

Like now. I can't fall asleep. It's too quiet here. I miss

coffee. I miss the smell of whiskey and smoke and the laughter of messed up people who *know* they're messed up. People who don't pretend.

I sit up from my bed and pace around my room. Then I hear something. The floors are so new that they don't even creak, but there most certainly is someone outside moving around. I get closer to the door. I've sneaked out of my house enough times to know what that sounds like.

Someone walks past my room. There's the soft hush of a door opening, and the slow click of a doorknob turning. I open my own door a crack. The hinges strain for a moment. I stick my head out in time to see Maddie tiptoeing down the hall.

I close my door behind me and follow her. I don't know why I'm following her. Part of me says to turn around. But my heart hammers in my chest with this new detail.

Maybe this place isn't all Pleasantville after all.

I bet she's meeting up with someone. I bet she's going to steal things from the kitchen where Lunchman Larry keeps the good chocolate (or so they say).

When she gets to the landing to go downstairs, I crouch down on the floor. She looks over her shoulder once to make sure no one is there. I'm pretty sure I haven't made a noise, but I haven't had to sneak around anywhere since I was sixteen and my dad gave me free rein, so I'm a touch rusty.

Maddie waves at someone downstairs. I can't see who it is from up here, and I can't stand up or I'll be seen. She walks over to where the shadow stands at the front door, and she heads outside.

When they're gone, I stand. I could follow her outside, but that's a level of creeper even my worst boredom couldn't lead me to.

Moments later, one of the younger girls who's even newer than me—I think she's a heroin addict—walks from the men's wing and down the stairs. I push myself against the wall that hides me in the dark. She isn't looking at me anyway. What's even more surprising is that she's holding a guy's hand. They're the worst at sneaking around. I can hear their footsteps, all heels against the ground and their failed attempts at holding back giggles. They race down the stairs and out the door.

"Huh," I say. Was there an activity I wasn't invited to? I vacillate between taking a step down to the main floor and going back to my room. Then I hear his voice.

"River?" Hutch says, standing at the bottom of the stairs. He's coming from the direction of the kitchen.

I nearly jump out of my skin. "Hutch."

"What are you doing up? Curfew was three hours ago." He has a flashlight in his hands. He's wearing a black tank and maroon sweatpants that say "Grizzlies" down one pant leg.

"Couldn't sleep. Are you living out your Hardy Boy fantasies?"

My lame joke is worth the smile he gives me. He rubs his hand over his bed hair. I want to jump over the railing and run my fingers through that thick dark hair.

"Depends. Want to be my Nancy Drew?"

"Careful, Counselor," I say. "That's against the rules."

He shakes his head. "I heard something. Seen anything while you were up?"

In the shadows, I can't see his eyes. He's daring me to rat out everyone I just saw. I'm not a snitch, even if I'm not their friend. Besides, I want to solve this mystery on my own.

"Nope," I say, and I wonder if he can tell I'm lying.

"All right." He waves at me. "Get some sleep, River."

I go back to my room and climb into bed. The next thing I know, the red and orange daybreak shines through my curtains. I miss my 100 percent blackout curtains. I miss sleep, too. I wish I hadn't thrown out all my percs.

But now I'm five days sober, and as much as I don't want to admit it, I miss a man who wasn't even mine to begin with.

CHAPTER 9

In the morning I watch Maddie's movements. She's spacey and doesn't want to talk. To stop myself from searching for Hutch everywhere I go, I decide to run. It's kind of like running away, except I have Ransom's permission, and I have to return at some point.

The last time I volunteered to go running like this I was running from a collector. Two years ago I had a hard time paying a bookie. I decided to place a bet on the Mets, because they were my dad's team. He had just been diagnosed, and I felt reckless.

I didn't realize it was reckless at the time—I thought I was being a good daughter. We're not a sentimental family, but I thought it was right. Five grand later, I remembered that even if I didn't know anything about sports, I should've remembered that the Mets suck.

I shake the memory from my head, and run the way I ran from that guy down Tenth Avenue. He didn't catch me, and I paid the money back. Here, there is no one chasing after me. There is only me, and the sound of my heart in my ears. I don't have an iPod, so I sing to myself.

The wind is delicious against my sweaty skin, and the sky is unbelievably blue. I get tired in about ten minutes. My legs hurt, and my lungs ache. I grab onto my knees and wheeze up a grassy hill. In the distance there's a dilapidated barn and a patch of trees that leads up a small mountain.

I can't remember what's still part of the property, but I keep walking. I haven't been this alone in forever.

I realize I don't really like being alone with my thoughts. I like noise and smoke and darkness.

I'm going to have to do something less exhausting. Maybe

finger painting will be more my speed. I wonder where Hutch works out. I'm sure he doesn't get those muscles by reading patient files, or finger painting, for that matter. All at once I'm thinking of his fingers and the way they felt against my skin.

It makes me run faster. One thing that sucks about this is that I can't run from my thoughts. Thoughts stay with you. They pop up, unwanted, and run laps around you.

When I get to the barn, I hang back a little bit. The grass grows tall up here. It's dry and tangled. I walk around the perimeter a bit and notice a worn trail.

Then the door flies open, and I throw myself into the grass. It pricks my skin, but I don't know if I'm supposed to be up here.

I hear a male voice talking on the phone, but a wind blows and cuts out his words.

"I've got it, all right? Last night was a great turnout, promise. It's at the pick up. Nope… Yep… I told you, you don't have to worry."

The voice sounds familiar. Male. Young. Perhaps one of the guys from group. I don't dare stand up and finish my run. I'll stay put until I've made sure he's gone.

"I need to get back." That's the end of the call. I hear the rumble of an engine starting up, and wheels on gravel. Dust billows high into the air as he drives away.

Now I know where everyone was sneaking off to last night. I sit up and pull the hay out of my hair. I finish my run (though by now it's mostly walking) back to HCRC. And for the first time since I got here, I wish I had someone to talk to.

• • •

"How was your run today?" Ransom asks me.

"Painful." I lean my head back in the chair. My muscles ache fiercely. "You know, I'm not really the outdoors type."

He laughs in that high-pitched way of his, surprising for someone so big. "This isn't a spa."

"There's still time," I say.

"Tell me. What did you think about while you were out there?"

"I don't know."

He stares at me for a bit. "I always replay the old days when I run. What about you?"

I look at my lap. I decide to tell him about running from the bookie.

"I can't lie. I've been in similar situations. Though, I'd never bet on the Mets."

For the first time during our sessions, I really laugh.

"When did your father pass?"

The question throws me off. I knew talking about my dad would come up eventually. I'm surprised Steven's waited so long. I'm a walking case study of the Electra complex. At least that's what Sky told me once. At first I thought she was talking about the shitty movie.

"A little over a year ago," I tell him.

"Is that when you first decided to change your life?"

"That's a funny way of putting it. Change your life."

"What would you call it?"

I shrug one shoulder. "I still worked at a bar. I just decided to drink a little less. I stopped going to games." I grab the book on the table beside me and thumb through the pages. The pages are thicker than a normal book's, so it almost sounds like a deck of cards. The sound soothes me.

"I'd say that's a change."

"Okay." I don't want to talk about my dad anymore. "Hey, what's that barn down the road?"

Ransom looks confused. "You must've run quite a bit."

"You can tell that to my leg muscles tomorrow."

"There are a few abandoned barns around here. I remember the first time I came out here. I didn't know the difference between a farmer and a rancher."

"Do you miss the city?"

"Sometimes," he says. "Do you?"

He's good at bringing the conversation back to me.

"I miss the noise. I miss real people."

"What makes you think the people here aren't real?"

I hold my arm out and point at the door. "Come on. You see them. They act like there's nothing wrong with them. Fucking Pete's back here because he's afraid of the world. It's like they're hiding."

He's silent, and I'm afraid I've offended him. "Do you think you're a real person?"

"I'm not lying to myself by thinking I'm okay. Sometimes I don't think I belong here. I know I've fucked up, but it can't be as bad as these people. I've never put someone in the hospital or abandoned my kids."

"What have you done?"

I shut my eyes and try to push away the thoughts that run through my mind. Who have I hurt? I hurt Pepe and Tony by bringing my mess to their wedding. I hurt Sky when I get so messed up that she has to take care of me. I hurt myself. I hurt myself most of all. And maybe I'm okay with that. Maybe that's who I am.

"I don't know," I tell him. I flip the pages of the book over and over again until Ransom stares at my hands.

"I want you to try something today."

"You're not going to make me run laps again, are you?"

He smiles softly. "I want you to have dinner in the main hall."

"You want me to make friends."

"Not necessarily. Being friends with people involves trust. Trust is hard to come by. I want you to open yourself up to the possibility of getting to know the people here. I think you might be surprised."

I don't tell him that I don't like surprises.

CHAPTER 10

The dining hall is bustling. It has the feel of a small-town diner and smells like burning oil and french fries. It's burger night and Lunchman Larry grills, while one of the patients mans the fixing stations.

I load up my burger with lettuce, tomatoes, pickles, onions, guacamole, and ketchup. I smile at Larry, and he gives me extra fries.

I feel nervous again. Sure, I like to think I have thick skin and a general New-York-don't-care attitude, but as I stand in the middle of the room, I get that terrible feeling of not belonging. I kept telling myself that I didn't want to make friends with these people. But for the first time I wonder if they feel the same way about me.

Pete and his table seem inviting, but I think I'm too dark for them. I don't see Maddie anywhere, which is weird because she's always here.

The counselors are spread all over. They don't separate themselves, but eat with the patients. The longer I stand here without somewhere to go, the more my hands start to tremble.

Get a grip, River Thomas.

"Hey, New York," Vilma, the Hispanic girl from Hutch's group, shouts at me. "Come here. Sit."

I'm so relieved that I practically sprint to sit beside her.

Then I realize Hutch is at the table, and I knock over my drink.

"I'm so sorry," I shriek.

"It's okay," Hutch says, grabbing a bunch of napkins to mop up the water.

Some of the girls giggle behind their hands.

"So," the dark-haired girl with the runny nose I met on my first day says, "you finally decided to come down from your lair."

"Yeah, we have a bet going," Fran says. "Julie thinks you're a vampire. I said you were maybe a cutter, but now that I look at you, you haven't got a scratch on you except that scar on your thigh. What's that from anyway?"

"Guys," Hutch says warningly. "Ease up, she hasn't even touched her food yet."

Vilma slams her hand on the table, and gives a telling look at Hutch and me. "Fran, what did I tell you not to say?"

Fran smacks her hand on her head. Then covers her mouth. "Sorry. Gambler. I'm sorry. We were just kidding."

I grab my burger with both hands. "I went for a run today. In the daylight. So your vampire theory is out. You're shitty at reading people."

Hutch cocks his eyebrow in my direction. Is he just going to sit there, or is he going to tell them to stop? Is he "off duty" all of a sudden?

Vilma flicks a fry at Fran.

"Vampires can go out in the daytime," Julie says. "They sparkle."

"I'm a vampire purist," I say, biting more of my burger than is polite. But if I have something to occupy my mouth, I'll have more time to think before I speak. I can't help but look at Hutch and think of something better to do with my mouth. I wonder if he's thinking the same thing, because suddenly he looks away from me.

"What about the scar?" Fran asks.

I look around the dining hall and try to catch Ransom just to give him a side-eye. My hand instinctually goes to my thigh where my pearly white scar is. I try to block the memory of it by replacing it with something better—Hutch's naked body walking away from me. *Damn*, he said. *Damn yourself*, I said. I think I damned us both.

"River, you don't have to answer that. Fran, what did we talk about this morning?"

"I'm just curious," she says. "Besides, she might just hide in her room all over again, and we'll never get the chance to know."

"It's fine," I say. "And the scar is from going through a window. Broken glass."

Fran widens her eyes. She's waiting for me to tell her the circumstances, but I smirk and keep eating.

"Is that all?" I ask them. "I have to say, I'm a little disappointed."

"For now," Vilma says. "Maybe you can help us figure something out."

"All right, enough," Hutch says, pointing a fry all around the table. Now it's his turn to be clumsy. He almost knocks his water over, but his reflexes are better than mine.

The girls hoot and holler.

"What's going on?" I ask.

"We're trying to figure out what Hutch's girlfriend looks like."

My daddy liked to tell his friends, "You don't want to go up against my baby girl. She's got the meanest poker face in all the city." I think he'd be really disappointed right now as I choke on a fry.

"I still have to learn to chew my food," I say self-deprecatingly.

"I don't have a girlfriend," Hutch says quietly. I don't know if it's for my benefit or to quell the rumor mill. "And I'm starting to feel pretty uncomfortable with this conversation."

"Come on, Hutch," Fran says. "It's just a game. It's not like you guys have bought any new gossip magazines in over a year."

Vilma turns to me to fill me in. "We think he's totally full of shit. He's been in lala land for a week now. Usually he's all quiet and cool, but lately there's something off."

"Yeah, I catch him grinning to himself when he thinks no one is looking."

Hutch shuts his eyes. "Okay, enough. Helen's going to kill me."

"No way, you're her favorite," Vilma says. "It's River's turn to guess. I say he's into Latin girls. You're part Spanish right?"

"That's another bet we've got going on," Fran says, then

clamps her fist over her mouth. "Sorry."

"I say he's into blondes," Julie says. "But the Playboy Bunny type, sorry River."

I roll my eyes. "You're all wrong."

"Okay," Hutch says, holding his hands up. "You're all going to get me fired. No bets. Especially you."

"Chill. I'm not taking a bet. I'm just going to state a fact. I see you with a pretty brunette. Someone small, but athletic. Someone sweet and polite. Someone nice. Someone you can trust. She probably rides horses and knows the difference between a dinner fork and a salad fork. Really put together."

I lean back in my chair and hold his stare. I can feel the other girls watching us. I can feel their giddy energy as they wait for one of us to blink. Suddenly, I feel like I'm back at a table again, confident that I have an excellent hand. Does he see what I'm doing? I want him to say yes. I want him to say that I've figured out his type so that no one will ever think he could be with a girl like me.

Hutch blinks. He smiles that heartbreaking smile of his and throws up his hands. "You got me."

The girls cheer and holler, patting me on the back. This time, Ransom looks over his shoulder and gives me a thumbs-up. I want to flip him the bird, but Hutch is getting up.

"I think I've had enough torture for the day." He glances my way, then busses his tray and heads outside.

"That ass is dangerous," Fran says, now that he's gone.

"Do you think it might be a patient?" Julie whispers.

My heart gives a guilty little thump.

Vilma shakes her head. "Doubtful. He's a total teetotaler. Remember when he got that last counselor arrested for smuggling in drugs?"

"Wait, what?" I ask. Also, considering I met Hutch at a bar, he is most definitely not straight-edge.

"About two months ago," Fran says, like she's reciting a story from People magazine, "there was a girl who overdosed. Hutch found drugs in the counselor's office."

"Really?" I ask. "That's something they neglected to put in

the pamphlet."

"Do you really think he's into brunettes?" Julie asks hopefully.

"Maybe." I smile. "I was just guessing."

"That man can have anyone in the world," Vilma tells her. "What would be want with an addict like you?"

Julie frowns, and eats her food.

Vilma is right. What would Hutch want with an addict? Still, hearing that he's had a smile on his face for a week, I get a funny feeling in my stomach. Because it was me. I put that smile there. And that's a bet I'd put money on.

CHAPTER 11

So maybe Ransom was right. Vilma, Fran, and Julie are okay. Fran is a terrible gossip, Julie is a bit depressing, and Vilma is painfully honest. But they're still real. They're unflinching about their addictions, and a part of me feels terrible for assuming they were in denial about themselves.

Maybe the one who's in denial is me.

They convince me to stay for the bonfire after dinner. A few yards behind the facility is a giant circle of stacked stones. Logs create a circle of benches around a roaring fire pit. The flames are the same color as the sunset. I inhale the smoky air, the smell of cedar. The air is so clean it *hurts* as it expands in my lungs.

"I've never made s'mores," I confess, taking a branch from the assembly table.

"What?" Helen says. She holds a branch with five smaller branches. It looks like a hand, and the marshmallows at the ends look like fat white finger stubs.

I shrug. "I've never been camping. I grew up in a city where the biggest park is manmade and the trees are transported from other places."

"Still," Stevens says. "I'm from Detroit and even I've been camping."

"I'm doing it now, aren't I?" I sass him.

"This isn't camping," Helen assures me. "We're doing a camping trip at the end of the month. You should sign up."

I make a face, and they laugh at me. I find a spot around the fire, and am just starting to toast my marshmallows when I notice Maddie coming down from her room. There's something different about the way she walks. She's trying to keep herself steady, and even though she's doing a hell of a job, I notice the difference. She slinks her way around the fire and settles onto a log bench. She huddles under her oversized hoodie and shivers. It isn't exactly cold.

"Maddie!" Fran shouts from the other side of the fire. "Missed you at dinner. Here, I saved you some marshmallows. What's wrong?"

"My stomach hurts. I think it was the bacon this morning." Maddie manages a weak smile. One look at her and I know she's high. But how could she be high?

"Yeah," Fran says. "I felt gross too. I think Lunchman Larry is trying to poison us."

I think back to what the girls said about Hutch finding the drugs with the counselor. She sneaked out two nights ago, but she's been fine since then. Maybe I wasn't looking…

I look at the counselors, and I wonder if I should tell someone. Sky would tell me, *Yes! Say something!*

But I've still got months here, and my self-preservation tells me that I can't be the girl who snitches. Maddie leans her head against Fran's shoulder and giggles as she eats her marshmallow. Maybe she really does have food poisoning. Maybe I just want to find something wrong because everything's too perfect.

"How's your first s'more?"

Hutch is standing beside me. His presence startles the thoughts out of my head. All I see and feel is him.

"Let's find out," I say.

Avoiding Hutch is going to be harder than I thought. I wonder if he's thinking the same thing. For me, it's that he's everywhere. He's as big as the roaring fire. He's the cool, end-of-summer breeze. He's the impossible blanket of stars and skies. He's the bearer of graham crackers.

"So what," I ask, "I make a sandwich?"

"It is so much more than a sandwich. It's a little bite of heaven."

"I don't know what heaven's supposed to taste like. Do you?"

"I do." For a moment, Hutch looks at me. He hasn't been

making much eye contact. Not the way he looks at everyone else. But now, he watches me, and his answer sinks into my skin. The implication is ripe with the things we are not supposed to be doing.

I clear my throat.

He breaks off a piece of chocolate, and instructs me to hold out my flaming marshmallow.

"Don't let it burn too much. You have to blow it out."

"Finally, something I'm good at."

He acts like he didn't hear me, but I catch the vein in his throat throb.

"Okay, pull."

"Why is making s'mores so sexy?"

"River."

"*Hutch.*" I pull the stick out, while he smooshes the sandwich together. It oozes down his fingers. I want to lick those fingers.

I bite down and let the sugar melt on my tongue. "That's the second best thing I've had in my mouth all week."

Vilma catches the last of my words. She saunters over in that cool way of hers. "Dirty girl. What was the first?"

Hutch looks like he's carefully waiting for my answer. I wonder if he thinks I'm that much of a loose cannon. Like I'm going to rat him out or put him in a precarious situation. I hope he knows I wouldn't do that. I hope he knows that I'll protect both of us.

"Whiskey," I blurt out.

"Damn," Vilma says. "I miss drinking. Not the hangover part, but right in the middle when you start to feel *nice*, you know?"

I nod. Why did I have to say that? Now Fran, poor girl, chimes in. "I miss the numbness."

More people catch onto what we're talking about. They gather around. What do you miss, River Thomas?

I miss the moment where I wait to see if my bet was a good one. I miss knowing I was right. I miss my friends and my dad and coffee with a kick. I miss my own bed and noisy Manhattan streets and shitty bars and rigged jukeboxes and rude waitresses.

LIFE ON THE LEVEL

I miss wishing I were somewhere else. I can't share any of these things. I hold them too close to my heart.

"I miss orgasms," Debbie says.

"I miss the high of not knowing if I'll live through the night."

"I miss my kids."

Ransom nods from across the fire. "I miss my friend."

"I miss my dad," I say, and no one is more surprised than I am that I'll admit that to a group of strangers.

There's a hush that falls over us. I've never been around people like this before. I've only surrounded myself with people who understand me. No judgment. Sky and Leti. They always love me and want the best for me. But in their love, even in their toughest love, they couldn't say no to me. Here, it's the toughest kind of love because it comes from strangers. Strangers who are going through the same thing as me.

If there was any doubt that I should be here, it's gone.

CHAPTER 12

The nights don't get better. And when I do sleep, the dreams get worse. I see a man with a hideous scar chasing after me. Taylor makes his way into my dreams, too. He mops blood from the floor and calls me "girly."

Some nights I can hear other girls on my floor crying. It must be loud because the walls are mostly soundproof.

Some nights I walk around the facility. I feel like a ghost wandering around. I'm not exactly supposed to be out of bed.

I walk down the corridor. I'm pretty good at sneaking around and not getting caught. I firmly believe you can't truly know what goes on in a place unless you see it when the lights are out. It's like seeing a show behind the scenes or the sausage being made. It might not always be pretty.

Once I saw the writer girl asleep in the computer room. Another time I saw the front desk clerk follow one of the rehab techs into a closet. I haven't seen anyone sneaking *out* of the building since that first time. Maybe it was a one-time orgy thing. Who knows what people do out here in the middle of nowhere?

I lie to myself in thinking that I'm not out of bed hoping I'll bump into Hutch again. I tell myself I just like being awake in the middle of the night. I've even gotten used to the taxidermy on the walls, although in the middle of the night it feels like the dead animal heads are watching me. I head down to the kitchen. I wear socks to keep my feet from making any sounds. When I get closer to the cafeteria, I hear a crunching noise. I take another step to the kitchen doors.

Then there's a shadow walking towards me. I duck behind the garbage can, and try as best as I can to be quiet. My heart thunders in my ears. Taylor comes strolling out of the kitchen with a black bag thrown over his shoulder.

Then Maddie stumbles out after him and loud-whispers, "Wait up!"

She has another black bag over her shoulder. They run into the back of the house.

Now, I can do one of two things: I can go back to my room and try to get sleep, or I can follow them. If they didn't have garbage bags flung over their shoulders I'd think they were just sneaking off to bone.

Before I can talk myself out of it, but after giving them a good enough head start, I follow Maddie and Taylor out the door.

Stepping into the cold night is almost enough to make me turn around. But the more steps I take through the grassy path, the more I commit. I get a terrible feeling in the pit of my gut. Even with what I've seen in my most terrible moments at backroom poker nights, I'm still not ready for what I might see.

What is in those bags? Are they stealing our entire supply of chocolate and Doritos? How bad could it possibly be in *Montana*?

Have I really spent my whole life thinking that people from the city are worse than people from the middle of nowhere?

Dear River, make better choices.

At least I'll get to tell Sky that my time here had a little bit of an adventure. Making my way up a hill in the dark to see what the sketchy ranch hand is up to, I realize that if this were a scary movie, as the non-virginal blonde, I'd die. I'd die so dead. And it might not even be the murderer that would kill me. I hear things—animals? I hope they're animals—making noises nearby. I mean, University of Montana's mascot isn't the grizzly bear because there's only one of them in the area. Did Helen even tell me how many bears were nearby?

I stop moving as I crest a small hill. From up here I can see the dilapidated barn, and a sense of relief washes over me. It's lit from the inside. If I wait for the wind to blow the right way, I think I can hear music. Suddenly, I know exactly what I'm going to find.

Then I hear voices coming from behind me. I recognize Vilma's bossy tone and Fran's panicked whispers. I throw myself onto the ground. I haven't done this much hiding since I lived with my mother. I forgot what hiding was like until now. I lie perfectly still, hoping the dark and the wild grass will shield me. Luckily, the women seem to be just as preoccupied with the lions and tigers and bears that prowl this countryside as I was. Fran squeals and complains about the dark, and Vilma shushes her, reassuring Fran that they're going to be fine.

I have to say, I'm a little hurt that I wasn't invited to this party. But as the new girl, I guess I haven't been trusted with whatever illegal activities are going on here.

Turn back, the little Sky voice tells me. You won't find anything good there. I'm not even sure what I'm looking for, and I mean that in both the literal and metaphorical sense of things.

All I know is that information is a powerful thing. My daddy knew that. Hell, even Hutch told me that. When the coast is clear, I keep walking toward the barn. I wonder if this can count as my daily hiking activity. (I know, I know—it can't.) I haven't had this much exercise since the summer in the city when my train stopped working and I had to walk everywhere for two days.

When I finally make it to the barn, I keep to the outside walls. Vilma and Fran go through the door. The thing is a safety hazard but there's no point in fixing something that's supposed to be broken, I guess.

"Splinters!" Fran cries out.

I stumble into something metal—I think it's a pail. I hiss through the pain in my foot. No one hears me over the terrible hip-hop music, and no one comes out.

What would they do if I just turned up? I find a big enough crack in the wall and crouch down. I feel like a creeper right now. Is this why I came to rehab? To stake out the illicit activities going on under the counselors' noses? Why am I surprised, really? I think it's just human nature to break the rules.

I look through the peephole. There's a wooden slab that passes for a table on top of bales of hay. Not everyone is from the rehab center though. People with gaunt faces lay on heaps of hay, staring at the ceiling. I see everything from joints to bumps being taken from the backs of hands.

Oh, Vilma. Don't do it.

I'm tired of hurting people. Isn't that what she said? Does she still mean it?

I'm not one to be all holier-than-thou. I'm not one to judge them. What would I be doing if I had been invited to join?

When I see him, my body is filled with rage. Taylor Patrick. His was the voice I heard on my run. Here, he's the king of the castle. He pats Maddie on the head as she lays out snacks on the table, along with cartons of cigarettes and other kinds of drugs. The only thing that's missing is syringes. It's hard to miss the bulge in his pocket where he keeps shoving money.

He takes a bottle of whiskey. The amber color is hazy in the dark. How much does he put away while taking advantage of the people he's supposed to be helping? How many people are in on this?

I watch Vilma go over to the table where Taylor is holding court. He's surrounded by girls in ripped shorts and trucker hats. They look like they're barely out of high school. One of them makes herself a drink in a red Solo cup. I feel like I'm stuck in a country song that doesn't end well. But do they ever end well?

Vilma looks over her shoulder. She scratches the inside of her wrists. I can't hear what Taylor is telling her, but I know how this works. First one's on the house, anywhere you go. He's giving her a little taste, making sure she'll come back for more.

I watch her indecision. She shakes her head, then takes one of his cigarettes instead. I want to beat the shit-eating grin off his face. I walk further along the barn wall and come across another hole. This time I see something that makes my heart skip. A poker table.

It looks brand new. The top is properly green, and I can see the plastic on the side of one of the table legs. There are five players. Four bearded dudes sit in a circle, their fat hanging out the sides of their sleeveless shirts. The fifth one chomps down on a cigar. He reminds me of my daddy, just in the way he holds his cards and puffs on that cigar. He doesn't make much chatter with the other guys at the table. That's where they're different.

My daddy might have been a lot of things to a lot of different people, but everyone loved him. I have his blue eyes, and his blonde hair. Some people used to tell us we looked exactly alike, but really I look like my mother.

I want to get closer.

I want to smell the cigar smoke and sit at the table and watch the other players trying to watch me.

Maybe I'm not as strong as I thought.

I can feel my insides waver even more when the dealer starts to shuffle. Crack, shuffle, crack. There's the small blind and the big blind, and someone else shuffling a second deck. It's clear they don't know each other. I bet they're truck drivers. Except one, who has a gun on his hip in a deep brown leather holster. He's got tattoos, and an emblem, and for the first time I notice the way his pant leg caves in at the knee. I bet he's a wounded soldier.

I realize my hands are shaking again.

I press them against the barn walls to stop it.

I start to stand when I see the pothead on the bale of hay looking at me. He squints to make sure I'm not some figment of his imagination.

"Hey!" he shouts at me.

My heart rises to my throat.

"Hey!" He points, trying to get Taylor's attention, but his words are failing him.

Luckily for me, I've already turned around. I run faster and harder than I ever thought I could, and I don't stop until I'm in my room. I run the shower, strip, and jump under the cold stream, afraid that if I don't, I might throw everything away for one more game.

CHAPTER 13

In the morning it feels like a dream. I'm cold, and my hair is still damp. I lie in bed for a long time, replaying last night. The pothead doesn't know me. Besides, the most he would have seen of me was an eye and maybe part of my face. My eyes feel swollen, but at least my hands aren't trembling. I've never reacted that way to a poker table before. It scares me how much I wanted to deal myself in. It scares me how much I wanted to throw everything away. I even considered giving Taylor my money.

Is my disdain for Taylor the only thing keeping me from gambling?

If that guy hadn't seen me, what would have happened?

I brush my teeth, then make my way downstairs. I've slept through breakfast, and I'm glad not to have to socialize. My skin feels too tight. My head throbs from all sorts of withdrawal. I pace around the first floor, unable to figure out what I want to do. It's my day off from sessions. I could go to the art room, where Vic from Iowa (cocaine and fire) is working on a clay sculpture. Or the library, where Linnette from California (alcohol) is working on her novel. I could go and get a riding lesson from Jillian, the equine instructor. I could go back to my room and hide under my covers until these feelings stop taking over my body.

"River!" Helen shouts at me from the entrance.

"Hey." I walk over to her.

"What are you doing?"

I shake my head and try to put on a smile. "Trying to find something to do."

"Great. Go put some boots on. We're going hiking."

I look down at my feet, then back at her. "Do you really think I own hiking boots?"

Five minutes later, I run back downstairs in my black, clunky military boots. I got them at Trash & Vaudeville back home. I feel incredibly out of place in my denim shorts and Fleetwood Mac T-shirt. Everyone else is in polo shirts and khaki shorts and Timberlands.

Except for Hutch. He's in cargo pants that highlight his massive calves and big leather boots. His T-shirt is white and well worn, and there's already a wet splotch on the chest where he's sweating. He looks me up and down and smirks. I want to lick that smirk.

"You guys are a fanny pack away from a Park Ranger cult," I say.

"Let's go, Joan Jett," Helen says. I think if she could pull me by the ear, she would.

Despite some side-eyes and general glares at my short shorts, I think this is going over pretty well.

On the way out, we pass Taylor. He's on his smoke break. He waves at everyone leaving, and promises Helen that he's going to work on the leak in the men's bathroom. I do my best to avoid looking at his face. If I look at him, my rage from last night will return.

"Bye River," Taylor tells me.

I can't help but look at him. It's a natural reflex when someone calls your name in public. He smiles. I decide I don't like his smile. It's artificial. It's makes his face squish together from trying too hard. He doesn't call anyone else's name, just mine. I give him the cool-person nod, and walk a little bit faster to catch up to the others.

Once we're out of Taylor's sight, I drag behind. Mostly because I'm tired from yesterday, but also because I keep stopping to marvel at the nature. Growing up surrounded by concrete, where the only bits of grass are in designated rectangular patches on the sidewalk, I'm amazed at everything I see. In New York, nature is sectioned off by blocks. Here, nature is wild. It reaches high into the sky. The trees and branches look like they're waking up from a long sleep and stretching. Birds fly freely, openly. Animals look at *us* like we don't belong.

Julie falls behind the group and walks beside me. "I didn't bring hiking boots either."

I laugh. "See? I'm not the only one."

She smiles meekly, then glances at Hutch. That's the reason she's here. She's got the biggest crush on him. I want to tell her that it's not going to end well, but I should be telling myself the same thing too.

I realize Julie and I have one thing in common. She wasn't invited to last night's barn black market either. I wonder if she knows anything about it.

"I heard you last night," she says. "I stopped crying after the third week. You'll get there."

Was I that loud or was she listening at my door?

I nod silently, then hop over a fallen log. "What was the one thing that made you cry?"

"Missing my family mostly. I know they hate me now. I messed up too many times. After a while, people stop having hope that you'll get better. That's the one thing I wish I could get back. Not even for me, but for them."

It's hard to believe that Julie is only nineteen. I'm twenty-four going on twenty-five, but sometimes it feels like I'm going on a hundred. I feel old and hard and withered and I don't know how to make it stop.

"What about you?" she asks. "What were you missing?"

Whatever I tell her, it's going to end up snaking its way through whomever she speaks to. Some people just can't help it. Some people just need to speak and don't realize that they might be hurting someone in the process.

"My dad," I say.

She pats my back. We've fallen behind quite a bit now. The trail is harder, and my breathing gets rougher the steeper the incline. My thigh muscles burn from sprinting last night, but at least there's a cool breeze.

Hutch turns around and walks over to get us. He's got a backpack full of granola bars and water bottles. His skin is shiny with sweat, and the closer he gets, the more I can smell it. I hate being sweaty, but I like being sweaty with him.

"You ladies okay?" he asks.

"Is he talking to us?" I ask Julie. "Where are these ladies he's talking to?"

Julie blushes scarlet, and walks past us like there's a fire at her heels.

I bite my lip. "See what you did?"

"Me?" He turns around to walk beside me. "What did I do?"

"Don't even."

"How can I even without knowing what I did?"

I look at him from the corner of my eye, but don't turn my face. "A blind man can see that girl has the biggest crush on you."

He shakes his head. "River."

"I'm just telling the truth. It's not like it's a secret."

"Is there anything I can do to let her down gently?"

"Give her a new counselor? Slice up your face to make yourself hideous? Stop being so understanding and kind? You know, be a regular man."

"I am a regular man." There's a branch in the way, and he pushes it down to let me walk first.

"The fact that you think you're a regular, normal man tells me that you live in some sort of fabricated world that isn't real."

"The fact that you *don't* think this is regular man behavior tells me—"

"That I live in the real world?"

"Are you always so contrary?"

"What do you think?"

He turns to look at me. I can feel his dark eyes searching my face, but I won't look at him. Looking at him does funny things to me. Looking at him will throw me back into a tailspin of missing something that was never mine to begin with. I made the choice. I picked him, and when it was over, I left him.

We fall into an easy stride. Too easy. Being with him shouldn't be this comfortable. I'm incredibly aware of his presence. He's too tall and too big not to notice.

"Have you been able to sleep?" he asks.

"Is this normal-man Hutch asking, or counselor Hutch asking?"

He pulls on the straps of his backpack. "I don't always separate them. Though… I want to when I'm with you."

Maybe he doesn't separate himself. But I do. There's the cowboy I met at the bar with his strong hold and firm kisses, and then there's the counselor with his easy voice and banter.

"I had some Percocets with me when I came in," I tell him. "In my bra lining."

He stops dead in his tracks. He runs his hands through his thick, dark hair. "River…"

"Relax, Officer Cowboy." I chuckle, and let him catch up to me. "I threw them out. I didn't have even one. But now I can't sleep. It's impossible. I haven't gotten more than four hours a day since I got here. My brain won't shut off, and it's too quiet all the time, and I'm tired."

"So hiking was the answer?" I can't tell if he's playing with me or just being sarcastic.

"You try saying no to Helen. She's already pointed out that I have the least amount of 'participation' marks. It's not like I'm getting a prize at the end. And if you tell me that the prize is some hippie bullshit like fulfillment, I will shove you down this hill and blame it on a mountain lion."

He chuckles for a long time. Now there's the kind of smile I like. "There aren't mountain lions around these parts. Only grizzlies and deer."

My fear of the wilderness from last night becomes acute. I look over my shoulder, but all I see are trees. Hutch just laughs at me.

"You're such a city slicker."

I reach out and jab him on his bicep. It's like hitting stone. I pull my hand back and massage my knuckles, ignoring the tickle I get in my belly after touching him. Meanwhile, he keeps his gaze on the trail up ahead, his thumbs hooked into the loops of his backpack.

"What do you do instead?" he asks after a while.

"Huh?" Sweat drips from my entire body. How is this supposed to be a fun activity?

"When you can't sleep?"

I walk around the facility, and discover black market dealings. Mostly I lie awake thinking about Hutch, the structure of his face, the feel of his hands. The memory is starting to fade away, so I have to concentrate to remember.

I clear my throat. "I think about the past. Things I can't change. Minutia."

"Tell me," he says. I remember when we first met, and he tried so hard to get me to divulge things about myself. It's the same now, only I'm not trying to remain anonymous. As much as I don't want to admit it, I want to tell him.

"Like, a few years ago I went to search for my mom. My dad warned me that I wouldn't find what I was looking for, but…"

"But no one tells you what to do," he finishes for me.

"Exactly," I say, laughing. "Except this time I think, what if I had listened to my dad *just that once*. He never told me what to do, so it was a big deal for me. I was just afraid that maybe she was sorry and didn't know how to apologize. Maybe she was too afraid to make the first move. Maybe she wanted me in her life but didn't know how."

We walk and walk, and the hill gets steeper. My heart races from trying to get up this hill and reliving this story. Why am I even telling him this voluntarily?

"Did you find her?"

I nod. "She wasn't hard to find. She still lived in our old apartment. Buzzed me right in. I guess she thought I was someone else, because there she was, my mother. I didn't recognize her at first. She just looked so… worn. It was like the life had been drained right out of her and there was just bad skin and bones left. But still, there she was, doing lines off her glass table. And you know what she said to me? Do you *know* what she said to *me*?"

When I turn to look at him, he's already watching me. "What?"

"'At least you didn't get your father's nose.' Can you fucking believe that? 'Hi Mom, haven't seen you in almost a decade. I'm your fucking spitting image.'

"You know, I would love to look like my dad. That way every time I look in the mirror I could look at someone who loved me."

He tries to grab my hand. I pull away. I feel like I'm getting strangled by the past. Hutch whispers my name. The compassion on his voice might just break me.

"I'm sorry," I say. "I'm not good at being touchy and emotional at the same time. And don't tell me it's okay."

We walk quietly. In this incline we can see the others again. Julie stops and waits for us to catch up, but she's too shy to rejoin us. It's just as well, because I don't want to be around anyone else. I don't like people seeing me this way.

I bite the inside of my lip until it's raw and bleeds a little bit. Hutch hands me a water bottle.

"I wasn't going to tell you it's okay," he says.

"You weren't?"

He shakes his head. "That's just something to say when you don't know what else to say. The other alternative is 'it could be worse,' but what if this is as bad as it gets? What I was going to say was, I know how you feel."

I finish half the water bottle in one gulp, then pour a little bit over my head. I hand it back to Hutch, and the first thing he does is drink from it. Look at that, he wants my germs.

"Let me guess," I say. "Broken home. Juvenile delinquent brother, alcoholic father. You went to shrink college to help people."

He laughs, then returns the empty bottle to the backpack. "Close. My brother was a juvenile delinquent, but the judge felt bad for him because he, unfortunately, knew my mom. My brother got himself straight, and now he's a fire fighter up in Washington. It's very impressive if you like tattoos and surliness, I guess. We see each other during Christmas. My dad wasn't the alcoholic. My mom was."

"Sorry."

"And you're right. I was going to join the Marines after high school. Then I changed my mind. I always think about how my life would've been different if I'd changed a single thing about it."

"Which part?" I realize I've slowed way down. My little toe is rubbing right against my boot. I can feel blisters forming on the bottoms of my feet. Still, this is all the time I get to spend with Hutch without it looking like we're on a date. When the breeze picks up and we're in a patch of thick trees, the heat isn't so bad.

"What if I stayed home? I was tired of seeing my mother destroy herself. It felt like no matter what I did it, no matter how much I told her that I loved her, that my brother needed her, it didn't matter. She was so young when she had us. My dad was her first everything. Some hearts stay broken and no amount of love will fix 'em."

We walk in silence. I no longer hear the others ahead of us, but I don't care about keeping up. I want to reach out to him and tell him that I understand how it hurts. I know what it's like to watch one parent wither away after being left. My dad just did it in a different way. Because words aren't enough, and okay, because I've wanted to do this since I walked away from him, I reach out and grab his hand. He seems shocked. He looks down at our hands, and I wonder if he thinks this is wrong even though it feels perfect. He holds on tighter. I never want to let go. He shines that smile at me, and nothing around me—not the trees or sun or sky—is this beautiful.

Fuck, I'm in trouble.

I squeeze, and let go. "So you think if you stayed home instead of going to college, things would have turned out differently?"

"I know in my heart that they wouldn't have. The unknown has too many variables. What if I did stay, and she kept drinking the way she did? What if I kicked out every boyfriend she brought home? What if she still ended up the same? What if… I flew back while she was still alive?"

"Hutch—"

He walks a little bit faster. He scoffs at himself. "I'm sorry, I shouldn't say things like that to you."

I have to run-walk for a few seconds to catch up to him. He has stupidly long strides.

"Hey wait up." I grab him by the back of his shirt and force him to stop. "You spend every day listening to other people's troubles. It's okay to speak about your own. Besides, if anyone is going to understand mommy and daddy issues, it's me."

He lets go of a long breath and turns his body completely toward me. His deep brown eyes hold mine for a long time. He looks at my lips. I look at his. I want nothing more than to kiss him. I bet—*I know*—he wants to kiss me back. I recognize the struggle that crosses behind his eyes, wrinkling his forehead; I recognize the frustration that makes his body stiffen.

Would it be so bad if I kissed him quickly? I could say I tripped and got up on my tiptoes and landed on his face. His lips were the perfect cushions. I could kiss him and then turn around and bolt, but I can't really run in these boots anymore.

Then, I notice an animal standing between the trees. I jump away and put my arms up defensively. What do I think I'm going to do? Karate chop a deer?

"Easy," Hutch whispers, putting his hands on my shoulders. "It's just a doe."

I straighten to see the creature. I've never seen one close up before. The closest I've ever gotten to a doe is Bambi's mom in the cartoon. This doe is the most delicate creature I've ever seen. Her neck is long, with the softest-looking fur. I freeze, and she freezes. Her head twitches this way and that, turning big brown eyes on me. Like she's the one inspecting me. Like I'm the one who should be marveled at.

"Wow," I sigh. I reach out my hand to touch her, but she's spooked and darts away into the thicket of trees. "Did you see that?"

My face hurts from smiling. I hold my arms out to the trees, feeling like the queen of the forest. I decide I like hiking, despite the sweat and blisters. I spin myself in place as stray leaves fall in the wind around us. One gets lodged in the mess of my blonde curls.

I stop right in front of Hutch. He's laughing at me. He frees a red leaf from my hair, holds it by the stem, and twirls it between his fingers. He holds it out to me, like he's presenting me with a rose. I take it, letting our fingers touch.

This is wrong. I know this is wrong. He knows this is wrong. That's why he doesn't want to be *my* counselor. But somehow, I've kept looking for excuses to be near him. Hear his voice. Touch his skin. Bask in the way he looks at me.

"You're incredible, River Thomas."

I laugh, then lick my canine. "Tell me something I don't already know."

I break away from him and walk up the trail. I feel a new surge of energy. Eventually, we catch up to everyone else at the top of a hill. Hutch hands out granola bars and water bottles.

I'm out of breath and I'm pretty sure my whole face is red, but I feel alive.

Helen smiles at me. Her hair is in a tight bun at the top of her head. I can't see her eyes behind those sports sunglasses. "You good?"

I nod, breathing heavily. I turn to the valley that drops below this cliff. As I stand closer to the edge, my heart is in my throat. *Maybe things will be okay,* I think as the wind sweeps across the treetops, the rushing river, and then envelops me. I feel like I could scream and everything below would hear me. I spread my arms wide open, smiling against the wind. I've never felt this before, as if the wind will pick me up and I could *fly*.

"River!"

I don't feel myself falling until his arms are around me, pulling me back onto solid ground. My head spins. My heart races. I'm on the ground, in Hutch's arm. The grass tickles my skin. I laugh and start to sit up, but he doesn't return my smile. His eyes are wide. His lips are a taut line. He runs a trembling hand through his hair, then stands.

"What's wrong?" I ask.

"What were you thinking?"

"I—"

LIFE ON THE LEVEL

The other patients and Helen have gathered around us. I look at the spot where we just stood. I see the way they look at me—wary, curious, judgmental. I don't understand what the big deal is. Then I realize—

They all thought I was going to jump.

CHAPTER 14

I sit on the floor outside Helen's office while Helen, Hutch, and Ransom talk about me. I can't hear what they're saying, but there's a lot of going back and forth. Is Hutch telling them the things we talked about during our walk?

I add another reason to the list of reasons why Hutch and I are a bad idea. Actually, it's the same reason, just amended. That he's a counselor is the main reason, and no matter how much I'm attracted to him, and no matter how much he's attracted to me, he has to be a counselor first.

I replay the way he shouted my name, the way he jumped for me, and the look on his face afterwards.

"Trouble?" Taylor asks, walking down the hall, his keys jingling from his belt loop.

"No, it's just cooler down here," I mutter.

He keeps walking, but his laugh echoes back to me. Others walk back and forth, too. Julie gives me her tightlipped, shy smile. She holds one sleeve of her sweater in her hand and waves. Vilma throws me a stick of gum and nods, Fran at her side. Maddie stops, rocking back and forth on her heels.

"What happened?"

I cross my arms over my chest. Is it even worth defending myself? Would I come off any better if I said, "I just felt like I could fly!"

What if I stepped too far? What if Hutch was a foot out of reach? What if he hadn't been paying attention to me? No one else seemed to notice me slipping but him. He was right there, watching me.

"I shouldn't be allowed in nature," I tell her. Then to change the subject I ask, "What are you doing tonight?"

She looks taken aback. "What do you mean? Like, dinner? Want me to save you a seat?"

I shake my head. "I'm okay."

I'm saved when the office door opens. Helen stands there. "River, come here, please."

I let out a long sigh, and give Maddie a wave goodbye.

• • •

Helen's office has a deep green rug and wallpaper the color of birch wood. There are diplomas and more taxidermy displayed high up on the walls. There's also the faint smell of cigar. I notice the ashtray, and a fancy pen, the kind that's heavy and engraved.

Hutch sits to the right. His arms are crossed over his chest and he's staring at a hole in the wall. Ransom leans against the wall. I wish they would stop looking as if I were threatening to jump from the Empire State building.

"River," Helen says. She's got that concerned adult voice. I suddenly have a flashback of sitting in the Principal's office every other month. *Riv-er. We have to talk about your grades. Riv-er, do you realize what you're doing to yourself? Riv-er, are you really going to bring down your friends with you? Riv-er, I can't keep giving you more chances.*

"Guys," I say, holding up my hands. "I wasn't trying to jump. I *didn't* try to jump!"

"Can you go over what happened again?" Helen looks from Steven to Hutch. "Chris?"

For a moment, I forgot Hutch's first name. He's become something completely different in my mind.

He looks flushed and concerned. He won't look me in the eye. "River was standing too close to the ledge. When I saw her tilting forward, I reached out and grabbed her."

"Because the wind was blowing hard," I say through gritted teeth. "I was just doing the thing you all told me to do in the first place! Now you're treating me like a criminal!"

"That's not fair," Ransom says. "We're concerned when any of the patients engage in harmful behavior."

I get up, my seat scraping behind me. "Then cross my name off the fucking hiking list."

"River!" Helen says. "This is serious. This is your life."

"Really? This whole time I thought I was living someone else's life. Look, I'm a lot of things, but I'm not suicidal. Yeah, apparently I suck at hiking, but if I fell off that cliff, it would have been because I'm a fucking idiot, not because I want to kill myself. If I wanted to die, I would have tried a long time ago."

They're all the wrong things to say, but my blood is boiling. I get up and don't wait for them to speak. I slam the door on the way out. I go right out the front door, where the receptionist gives me a peppy "hello!" My response is a growl. It's not her fault. Why am I doing this? I run my hands through my hair and hold on. How can I be surrounded by wide open space and feel like the walls are closing in?

I weave through the parking lot, then remember I don't have my keys. I keep walking straight into the small patch of woods in the area. I find a huge rock and sit with my head between my knees. I take deep, long breaths. Then, I lie back and watch the sky change colors. When I close my eyes, I can picture the valley. I really did love it. I really did feel like I could fly.

I wasn't trying to jump. What if they don't believe me? What if, after my outburst, they decide to send me away?

I snap up at the sound of crunching twigs. In the amber sunset, the doe looks like her fur is made of fire. She lowers her head and eats the greens around the tree. Her long, pink tongue pushes leaves into her mouth. I was wrong. She isn't delicate. She's unafraid. She gets closer still. This time, when I reach out my hand, she licks it.

"Next time, I'll bring you an apple or something. Or is that only for horses?"

The doe nudges my hand, then, realizing it's not going to produce anything edible, walks back into the trees.

"I should go back, too."

But I don't. I sit and play with blades of grass. I braid them into long ropes that I string around my wrists. I'm making things worse by staying away. I'm just embarrassed. I don't want people looking at me like I shouldn't be playing with scissors. Besides, isn't everyone here because they've done damage to themselves or others?

Once the sun has completely set, and the temperature drops, I want to go back. But in the dark, everything looks the same.

Good going, Riv.

I get up, dust the back of my shorts and pick a direction. I don't have to go very far before I hear my name being called out in the dark. The beam of a flashlight shines around the trees.

"Here," I say unenthusiastically. "Did you send a search party?"

"No," Hutch says, walking through the trees. "Everyone's at movie night. Besides, you're not even in the woods yet. This is technically part of the parking lot."

I scoff. "River Thomas: lost in a parking lot."

He turns off the flashlight. There is only the light of the moon. "I talked to Helen. I convinced her you weren't trying to jump. I know you're not—I know you don't want to harm yourself, but Helen's lost people here before. One more sign, and she'll recommend you to psych."

"Right, because she can't trust the word of an addict so you have to vouch for me."

"Stop. You have to understand what it looked like to her. You don't exactly walk around here full of pep."

"So my general jadedness is code for suicidal? You should never go to New York."

"River."

"*Hutch.*"

He paces back and forth. I can feel his frustration radiating like waves.

His voice drops to a whisper. "You scared the life out of me. What if I'd been just a foot further away? What if I couldn't hold onto you?"

"I didn't realize I was falling forward until I felt you grab me. It's a good thing you were paying attention to me."

I let the words hang. I want him to tell me that he was watching me. I want him to admit that there's something here.

"How can I not?"

I reach out and grab his arm. His skin is hot to my touch. His muscles tense.

"Thank you." I run my hands down his arm. Our fingers entwine. I know I should pull away, but I can't. I can't let go of his hands.

"Promise," he whispers. "Promise you'll be more careful."

I nod, but he can't see that. I tug on his hand, and he edges closer. I press my other hand over his heart. It's beating as fast as mine. I move my hand up, around his neck. I run my fingers through his hair. He grabs hold of my wrists.

"We can't," he whispers.

"I know."

Still, he walks right into me, pushing me against the trunk of a tree. In the dark, I search for his lips. I kiss his chin; he kisses my nose. I hold his face with both of my hands. He grabs my waist and lifts me inches off the ground. I wrap my legs around his waist, and he keeps me pinned in place against a tree.

He kisses me. The stubble on his chin rubs my soft skin raw, but I don't ever want to stop kissing him. This feeling is like the wind when it pushed me off that cliff. My head spins, free falling. I'm not ready to fall like this, but I can't stop. I press him tighter against me. It's been two weeks since the last time we kissed. Two weeks that I've dreamt of this.

He pulls back to catch his breath. "River."

"Please don't stop."

I feel him nod against my lips. His tongue searches for mine and I push back. I bite his bottom lip. He hisses and presses me so hard I think I might melt right into the bark.

The sound of an engine revving makes us jump and break apart. We hide against separate tree trunks. Headlights shine into the area where we were kissing. I can feel my heart throbbing in every part of my body. I lick my swollen lips, then I laugh.

Hutch sighs. "I'm glad you think it's funny."

The car pulls out of the driveway. We wait a few minutes to make sure it's safe. Twigs break under my feet as I walk to him. He grabs me by my arms.

"This is wrong for so many reasons," he whispers. His

fingers play with the end of my curls. "But you make me crazy, River Thomas."

I press my finger to his lips. "Stop right there. Please. Please don't ruin it."

He takes my hands in his. He kisses each one, then presses them to his chest. It's the strangest thing a guy has ever done, but I decide I like it. "We'll talk tomorrow."

I find his face in the moonlight. I kiss him. I etch this moment into my mind. It's my first sober kiss with Chris Hutcherson, and it feels so good.

CHAPTER 15

Dear Sky and Leti,

I'm writing to both of youse to save time. Also this connection might as well be dial-up.

Yesterday I almost fell off a cliff. No big deal. My beautiful cowboy counselor saved me. The camp director has unofficially told me that I need a "buddy" the next time I do any physical activities. I feel like I'm in fucking kindergarten.

I think you'll be happy to know that I've made friends. Clearly, not one will compare to my ride-or-die bitches, but then again, no one could. I've discovered an underground black market. And by underground I mean in a barn. When in Montana, do as Montanans do. I swear on everything that I haven't gone in. The guy that runs it is a dirtbag. He should literally be made of shit. He keeps making snide comments about me. I feel like if I get enough dirt on him, he'll have to back off. I know how these guys think.

He's not the friend I was talking about. So far the person I like the most is Maddie. She's a bit annoying sometimes, but I think she's just lonely. It does gets lonely as hell. I'm lonely right now. Then there's Julie, Fran, and Vilma. Vilma has three kids she's not allowed to see. Fran and Julie aren't even old enough to drink. Can you believe that? Granted, we were drinking when we were thirteen, but at least two out of the three of us turned out well. (Don't look at me like that, Sky Lopez.)

Now, for the real reason I'm writing.

HUTCH AND I TOTALLY KISSED.

He's been trying to keep his distance, but failed. I was really upset after the director (Helen of Troy) suggested I wanted to off myself. I don't. I promise. Don't even think about it. I just failed at being a nature person. Then I was in the woods and saw a REAL DOE A DEER A FEMALE DEER. It was amazing. It was like looking at the most perfect creature, because it was just innocent and pure and not terrible like people. Then Hutch found me and we just started kissing. I'm avoiding him because I know what he's going to say. He's going to try to put a stop to it.

How can something so wrong feel so right?

Are you guys back in the States? There's a family visit thing in mid-October. It's lame, I know. And I'm in the middle of nowhere. Bring me a deck of cards and a carton of American Spirits. Kidding. Kidding. (About the cards, not the cigarettes.)

There's someone waiting to use the computer giving me a nasty look so I have to go.

Love you,
Riv

• • •

I hit send and move the arrow to sign out, but something catches my eye. I have a new e-mail address. I made this one specifically to keep in contact with Sky and Leti. No one has this address except the two of them.

But here it is, a new e-mail from king0fklubz999@gmail.com.

"Come on," Debbie mutters from the door. "I have to e-mail my boyfriend."

I roll my eyes at her. "Do you even know how to use a computer?"

"Don't you sass me, Miss Thing!"

I'm instantly sorry, but I turn back to the screen. The e-mail is marked NO SUBJECT. I click on the mouse with a clammy finger.

> I know ur hiding. I know how 2 find u.
> -K

"Are you okay?" the counselor on computer duty asks, looking up from her desk.

"Fine! Screen just froze."

Debbie huffs behind me. "They only stopped using dial-up

two years ago, what'd you expect?"

I delete the e-mail. If I could delete it a hundred times I would. I clear the inbox, then add the e-mail address to my blocked list. I close out of the browser and give my seat to Debbie. As I run out of the computer room, I bump into Hutch.

His smile vanishes when he gets a good look at me.

"River, what's wrong?"

I slap his hand away. I didn't mean to, but I just don't want to be touched right now. He pulls his hands back. He repeats himself.

"I, um—" I'm being stalked by the man whose face I scarred. "I have to go to group."

I run down the hall and shut the door behind me. I get in my seat and watch the doorways. Where is he? Is he in the state? How could he possibly know where I am? He doesn't look smart enough to be a hacker, but people always surprise you. I know someone who can help, but I need to get my cellphone and get a number. The problem is, my phone is locked away in a metal cage.

There's no one I trust enough to help me. Maddie's close with Taylor, but Taylor is the last person I want to owe a favor to. Favors are blank checks. They're get-away-with-murder cards, if you get one from the right people. My daddy used to rip up thousand-dollar ledgers in exchange for favors.

"Someone's a little tense today," Ransom says.

I try to play it off with a smirk. I have no control over my fingers, though. Two weeks without gambling and I've completely lost my cool. "I'm just sore from that nature walk."

Vilma laughs. "That's the worst kind of sore. The *best* kind of sore—"

"Come on now," Ransom says. "Let's get this show on the road. Today I want you all to think about one of the worst things that's happened to you under the influence."

There's a collective groan.

"Hear me out." Ransom paces around the room. "One of the things that helped my recovery was forcing myself to relive a lot of the terrible things I'd done. It helped me realize that I never wanted to go through that again. Facing your past is the same as facing your fears. You have to keep your eyes open." When he stands directly behind me, I know he's going to ask me to *volunteer*.

I've been pretty quiet during these sessions. I can't help but keep my thoughts to myself. I do like listening to the others. Sometimes I feel bad for thinking, "At least I'm not like that guy."

I watch Ransom watch me. I bet he's thinking about yesterday, and my outburst. The smart thing to do would be to play along. Take the heat off me so they stop thinking I belong in psych. Besides, I don't want to get stuck with the buddy system. Unless the buddy system involves making out with Hutch in the woods.

Hutch! I was a dick to him. Another reason we probably shouldn't be together. I'm a wrecking ball. I destroy everything around me after I get one good push.

I get up and play with the wrinkles on my shirt for a little while. Everyone stares at me. People here are very good at waiting.

"I'll spare you the mommy never loved me stories," I say. No one laughs. Tough crowd. "After my dad died, I told myself I'd stop. Stop everything. Gambling, partying, drinking. It's kind of hard when you work at a bar, but I did pretty well. Then a couple of months later, I started dating this guy. He grew up around the tables, just like I did. When we'd go to games I'd always hang back, smoking, and watching the other players for him. It was *indirect* gambling. Anyway, I had this chip. Just a regular blue chip, but it was my dad's favorite. Told me it was the first time he ever won and he kept it as good luck. Now it was mine.

"Eventually I got tired of just hanging back because I knew I was better than him. I got sick of watching him lose. Sometimes, I'd tell him to stay in the game, and he'd fold just to do the opposite of what I said, because he didn't like being told what to do."

"Dick," Vilma mutters, and Ransom silences her with a stare.

"Toward the end of our relationship, we went to this game in Boston with guys you don't want to fuck with. I didn't want to go, and I kept drinking because I was so nervous. They made me sit at the bar along with the other girls, and I was so *pissed* because he still wasn't *listening* to me. He was down six grand. In the scheme of things, he'd make that money back. You always make it back somehow.

"I don't know when it happened. I went to the bathroom, and he'd lost his whole hand. He started yelling at me in front of everyone. Told me I'd made him do it. I was the reason he lost. I swung at him, and he swung back. One of the bouncers threw him out. I was so pissed, and I couldn't leave like that. So I bought myself into the game. Played until sunrise. I was up about four grand. I was feeling really baller, so I went all in. It was the biggest pot of the night. I don't even remember the cards that I had, but at that point I just couldn't get out of that chair, because I had nowhere else to go.

"Did you win?" a guy asks.

I scoff, shaking my head. "Nope. I made back nine hundred bucks to get back home, but by then I just felt like I was this thing crawling from the sewers. When I left, I didn't see him until I was on the ground. I just remember glass and an alley. Some asshole must've thrown out a broken windowpane and just left it in the alleyway. There was blood everywhere. I thought I was dying. I just laid there, my leg all cut up and him standing right there, holding my dad's lucky chip."

I can see every single moment in my head. My mouth is dry and the scar on my leg is throbbing. I look at Ransom and shake my head. I can't finish the story. It's not because of what Kiernan did to me; it's what I did to him when I stood back up. We both walked away with scars. I thought I'd run as far from him as possible. Everyone I knew in New York made it clear that I was off-limits. But after that e-mail today, I know it's not over.

"Now I'm here," I say, but I won't finish the story.

There's a barrage of questions.

What happened to the chip?
What happened to him?

LIFE ON THE LEVEL

Did he go to jail?

Even if I finish the story, people have already let speculation make up the rest.

"Thank you for sharing with us, River."

I sit back with a falsely triumphant smile. Vilma goes after me. She starts to tell a story about passing out drunk in the middle of cooking. Something must've happened with one of her kids. But she can't get through the story, and it's left hanging in the air that they took them away from her.

Vic from Iowa shows us the scars he got from burning himself on purpose, and waking up to an accidental fire that killed his dog. The dog is what really gets people to say *awww*.

I don't see him until the end of the session, when Ransom is giving a pep talk that's better suited for Friday Night Lights. Hutch is leaning against the wall. Has he been there this whole time? Did he hear everything I said?

Before I can go to him, Ransom beats me to it. Hutch gives me one last glance as they exit the room.

CHAPTER 16

TWENTY DAYS SOBER

I wake up to Maddie standing over my bed.

I instinctively slap her away. "What the fuck?"

"Ow!" She dramatically holds her hand over her eyes, like I just bludgeoned her. "Is that the thanks I get for checking in on you?"

My head pulses. How can I feel hungover when it's been almost three weeks since my last drink? I blame it on the jogging and general physical exertion.

"You told me to wake you up for horsies." She says "horsies" the way a five-year-old might say it.

She's slicked her hair back and painted two stripes of pink on her cheeks. Is that an attempt at blush? I sit up on my bed and make a face at the terrible taste in my mouth.

"I'll be right down," I mutter.

"You are seriously not a morning person. I'm totally a morning person. I'm pretty sure I was born in the morning, too."

"Well, I'm pretty sure I was born at midnight."

She makes a face. I wonder if she's gone back to the barn since the last time I saw her there. I'm sure she has, but she hasn't showed any signs of using. Maybe she's getting a cut from Taylor just for being there. "Midnight in hell, apparently."

"I said I'd be right down, okay?"

"See if I ever play at being an alarm clock for you ever again."

I haven't been a morning person my whole life. My daddy used to tell me that I would sleep through the day, and as soon as the sun set, I'd be ready to play. He worked most nights as a bartender, or played the tables, and eventually he just took me with him.

Horseback riding has been a secret dream of mine since I was a little girl. It's taken me a while to warm up to actually doing it though, because up close, horses are terrifying. They're massive, powerful creatures that somehow manage to be gentle at the same time. I like to walk near the stable and brush them. Jillian Montoya runs the stables. All the patients are assigned shifts to water and feed the horses. My favorite is a white one with golden brown splotches on his sides. Jillian calls him a paint horse. His name is Apollo, and today I'm going to ride him.

Because I'm the least prepared out of everyone here apparently, Helen volunteered to buy me a pair of cowboy boots. I told her to put it on my tab, but she didn't exactly find it funny.

In my jeans, boots, and long-sleeved plaid shirt, I feel a little bit awkward. It's like I'm wearing someone else's life. Sure, I've gotten used to the routine, and I'm getting better at the talking thing, but something is off. It's like I'm a stranger to myself.

I smile like an idiot when I see Hutch in his cowboy hat and boots. We haven't spoken since we kissed, and then I hit him, and then he heard that story I told. He's certainly been making himself scarce. He hasn't even slept at the facility since the kiss happened. It's like he's getting ready to break up with me, and we're not even together. But if anyone is going to break up with anyone, I'm going to break up with him. He can't just kiss me and say nice things to me and save my life and then act like it doesn't mean anything.

"Morning," he says, while brushing his horse. Her name is Elphaba, and she's pitch black from head to toe.

"Hey."

"Hay is for horses," he says.

He's such a sexy goof, and I love it. I roll my eyes at him, but feel a twinge in my heart from this small, playful exchange. I gather around Jillian with Maddie and some of the other patients.

I feel like I'm the only one that looks nervous. For the past week I've been allowed to feed, water, and brush Apollo. It's a show of good faith, building a connection—more hippie stuff.

The worst part was getting used to the smell. The second worst part was waking up early enough to do it. Jillian is up at five a.m. and somehow manages to look peppy and bright five hours later. I envy her dark-circle-free eyes.

She claps her hands and smiles. She's on an exchange program with some equine group from Spain, and I'm pretty sure she was born riding a horse, the way she does it.

"Okay everybody. Today is the moment you've been waiting for. Some of you have ridden before, but for some of you it is your first time. No matter what, it is important that you stay calm. Horses are very sensitive to their riders. Trust your horse, and your horse will trust you, my father always said. Christopher is going to help you with the saddles. Take deep breaths if you're nervous."

"Of the horses, or of Hutch?" Maddie asks.

Jillian chuckles, and Hutch just shakes his head.

We get helmets and gloves. My gloves are a little big, but it's all they've got. Hutch throws saddle pads, then the leather saddle on Apollo's back. Suddenly, the horse seems too tall, too big. My heart starts to race, and I don't know if it's my nervousness about riding or that Hutch is standing so close.

"Why are you avoiding me?" I blurt out.

He looks over his shoulder. I'm the last one—again—and no one heard me over the horses neighing and stomping their hooves.

"We can't do this now," he says.

I'm hot with anger. I still have to hold onto his shoulder as he helps me onto my horse. Once I'm up there, I sway.

"Whoa," I say, as Apollo moves a few paces back and forth.

"River," Hutch says in his calming way. "He's just getting used to your weight."

"All hundred pounds," Maddie mutters, already mounted and trotting to my side. It only makes Apollo skittish.

"Hundred and thirty," I correct, gathering my reins.

"Whatever," Maddie mutters.

Jillian whistles to grab our attention. She rides up and down our line, inspecting every one of us, even Hutch. He looks like he's been pulled out of a John Wayne movie, in his denim shirt with pearl buttons. His jeans do something fantastic to his thighs.

Turn around, I tell myself.

"Chris," Jillian says. "You take the rear, yes?"

Hutch tips his hat. I'm the only one who thinks this is hilarious. But then, I'm the only one who freezes up. I can feel my whole body hunching forward. Every step sends a pain up my tailbone. How do guys ride these things without crushing their balls?

"You're not riding a tiger," Maddie says, turning around in her saddle. "Relax."

Easy for her to say. This isn't her first time. I watch the way they all do it. They don't bounce, but move with the horses. They also dig their heels into the horses' sides. I'm not exactly a member of PETA, but I feel bad about kicking Apollo. He seems to be enjoying lagging behind and snatching up the leaves along our path.

Hooves sound behind me. "You've got to pull on the reins. Don't let him eat. It'll spoil him."

I pout my bottom lip and brush Apollo's mane with my fingers. "Maybe I didn't feed him enough before."

"Or maybe people say 'hungry as a horse' for a reason."

Hutch holds his reins with one hand and lays the other one on his knee. He looks like he was born on a horse, too. I wonder how long it would take for me to be that comfortable riding. I sigh, and do as Hutch tells me. I squeeze my legs, and suddenly Apollo starts walking forward on his own.

"They're used to following each other, but they don't have the best attention spans. Like people."

"Says you," I tell him.

"Oh, you don't have a short attention span?"

"Maybe I do, but I don't generally like to follow anyone."

He nods in silent agreement.

"How come I don't have a cowboy hat?"

He smiles, and rides beside me instead of behind. Even though things are inexplicably weird, I don't mind. I feel calmer just talking to him.

"Because if you fall, you're going to need the helmet."

"And here I was doing such a good job of staying calm."

"It's funny," he says, "that you're so nervous."

"Oh yeah? Why's that?"

All I see is a huge smile, and the blush on his face before he tilts his hat forward. "You just make a mighty fine cowgirl, is all."

I take a deep breath and shut my eyes at the memory of me straddling him. He's so big that when he stretched out he took up almost his whole bed. I've been surviving off that memory like a super model on a single slice of toast. My skin tingles as I remember moving with him, back and forth and back and forth. Is he thinking about it too?

"You don't get to flirt with me after ignoring me for a week." I hate that it takes his smile away, but it needs to be said.

"I know, River. I'm all turned around. So let's talk about it."

"Now?"

Except we can't. Up ahead, Jillian whistles. There's a truck driving by. The old man waves at us as he drives up ahead to the road. I realize it's the first car I've seen in days outside of our parking lot. Growing up in the city, cars and sirens were just part of the ambiance. I never thought I could get used to a place without that kind of noise. I wonder, when did the shift happen?

"Are you guys ready to try trotting?"

I shake my head. "Nope. Nope. Nope."

Apollo walks in a circle as I pull his reins too hard to one side. Hutch catches up with me.

"Easy," he says. "Don't psych yourself out."

I take a deep breath. "No, I'll leave that to you."

"Funny," he mumbles. "Here, I'll go ahead. Shorten your reins and give him a kick. Not too hard, but just enough."

"That means nothing to me," I say.

Still, I do what he says. I squeal and make all kinds of scaredy-cat noises as Apollo trots behind everyone else. I can't remember if I'm supposed to squeeze my thighs or not. Either way, this is going to hurt like a bitch tomorrow morning.

Hutch makes a clicking noise with his tongue and kicks the sides of his horse. There's a challenge in his smile. He canters beside me. His body moves *with* the horse, not against her. Meanwhile, I feel more and more like a turtle. If I could retreat my head into my body, I would. I'm so tense, and I don't know how to let go. The further we go, the better everyone gets—except for me. I bring my horse to a stop. He stomps around and makes a noise that sounds a lot like a laugh.

Hutch pulls on his reins and comes to a stop beside me. "What's wrong?"

"I don't know, it just doesn't feel right. I always thought I'd be a natural, you know? But I think I'm starting to realize that I'm not really good at anything other than poker. What am I supposed to do when I leave here?"

"River—"

"Don't River me, Hutch. Let me freak out, okay?"

"Okay. I'll freak out with you."

He lets me ride ahead. The others have stopped trotting and now race. Apollo makes a raspberry sound, and I fear even my own horse is laughing at me.

"Is it weird that I felt more at ease stealing my dad's car when I was fifteen than this?"

"That's a hunk of metal," he says. "This is another living thing. Riding requires more trust."

Hutch leads my horse with his. They walk side by side. As the trees fall away, and we come onto an open field that goes on as far as I can see, I commit this moment to memory.

"When I was a kid we lived up at Flathead Lake," he tells me, "we lived near a stable. I'd ride my bike five miles to go look at the horses. My dad didn't send any money and my mom drank up whatever we had. One of the stable hands would see me standing there with my bike, staring. One day he called me over and put me to work."

"How old were you?"

"Thirteen. The first horse I ever rode threw me right off. Damn thing was skittish as hell, but he was my favorite."

I laugh, trying to picture what Hutch would have looked like as a kid. "At least my dad's Chevy never threw me off its back."

"See, you've already got one up on me."

Out of nowhere, I realize we're going faster. I swallow a gulp of air and relax my back. I feel more confident, so I kick Apollo. He picks up speed. I let out an excited yelp.

"Atta girl," Hutch shouts behind me.

I don't look back as we race across the green grass. There isn't quite a feeling like this. The wind beats against my face. The sun shines, peeking from behind clouds that resemble mountains. The other patients ride freely, zigzagging back and forth in the clearing up ahead. There's still too much space. So much so that I can feel like I'm riding all by myself.

After a while, I pull on the reins. Apollo comes to a halt in front of a leafy bush and starts chomping away. I rub his neck, and pull at bits of hay stuck in his mane.

"I did it, Apollo," I tell him.

While Apollo eats, I get to watch Hutch ride. His shirt's come undone a few buttons, so it blows open to reveal the glory of his chest hair. I never used to like chest hair, but on Hutch, I got used to it in seconds. He snaps the reins. The black horse zooms across the field with him, the mountains and sky their backdrop. His hat flies right off his head. Even as far away as he is, he looks up to where I'm resting, like he knows I've been watching him all along. Like he was showing off just for me.

I wonder, how different would my life be in a place like this? Is that all it takes to change the way you live? Pick up and move somewhere new. Put on new clothes. Be a different person. I wonder.

As we ride back, I fall somewhere in the middle of the line. This time Hutch takes the lead, and Jillian takes the rear. I feel myself getting tired and hungry. How do people eat granola bars like it's satisfying to munch on something that leaves the roof of your mouth raw?

When we get back to the stables, Jillian and Hutch help us get down. I wait my turn, intending to help put the saddles away because I want to be able to do this again.

Taylor comes out of the stable. His shirt is drenched in sweat.

"Need some help?" he asks.

"I'm good."

"If you'd rather wait for Hutch, just say so," he says, smirking.

Guilt and anger make me speak before I can think better on it. "I'd rather wait for anyone but you."

His face gets scrunched up and mean-looking. He runs off with the pail he's carrying. Deep down, I know Taylor's not someone I want to cross around here. No matter what brave face I want to put on.

Apollo goes crazy, neighing and bucking under me. I've let go of the reins, and now I can't get them back.

"Easy," I shout. "Whoa!"

But none of my words calm him down. Something's spooked him. I grab a handful of mane to keep myself on his back, but that makes it worse. He rears his front legs high in the air. I hit the ground hard, on my back. My whole head rattles.

It takes three tries before I can breathe again, and two more before I can open my eyes.

My name is shouted from all different directions. Then I'm floating. I'm on a cloud.

"Don't close your eyes," Hutch whispers. "Please, River. Look at me."

I shake my head, and instantly wish I'd kept myself still. "I can't. There's five of you."

My head rolls to the side. The last thing I see is Taylor, standing at the fence with a great big smirk on his face.

CHAPTER 17

"What. Is. That?" I hiss.

"Good morning, sunshine," a male's voice tells me.

I grab for my covers and try to pull them over my head, but they get snagged on my neck brace. "Can you close the drapes?"

"They are closed," he says.

The pain in my mind is *crushing*. I've never felt pain like this before. A few seconds later, as I try to sit up, I realize that every inch of me is in pain. Muscles I didn't even know I had are throbbing. I, River Thomas, whimper.

"Who the hell are you?" I mutter.

"I'm your nurse."

"Hey, Nurseman," I say, "get on with the painkillers."

He shakes his head. His smile is youthful. I bet he's younger than me. Fresh out of school. His cheeks are flushed, and his brown eyes are—I can't look anymore. It's too bright in here. My people assessment is going to have to wait.

"Sorry. We can't give you anything for the pain."

"Are you fucking with me? I fell off a horse!"

"And Debbie broke her foot trying to run away. You should've heard the things she called me."

"What does she have to run away for? It's not like she's in prison."

He doesn't answer me, which tells me all I need to know. Some people, like me, are here voluntarily. But most of them are here because otherwise they'll lose their kids of end up in jail.

"How long was I out?"

He checks some stuff off a clipboard, then comes to my besides and fluffs my pillows. Even the slightest shake of my bed sends needle prick into the inside of my skull.

"You've been in and out of it for a day."

"I can't even remember," I say.

"At least you're finally catching up on your sleep."

"Who says I haven't been sleeping?" I tell myself to calm the hell down. But when have I ever not been confrontational? I sink into my bed, deciding I do feel well-rested. Who knew the answer to insomnia was getting a concussion? Somewhere Nurse Sky Lopez is shouting about my faulty science knowledge.

"You've had visitors," my nurse tells me. He points to the table on the other side of my bed. There are wild flowers picked from the garden, hand written notes folded up. There are latex gloves blown up and scribbled on with Sharpie. One says, "Ride 'em, cowgirl!" and another says, "Get well soon!"

"Are we still at Horse Creek?"

"Nope," he says. "Welcome to Hamilton Hospital. We're the sister hospital to the recovery center."

"Why does that sound familiar?"

He gives me a pitying smile. "This is where we treat patients who require psychiatric help."

I jolt up and swing my feet off the bed. Helen really did it; she sent me off!

"You're not in psych," he tells me.

Blood pumps adrenaline to my heart.

"Maybe you should *lead* with that!" I shout.

He's looking around the room, looking for help, when Hutch walks in. Hutch is wearing black cowboy boots covered in dust, his jeans tucked into them. His gray T-shirt stretches across his broad chest muscles. The vein in his throat throbs, and his jaw tightens. He looks at my nurse, then he looks at me.

"Are you okay? I heard shouting."

Despite how painful it is, I laugh. "Did you know that Nurseman over here wants to be a comedian?"

My nurse turns scarlet, mumbles something under his breath, then leaves. Hutch shakes his head, chuckling. He tucks his thumb into the waistband of his jeans.

"Already causing trouble?"

I pull the covers over my head and groan. I don't want him

to see me like this. My mouth tastes gross, and I think that stale smell is coming from me. I hear a chair being dragged from one end of the room to the other. Hutch's heavy footsteps march back and forth.

"There," he says. "Better?"

I pull the covers down, ready to squint. The room is a shade darker now that he's hung an extra bed sheet over the window.

"Thank you," I say, feeling myself blush.

River Thomas does not blush.

River Thomas also does not ride horses.

River Thomas should stop referring to herself in the third person.

Hutch pulls up a chair and sits in front of me. He rests his elbows on his knees, leans forward a bit. I sink into my pillow, hating this brace around my neck. A wave of anger and frustration washes over me.

"Why are you crying?" he whispers. He grazes his finger across the top of my hands. It's the softest touch, like he's ready to pull away if anyone were to come in.

"I just feel stupid. I don't know what I did that made Apollo kick me off." I pull the covers over my face so Hutch doesn't have to see me blubbering. I wish I could knock myself out so I would stop crying. I hate crying. I hate the tightness in my chest and the way my eyes swell. I haven't cried since my dad died, and that was the first time since my mom left. I make it a point to not cry when I fall down, or get dumped, or a guy treats me like shit, or when I fuck up. Most importantly, I don't let other people see me cry. "Don't look at me."

Hutch pulls gently on the covers. I let them fall. I tell myself I'm too tired to be contrary. I let him see the worst of me.

"You're not stupid," he tells me. "Something spooked Apollo. Maybe a snake."

I hold his hand like a lifeline. My thoughts feel fuzzy, but there's one image that stays with me. Taylor grinning while Hutch was carrying me away. Could Taylor have spooked my horse from so far away? That's a pretty big accusation without having proof. I'm a newbie on a horse; they expected me to fall.

Maybe it was a snake. *A snake named Taylor.*

"When did everyone bring these in?" I point to the gifts on my bedside table.

"Last night." He thumbs the side of my hand.

I can feel my eyes start to flutter shut. I could fall back asleep with his brown eyes watching me. Something inside of me feels all tangled up, like I'm caught in a net and can't get myself free. I pull my hand away and drink from the glass of water at my bedside.

"Thank everyone for me," I say.

"Thank them yourself." He smiles ruefully. "Now that you're awake, we're going to transfer you to our medical wing."

"Oh, goodie," I say. "Now everyone can visit me and stare."

"And take turns taking care of you. Including me."

The tickling feeling spreads from my belly to my toes.

"Before you start saying any more cute things, let's have that talk you mentioned during your ride."

He raises his eyebrows. "You really want to talk about that now?"

"Why not?" I sit up and mold my pillows to my back. This bed gets less and less comfortable by the minute. "I've got nowhere to be and you're supposed to take me back, aren't you?"

"Let's go, Trouble."

• • •

I check out. There's paperwork to fill out, and when I write Sky's name as my emergency contact number, the nurse at the counter gives me an off look.

They insist on taking me out in a wheelchair, despite my protests that I'm perfectly able to walk. I hold my cardboard box with my wilting flowers and my notes. I still have to read them.

"It feels like I got fired from the hospital," I say.

Hutch pushes my wheelchair. Nurseman opens the door for us. I wave at him on the way out. In hindsight, I should've been nice to him. Sky always complains that she gets rude people who think they're at a hotel instead of the E.R.

"You're the only person I've met that doesn't want to be taken care of."

"That's right," I say. "I can take care of myself. Been doing it all my life. Why should I stop now?"

"I don't know. Some people like accepting help. Some people like being doted on."

"Is that how you treat the girls you date?"

I wish I didn't have this stupid neck brace so I could see the reaction on his face.

"Not that we dated," I tell him. "Just had the one night of passionate sex all strangers have."

Stop. Talking.

When we get to the HCRC van, Hutch turns around. He leans against the door with his arms crossed over his chest.

"Did you shrink your shirt in the wash on purpose?" I ask. "Not that I'm complaining. I can just count all your abs underneath." I grab the wheels of my chair and push myself forward. "One, two…"

"River, stop deflecting."

I sigh. "Stop studying me. I'm not your case, okay?"

He shakes his head, and now I know I've done it. I've pushed him as far as he can go, which isn't very far. It's not that I want to push him away.

Well, yeah, it is.

I want him. I want Hutch so much. But I need to keep him at a distance. A distance where I can admire his rough-and-tumble hotness, and the softness of his lips and eyes.

He helps me into the front seat and buckles me in to wait while he goes to return the chair. In the van, I flip through the stations. Country, bluegrass, country, top forty, rap and country, and finally classic rock.

When he comes back in, I can only glance at him without stretching my neck. I sing off-key to Sweet Child O'Mine.

"Can you explain why Horse Creek is called Horse Creek if I haven't seen a creek?"

Hutch pulls out of the driveway. He taps the wheel with his fingers. He clears his throat. He fiddles with the rearview mirror even though it's fine. He's a study in nervousness, and I love it. I don't know why it sends a thrill through me. True, he has reason to be nervous. Everything that's happened between us could cost him his job. It's more than a job to him. It's his life. I've never had that. My life includes drunks and people who gamble their rent money away. Hutch is the one who saves them, while I make them worse. Whatever is happening between us, I know I want him to keep that life.

I never went to college, but I'm sure he wouldn't want to throw away everything he's worked for just because of our little tryst. What would happen to me? I might get kicked out. I could go to another facility. What would happen to Hutch? He'd be fired. It could go in his files. How would he ever find a job again if his references said, "Inappropriate conduct with patients"?

The thought of Hutch losing everything because of me is sobering. I stop singing, and watch the road stretch before us. I wish I could turn my head to the side and look out the window to avoid him.

These highs and lows are killing me. I know I need to get a hold of myself. I still have a little over two months to go in my program. Those months will get awfully uncomfortable if we can't make this right.

Then Hutch makes a left where we're supposed to make a right.

"Where are you going?" My heart thumps in my chest.

"You'll see."

Five minutes later we're in, surprise, more woods. He stops the van, then comes over to my side and opens the door.

"I know, I know, you can handle it yourself." His dark eyes stare sternly at me, leaving no room for argument. "But the path is rocky. I don't want you to hurt yourself again. Let's face it—you and nature aren't on good terms yet."

"Jerk," I mutter, as he scoops me up from the passenger seat and into his arms. Actually I'm thinking, let's keep going. Let's get as far away from here as possible. Just keep holding me like this.

The cool breeze blows my hair over my face, which does a

great job of concealing my smile.

"You know, being a New Yorker, I should be afraid you're going to take me to your secret cabin and turn me into taxidermy."

"Oh yeah?" he huffs and puff as the incline steepens. "Why aren't you?"

"Because I don't think you're into taxidermy."

I feel the vibration of his laugh go right through me.

Then, I hear it. The trickle of water against rocks, the chirping of birds I could never name, the chatter of wild squirrels. Hutch sets me down at a tiny waterfall.

"Welcome to Horse Creek." He says creek like "*crick*."

"Crick?"

"That's right, creek."

"You're saying crick."

"Cree-eek." He sits beside and a little ahead of me, so I've got a perfect view of him flanked by trees and far-away mountaintops. As pristine and beautiful as this place is, untouched by man, like we're the only two people in the world, I think I prefer the gorgeousness that is Hutch.

"Much better," I tell him. "I'll teach you how to speak, and you can prevent the wild from devouring me."

"They were originally going to build the Center closer to this. But the locals were afraid it would damage the ecosystem."

"It's nice that there are still some sacred places left. Imagine what the world is going to look like in the future. All cement blocks. Food probably won't be real. We'll get those freeze-dried foods like the astronauts get."

He makes a face. I reach out and touch his nose. Then I find my hand has gotten away from me, and I'm caressing the side of his face. Traitorous arm. What were we just talking about?

"I'd like to be frozen one day," he says, "like Han Solo in carbonite. I'd give instructions to unfreeze me in a hundred years, so I can see if the future you're envisioning is real."

"Then I'll freeze myself too. Just so I can gloat about being right."

He laughs. A dragonfly buzzes around his head. "That the only reason?"

Nope. Then I'd get to be with you in a hundred years, too. Instead I say, "Yep."

He looks down and yanks grass from the ground. "We can't stay here long. Helen might think I kidnapped you."

"Have you ever kidnapped anyone before?"

He looks mortified. "God, no."

"Then why would she think you started now?"

"River."

"Hutch."

"You wanted to know why it felt like I was avoiding you."

I roll my eyes. "It *didn't feel* like you were avoiding me. You were."

"That was a dick thing to do."

"The dickest."

"What do you want from me, River?"

"Well, Hutch." My butt cheeks are falling asleep from sitting cross-legged. I'd rather lie down, but that wouldn't be any better. I fidget and look at his face and fidget some more. Isn't that the question I keep asking myself? Isn't that the question I can't answer? What do I want from Chris Hutcherson?

"I don't know." I shrug one shoulder, sending pain across my back. "What do *you* want?"

He licks his lips. His eyes search my face for something I might not be able to give him.

"I want more than this."

My insides feel like they're collapsing. I feel like I'm at the top of a building, and it's breaking apart beneath me.

"What did you expect?" I shake my head and narrow my eyes. "That first night we were together. What did you think was going to happen? Did you think we'd wake up and you'd make breakfast and I'd tell you my name? That's not how happily-ever-afters start. It's not like we can go to the movies or to dinner. That's not my style, Hutch."

"What is your style? Getting smashed and waking up with some guy you barely know, only to leave him without a word? You *left* me, River."

If I pretend Hutch is an opponent at a poker table, then I

can keep a straight face. I push away the dull pain in my heart. I push away the sting of his words and focus on his eyes, the pleading in his voice. He wants more from me. I don't know how to begin.

"You have a problem with the way I live my life? You didn't seem to mind when you were fucking me."

He looks away, frustrated. "Why do you talk like that?"

"Because that's who I am! You have to know that. I'm not some broken little girl waiting for Prince Charming to ride in and fix her life."

"I'm not trying to fix you."

"You are a counselor at my *rehab* center. That is literally what you're trying to do."

He sighs, and the beauty of what this moment could have been is broken. "I don't want to fight with you."

"Then stop telling me the things that are wrong with me. I know who I am, and I can't pretend to be someone else for you."

"This was a mistake."

"You're preaching to the choir."

We sit in a painful silence. I hurt from the inside out. My tear ducts sting, but I won't cry.

"Answer me this," he says. "Why did you kiss me in the woods?"

I replay the kiss in my head. Kissing Hutch for a second time was like breathing after drowning.

"Because I wanted to," I say.

"So we're fighting because I want you and you want me. But I want more than you want."

"You want," I argue, "someone sane and put together. Someone like Jillian or Helen or that secretary girl who looks at you like you're a Christmas present she wants to unwrap. You want something that I can't give you. Something I don't know how to give. My daddy taught me how to win, not how to be somebody's prize."

"The world isn't a poker table, River."

"How would you know? You've lived your whole life in one safe little corner of the world. Fuck you. You're not one to get self-righteous with me." I shove him, but he barely budges.

He reaches for my hand, and I pull it away. He gets on his knees, taking up my whole view. He holds his hands to the sides of my face, like he's afraid to hurt me. I shut my eyes. It's hard to be reasonable with him looking at me like this.

"Fuck you too. Stop telling me what I want. I want you, River. I want *you*."

"You won't want me after you've heard everything I have to say. Isn't that why you stayed away? Because you heard me tell that story about Kiernan?"

"No," he says. "I tried to stay away because if I'm not careful, I'll walk right up to you and kiss you every moment I can find. I'll spend every activity trying to make sure you're okay. If I spend each night at the facility, I'll find myself walking the halls in the middle of the night to get to your door."

"And I'd let you in."

He presses his lips to my forehead. He kisses my nose. He kisses my lips. I open my eyes. I can see the struggle on his face.

"How can you want all those things?" I ask. "You don't even know me. If you did, you'd run for the hills."

"Then it's a good thing I'm a lot better at hiking than you."

I punch him in the chest, and he laughs. That hurt me way more than it hurt him, but at least we're both smiling again.

"I wish I'd met you so much sooner," I whisper.

"Would you have left in the morning?" His smile is devilish, and daring me to contradict him.

The thing he wants to hear is "no." But, honestly, I'm not sure. I left because I didn't want to get attached, but I can feel how everything inside me wants to reach for him. Meanwhile, the only thing keeping us apart is me (and the whole patient/counselor thing doesn't help). Giving your heart to someone is the worst thing you can do. It's like betting it all on a high card.

"We should go," I say.

He nods. I can tell he's hurt, but he isn't going to pressure me. He scoops me up and takes me back to the car. We've already been gone for too long.

When we get back to HCRC, I go right to our infirmary.

Hutch places my flowers on my new beside table. He waits for the nurse to check me in. It makes me nervous that he's staying so close. He's paying too much attention. He's straddling the border the way an adrenaline junkie might, seeing how far he can go before getting caught.

He pulls my curtain divider. Lingers.

"We're not done yet," I whisper.

"I know. I don't think I'll ever be done with you."

CHAPTER 18

That night all I can think about is Hutch. What does "I'll never be done with you" even mean? The second thing on my mind is the pain in my body when Helen comes in.

"You scared us back there." Helen sits at the side of my bed, brandishing a dinner tray. The Tuesday night special is a sandwich and apple juice, with a brownie for dessert.

I forgot how hungry I was.

"You know what would go well with this fantastic dinner?" I ask sweetly.

"We can't give you painkillers, River."

I grumble, but dive right into my sandwich.

"I wanted to apologize for the day of the hiking trip."

"That was, like, a week ago," I tell her with my mouth full. "You have apology issues. You might want to talk to someone about that. I know a couple of shrinks, if you're interested."

"It's a good thing that concussion didn't hurt your sense of humor."

"I know. I was really worried about that. And I accept your apology. I get it. You have to be on the lookout for dangerous behavior and all that."

"Coming to a place like this isn't easy," she says. She leans back into the chair. I kind of want her to leave. I want to be alone and replay my conversation with Hutch over and over again. "Sometimes people who feel like they're alone in the world feel like there's nothing left to live for."

"I'm not alone, doc. I've got family. Not blood family, but still, family." Besides, my mom is blood and she's as good as dead to me.

She looks down at her lap. She doesn't seem to mind my

terrible table manners.

"I lost a girl a few months ago. A patient. She was this bright, shiny thing. She was in here for drug abuse."

"What kind?"

"Everything except for meth."

"A girl's gotta have standards, doc."

Her laughter is mixed with sadness. "She was a budding country singer, but she didn't have good people around her. She crashed her car and did terrible damage to her hand. There went her music career, and all the people who pretended to love her."

"Why are you telling me that?"

"Because you remind me of her."

My appetite goes away. "Do you pick on me or do you give these pep talks to everyone?"

"I don't want you to feel like I'm picking on you, but I do want you to understand that there's a difference between getting well and pretending that you're well. Being here means you have to be present."

"I am present," I protest.

She arches her eyebrow, challenging me to admit otherwise. "Part of you is still resisting admitting you have a problem. You don't share in group therapy. You can take your time, but the point is to get to the root of what's in that pretty head of yours."

"Ransom's a total rat," I say. But I know that she's right.

"It's his job to report back to me. We all want to see you get well, River. No pretending. No holding back. We're here for you."

"When I got here I wasn't sure I belonged with everyone here."

"Have you changed your mind?"

"I know I want to get help. I know I still make little bets with myself because it's a compulsion, a tic, like ripping up receipts or tapping my foot or biting my nails. It's ingrained in me. I don't know if that's ever going to stop. I know I miss the nightlife and partying and that rush that comes with dozens of little chips and the uncertainty in the turn of a card. I miss it. But I haven't left this place, and there's no one keeping me here but me."

She smiles. "Good. Get better so you can get back on

that horse."

"You're so awkward," I tell her, and she leaves me alone to eat dinner. She pauses at the door. "Hutch mentioned you believe something spooked your horse. Did you see what it might've been?"

This is the part where I tell Helen about Taylor. If I tell her I think Taylor spooked my horse, she'll investigate. He'll take it out on me. Or worse, Hutch. Taylor suspects something between Hutch and me. I can feel it in my bones. I can tell her about the barn, but I don't have any proof.

"No," I lie. "I don't remember anything."

...

But I do remember Taylor's face. The contempt in his eyes, the smile on his face. I lie in bed replaying my fall. Before that, the cliff. The wind in my face. Hutch's perfect kiss by the creek. To get him off my mind, I read the cards everyone made for me.

Most of the "cards" are folded pieces of printer paper. Vilma drew me a stick figure sequence of what I looked like falling off the horse. So sweet. Maddie wrote me a poem.

> *There once was a girl named River*
> *She was so wild, you shoulda seen 'er.*
> *She fell off of her horse*
> *And we all felt remorse*
> *Maybe some sleep will make her less meaner.*

Cute, real cute. I'm not really mean, am I?

There are a few more drawings, and a "get well soon!!!" from Julie. The one that really shakes me is one written in marker. The letters are little more than chicken scratches, but I can read them plainly.

DONT MESS WITH ME BITCH.

First, I think, there should be a comma before "bitch."

Then my head begins to throb. I crumple the paper in my hands. I'm shaking. I get up and lock the door from the inside, but then I realize Taylor has the keys to this whole place. I place a chair under the doorknob. If someone opens the door, I'll hear them. Would he really hurt me inside the facility?

I lie awake for hours before I finally fall asleep. I jump at the way the wood creeks and groans, like there are ghosts prowling the halls. When I start to close my eyes I pinch myself.

SLAM.

I jump up so hard I give myself whiplash. Just what a girl with a neck sprain needs.

"What's going on?"

Grogginess and pain pull me back against the pillow. I'm seconds away from begging for drugs. That won't make me look like a junkie at all.

Nurse Jean walks over the fallen chair. She's small and plump, with light brown skin and dark curls.

"Are you trying to kill me?" she asks.

No, I think. Someone is trying to kill *me*.

"Sorry. I was scared."

She rests her hand on her hip. She purses her lips, like she doesn't have any patience for me. She rights the chair and busies herself checking up on me.

"How long do I have to wear this thing?" I ask.

She smells like Chanel Number 5. I used to do the door at this burlesque club in the East Village, and the manager always wore it.

"A few more days. Just to be safe."

I smile, remembering to be nicer to this nurse than I was to the other. "Thank you."

"Has anyone made you feel unsafe?" she asks. "The door just locks."

"This place just makes a lot of noise at night."

"Aren't you from New York?"

"It's a different kind here. Did you know there are bears?"

She throws her head back and laughs. "Welcome to Montana, girlie."

After she leaves and my heart goes back to a normal rhythm, Maddie comes in with my breakfast.

"Morning, sunshine!"

"I didn't know you wrote poems."

She blushes, and sets the tray down in front of me. "A little bit. I just have all these feelings, you know?"

"Feelings about me being mean?"

She shrugs, and it makes her look younger. "Not always. But you don't have a lot of patience with me. I know I'm hard to deal with, but I'm trying."

Suddenly, I feel sorry for not having more patience. The people here are trying just as hard as I am. Well, probably harder. They've been at it for longer than I have.

"I'm sorry, Maddie." I watch her. I can't imagine this girl, only four years younger than me, doing the things she says she's done. Ransom was right; I've avoided making friends, maybe for the same reason I'm avoiding the feelings I have for Hutch. Then it hits me: Maddie is part of Taylor's black market barn. I think of the ways my dad used to get people to do things for him. "People will believe what they want to see," he used to say.

I go to take a spoonful of cereal. The yellow flakes are soggy, but at least it's sugary. I grit my teeth and hiss.

Maddie stands. "Are you okay? Should I get someone?"

"It doesn't matter if you do," I say, piling on the pathetic. "They won't give me any stinking pain meds."

"That sucks."

I hold my head with my hands. "It's fine."

I push away my food. Maddie reacts just the way I want her to. She pulls her chair closer to me and leans in for a whisper.

"We're friends, right River?"

"I think so."

"Well." She looks over her shoulder as someone walks down the hall. "I think… I think I might be able to help you."

I set hopeful eyes on her. "How?"

She shrugs one shoulder. Maddie seems loyal enough that she wouldn't rat out her source. But all I need is an in, a crack, and I'll figure the rest out. If Taylor thinks he can intimidate me, he's wrong.

"I'll come back. Tonight. Just, don't ask too many questions."

"I promise."

Later in the day, Julie brings me a bunch of flowers. She's scratching at the inside of her wrist. I'm still not sure what's wrong with Julie, because she doesn't talk much. She doesn't strike me as a druggie, but sometimes it's the people least likely that take to it the most.

"How're you feeling?" she asks.

"I'm better. My head hurts a bit."

I take the flowers from her and sniff them. The pollen is thick and yellow, and makes me sneeze. Looking at them makes me happy, though. It's a strange feeling to get flowers from someone I hardly know. The attention that everyone here is showing me makes my heart twist and turn. It's like I'm being rinsed out from the inside. How can these people give themselves so easily to others? Isn't it emotionally taxing?

"Everyone was so worried. They thought you might be—" She looks over her shoulder and whispers like she's telling me the latest gossip. "A vegetable."

I chuckle, and share my chips with her. "Thanks for coming to see me."

"River," Julie asks shyly.

"Yes?"

"Do you think you can help me make a dress? A costume really."

"Costume for what?"

"Halloween, duh. Helen says we can have a party. I want him to notice me."

I swallow the lump in my throat. "Who?"

She turns bright red. "No one. Just. Someone."

"You don't have to tell me." But I already know.

"Good. Anyway, can you? None of the other girls dress like you."

"Like what?"

She shrugs. "In all black. Mysterious and stuff. Like you're ready for it to be Halloween all the time."

"Thanks, I think."

LIFE ON THE LEVEL

Halloween is at the end of the month. Have I already been here for a month? If I were home, I'd be planning my group costume with the other bartenders. Last year we were zombie Disney characters. I was a zombie Alice in Wonderland.

"We get stuff from Goodwill and some thrift stores, and they let us make things out of what we've got. It's kind of stupid."

I hold her hand. "It's not stupid. It'll be nice to have one day where we can have fun and pretend to be someone else. That's the point of Halloween right? Besides the candy?"

When she smiles her whole face widens, revealing dimples I've never seen before. She gets up and throws her arms around me.

"Thank you, River. I'm really glad you're okay."

CHAPTER 19

Dear Sky,

I have to wear a neck brace because I fell off a horse. Don't worry! I'm fine. Or worry, and come visit me instead of traveling with your handy man tool. (Don't tell Hayden I called him that.)

There's something going on that doesn't feel right. Remember the guy I told you about that runs this black market barn? I think he spooked my horse. What's that, you say? You want proof? Even I know that I can't just accuse someone like that. Who is everyone going to believe? The hand that's worked here for years, or the newbie addict? It's funny that everyone wants to helps us become better people, but when it comes down to it, our word means shit. So I have to get proof. I know what you're going to say. Do you know that every time I do something bad, or get ready to do something bad, I hear your voice? I think you should be Jiminy Cricket for Halloween. It suits you.

P.S. Where are you?

P.P.S. You're a nurse. They tell me I have to wear this brace for another week. Is that true, or are they just doing it to make me look stupid?

Love,
Riv

・・・

While I prefer being in my own bed, I still want to rip my neck brace off and set it on fire. I made the mistake of saying this in front of Ransom and everyone else during a group session. I'm not used to checking what I say all the time. I also never realized that all of my crazy threats tend to be explosive. The pyro kid has started sitting next to me ever since I said that.

"My name is River Thomas." I wave at some of the new people. It's getting easier to speak to everyone. It's like I'm watching a movie of myself. If I look at all of this as an out-of-body experience, it feels easier. "I'm an alcoholic and I have a gambling problem."

There are two new people in our group: Jermania Nelson (will snort anything in powdered form) and Randy Rider (prescription drugs, and from the smirk on his face as he undresses me with his eyes, sex).

"Spend too much time at the slot machines?" Randy asks. He's sitting on his chair like he's the coolest cat in Cool Town. He's got a taut, swimmer's body. He scratches his crotch, and I can tell he's not wearing any underwear. His ash blond hair falls around cheeks that were chiseled by Aphrodite, goddess of sex herself. Too bad a nice body and an even better face can't make up for how annoying he is. He's like Disney's John Smith without the compassion, Jamie Lannister without the quick wit.

Ransom reprimands him, but I can hold my own.

"Yeah, I sit right next to your mother."

There's a flurry of "Ohhhhhhhhhhh," before Ransom decides to reprimand me instead, because I should know better.

"Anyway," I say. "I always thought that everything I did was normal. When I was in elementary school, I was teaching kids how to make Go Fish more interesting." That one always gets a laugh. "As I got older, I never thought there might be something damaging about staying up for two days straight, sitting at a poker table surrounded by people with bleary eyes and down to their last dime. It's just something I grew up with."

"What made you decide to change?" Ransom asks me.

I look around the room at the other patients. I've always been worried that people here would judge me. But I think the only person actually judging me is *me*. They quietly wait for me to answer the question. I stall by digging my fingers under my neck brace to scratch where it itches the most.

"After my dad died. I mean, he was the one who taught me how to play. Learned everything I know from him, even the things he hated about himself."

"Time out," Randy says. "Your own pops had you playing poker?"

I walk away from my chair and stand right at the center, facing him. I don't look very menacing with this thing around my neck. "Do you have a point or do you just like to hear yourself speak?"

He shrugs one shoulder in that way slackers have. All, *I'm just saying, man.* "I'm just saying, man. It's kind of obvious why you've got a problem. He's, like, the one that got you started."

"You need to shut your mouth if you know what's good for you," I tell him.

"Randall," Ransom warns him.

"What?" Randy says, putting on an innocent smile. "We're supposed to talk right? I just feel like telling it how it is."

I scoff. I'm going to tell Helen that *this* is what I get for sharing.

"River, please continue," Ransom says.

Everyone looks between Randy and me. The mix of excited and worried faces is a blur.

"I'm done." I start to return to my seat.

"Don't worry," Randy says. Ransom is asking him to be quiet, but he just keeps talking. "I know how it ends. Pop starts her working the poker table at seven and by seventeen she's turning tricks. I think I saw that on CSI."

I laugh. It's strangled-sounding and ugly. I'm not hurt. He's as far away from the truth as Pluto is from Earth. But something snaps inside me. Fire runs down my body, and pain flares in my neck as I lunge at him. I smash my fist across his cheek. His scream is high-pitched; he's holding his arms up. Hands land around my waist and yank me away. I'm still punching and kicking. Chairs scrape back, and people stand. Someone runs out the door.

"Put me down!" I scream. "Let go of me!"

But Ransom is holding me the way I would hold a pillow over my shoulder. He walks me out the open door, into the hall, and towards the medical wing before finally setting me down.

LIFE ON THE LEVEL

Nurse Jean comes running out of another room with her stethoscope around her neck. Her dark eyes are wide, then become soft when she sees me. Everything about me is tense. My hands are balled into fists, and I hunch forward. In my next life, I'd like to come back as an armadillo. I want to be able to curl up into a ball. I want to have the toughest skin.

They take turns saying my name. River. River. River.

My thoughts are dizzy. I feel like that time I was thirteen at San Gennaro's fair back in Queens. I gave the carousel operator a twenty to make it go faster than normal. I held onto that chipped pastel horse for dear life and screamed the whole time. Sky and Leti and my dad just stood there, watching me giggle and scream. Everything was blurry and colorful, and when it was over, I stumbled dizzy and giddy off the ride and held out my arms and my daddy caught me.

My daddy always caught me.

Finally, I look up at Ransom and Nurse Jean. I shake my head but don't smile.

"I'm fine."

"You're not fine," Ransom tells me.

I hold up the hand I hit Randy with. It's pink and throbbing. "You're right. I need some ice."

"We don't deal with our emotions using violence," Ransom says.

"You don't," I say. "But if he talks to me like that again, his face is going to be the least of his problems." Talking big makes me feel big. I think of all the times I've thrown out threats to guys who try to cheat at the table or treat me like a waitress because I'm a girl. Back then, I had even bigger guys at my disposal—my godfather, and bouncers who watched me grow up. Here, I don't have anyone. Here, I'm alone.

"No," he says firmly. "You won't. Listen to me, okay. I need you to *listen* to me. You will not raise your hand to another patient ever again. Don't jeopardize your place here for some punk who gets off on getting under your skin. I expected more from you, River."

"Maybe that was your problem. Expecting more from me.

This is all I've got. This is all you're getting."

I turn away from him. I don't want to leave things like this. I tell myself to say more, but I'm not thinking straight. I'm angry. I'm angry down to my bones, and there's nothing anyone can tell me to make it any different.

Ransom leaves the room, and I deflate. I can feel tears stinging my eyes. I pace around the room, my head throbbing with pain. I've never had to stop myself from crying so often. It's not that I'm dead inside; it's that I don't usually let people like Randy get to me. I know where I come from and I'm not ashamed. Being here won't change that. I still know myself. I'm the kind of person that loves fiercely and completely. I love my friends, and I loved my dad. My emotions are black and white. I either like someone or I don't. I never learned to pretend to be nice. I care what someone thinks, or I don't. I've always been straight up. That's how I've protected myself. It's easier to leave than to get left.

Randy doesn't know what he was talking about. That's what I get for "sharing" in the first place.

Nurse Jean returns. "Sit still for once."

"I can't. I don't know how."

"Try." She takes my hand and holds it in hers. It's a friendly touch. She places an ice pack across my knuckles.

A single tear falls down my cheek. I turn my face to the side so she can't see it. I'm sinking into the cooling feeling of the ice pack when Hutch comes in. My heart flip-flops when I see him.

"What's going on?" He looks around the room, like he's expecting a crime scene.

"What are you doing here?" I don't hide my annoyance. It's not that I don't want to see him. I just don't need another lecture like Steve's. Besides, he's not my counselor. He's going to get us both kicked out if he keeps acting so reckless. Says the girl who just decked a guy.

Even though I try not to look at Hutch, my eyes flick to his face. I see worry and fear and something like love.

Just then, Ransom comes back with Randy. Randy holds a wad of napkins to his nose. His piercing blue eyes glare at me.

He's mentally punching me back.

"You're lucky I don't hit girls," he spits.

"You're unlucky I do," I sing song.

"Enough," Steve says. "Hutch, can you help me out here, please? *You* two are lucky Helen went to town this morning."

"I would like to file a complaint," Randy says.

"I got it, Jean," Hutch tells the nurse. He takes the icepack from her. She purses her lips and goes to put on latex gloves.

Hutch gives me a look that asks, "are you okay?"

I nod lightly and a tiny smile escapes my lips when he takes my hand in his.

"Seriously," Randy says, since no one is paying enough attention to him. "I fear for my life."

"You should," I whisper.

"She's a nut job. Why isn't she in the loony bin instead of here? My parents are paying top dollar to have me here, and this is the kind of service I get?"

"This isn't the Four Seasons," Ransom reminds him.

I turn to him. "Me in psych? Which one of us is the sociopathic narcissist? You're lucky I'm not wearing any of my rings, pretty boy."

Randy smirks. "At least you admit I'm pretty as fuck. If you wanted to touch my face, all you had to do was ask. I'm in room 3F if you want to look at the rest."

"Thanks, but I'd rather stay STD free."

"Randall!" Hutch shouts. I've never heard him shout. "Enough."

"Maybe we should get Apollo's muzzle," I say.

Ransom looks like he might just have a heart attack. I decide to keep my mouth shut.

"Listen, I know you broke my nose and all," Randy says after a minute's silence. "But I can really feel this energy between us. I've never felt this way before."

"I think that energy you're feeling is disgust," I say.

Hutch gets up and draws the curtain between our beds. I break into a smile and shake my head. I mouth, "thanks."

He sighs. He takes off the ice pack. Looks over his shoulder.

Kisses the red of my knuckles, then places the pack back. I shut my eyes. Suddenly, I take back the wish about being numb. Hasn't numbness led me here?

Nurse Jean returns with a tampon and scissors in her hand. I let out a barking laugh, then clap my free hand over my mouth.

"What the hell?" Randy shouts.

"Best way to stop the bleeding." She cuts it in half.

I pull the curtain back just in time to see her insert the split tampon into Randy's nostrils. I don't think he can hate me any more than he already does. Nurse Jean feels the bridge of his nose. It's not broken, otherwise I'd probably be in more trouble. But when Ransom looks at me, I know I'm not off the hook just yet.

• • •

I take my dinner tray outside. It's a little cold, but there's a fire and I've got my Mets hoodie. A few patients watch the sun set from the wooden lawn chairs lined up to face the mountains. I pull my chair towards the flames. My right hand is stiff, and Nurse Jean insisted on bandaging it. After everything was said and done, Ransom made a point of telling me I have a good punch, but not to use it on anyone again. He invited me to his morning kickboxing sessions once I'm all healed up.

I grab my sandwich with one hand, most of the meat falling out of the bottom. I am a pathetic baby bird who can't feed herself. I push the food tray down and watch the fire until the light dances in my vision even when I look away.

"Hey, Trouble," Hutch says.

"You again," I say, feigning disgust.

"I keep cropping up like an old weed."

"You know what they say about weeds?"

He shakes his head.

"You just give them a good tug."

He laughs. "That was terrible. Don't quit your day job."

"My day job right now is being an addict."

He sits beside me and rests his elbows on his knees. "Your

day job is being a recuperating addict."

"Do you always have to be objective?"

"No. I just don't want you to be so hard on yourself."

We watch the fire crackle. He takes a stick and throws it into the fire. The log is one of those chemical ones that burn for three hours, but he does it anyway because he needs to keep his hands busy. He crosses his hands back and forth. He cracks his knuckles. He's trying to keep a cool, professional persona. He gets up and turns around on the log to face me.

"Do you want to tell me what happened?"

"Didn't Ransom tell you?"

"I still want to hear your side of it."

So I tell him. "When I was little people used to tell my dad to get a babysitter. To not take me to *those* places because I'd turn out bad. I'm not a bad person, though. I happen to make bad decisions sometimes, but doesn't everyone? I can't be the only fuckup in the world. I also happen to drink like a fish and gamble long after I should've folded. It's not like my dad forced me to learn how to play."

"How did he teach you?" In the firelight, Hutch's skin looks warmer. The shadows make his face look more angular, his hair darker. In this moment, I have to catch myself from falling into his deep brown eyes.

"Before my mom left us for good," I say, "she used to go on these benders. She'd be gone for days, sometimes weeks. I was little. Maybe five. My dad had to work, and his work was at a bar. He didn't trust me staying with neighbors, because he didn't trust people in general. Plus, I was really talkative and friendly."

"Wow, you've changed."

I jab his leg, and he laughs. "*Anyway.* He was probably afraid I'd talk to strangers. Or that one day I'd be gone like my mom. So he took me to the bar, and the waitresses watched over me. Most of them were old and had their own kids. Those were the ones who would give me my own bowl of peanuts, and milk or juice. Sometimes he'd be at a game and I'd want to sit on his knee. I was instructed not to talk. It was the only time I ever listened, watching my dad check his cards. My favorite card was always the Ace of Hearts, because it was red and I liked hearts."

"No one minded you there?"

I shrug. "I don't really remember. It wasn't a casino or anything. It was one of those backroom games that are definitely not legal. Sometimes strangers would come in and look at me like I was a sewer rat. Only one guy ever accused my dad of cheating through me."

"What happened to him?" Hutch asks. When he looks at me, I find myself embarrassed by the things I say, or the things I've seen. I'm never embarrassed about this. I just don't want Hutch, of all people, to think of me differently. Should I lie? Why does he need to know the truth? It's not like he's my boyfriend. He's just a guy. Just a counselor. Just the only man whose kisses make me dizzy.

A long sigh leaves my lips. This honesty thing is painful. "The guy who accused my dad of cheating was taken out back and beaten to a pulp. I didn't see it, but I heard it. They played music, but it didn't cover up his screams."

"That's horrible," Hutch says.

"That's my life," I say coolly.

"That *was* your life. You're giving yourself the chance to start over. I want to take you away from all of that and keep you safe."

I'm about to say "I'm fine." But now, more than ever, I accept that I'm not fine. I haven't been in a long time.

"I don't need saving," I tell him. "That's not your job." I look around the courtyard. The sun is a perfect orange, sinking behind the mountains. No one is paying attention to us. If I start walking into the woods, would Hutch follow?

"Actually," he says. "It is my job. You said so yourself at the creek."

I groan and stare at the flames.

"River, look at me."

My heart is going crazy in my chest. If I look at him, I know I'll lose some of my nerve. He's just got a stare that makes me weak, and weakness has never been an option for me.

I look at him nonetheless.

"Ransom and I spoke to Helen."

"Is she giving me the boot?" My heart races at the thought that Helen might be kicking me out. I don't want to be kicked out. I want to stay, and I don't know if I want to do it for myself, or because I'm not ready to stop being near Hutch.

"Of course not." He frowns, and I'm glad he's just as surprised at the thought of me leaving. "Randy is going to stay with Steven's group. Because the other counselors have more new patients on their plate, Helen thought it might be a good idea to… give you to me. I mean, to my group. We can give us another shot."

"Give *us* another shot?"

He looks down at his lap and smiles. "You and me. Counselor and patient."

I lean back on the lounge chair. My sandwich is probably stale by now. Either way, I've got no appetite. I'm going to be Hutch's patient again. It is both thrilling and terrifying. I get to see him every day and listen to him speak. I also get to be on my best behavior, because all I want to do is jump on top of him and kiss every inch of his perfect face.

"The decision is yours. We want you to be comfortable."

I nod. "You're the one who didn't want to take me back in the first place."

"River…" He looks over his shoulder and takes my hand in his. My hand belongs in his, and his in mine. But I hate having to be on the lookout. "I did that because it was too hard to be near you. We spent one night together. One. And it was the best night of my life. This isn't easy for me, watching you run around here and not be able to—not be able to hold you, or *feel* you. You don't know what it does to me."

"Yes I do."

We're quiet for a moment. The dying flames crackle beside us. The patients who were watching the sunset wave as they return to the main building—not that the sun has completely set. We're the only ones left, which means we have to go back soon, too.

"So, River Thomas. Will I see you in group tomorrow?"

I'll never be done with you, he told me. I get it. There isn't enough time.

"No," I say. He looks as stricken as I feel.

"Look, I want you, Hutch. Maybe more than I've ever wanted anyone. But I realize I'm not okay. I don't want you to see that part of me yet. I don't want you to think less of me because of what I've done."

"River, I would never. You have to know that. I can't help but want to shield you from anything that's bad." He hooks my fingers with his.

I press my hand on his cheek. "Me too."

He presses a kiss on my nose. I hope he'll continue to kiss every part of my face, but he doesn't. It's so easy to forget where we are. I wonder if it's too late to change my mind again.

"There's one more thing. You and Randy both have to do some volunteer work."

I scoff. "On top of the chores we already do?"

"You get to choose. One is a day at a soup kitchen in town. The other is visiting the children's hospital wing to read them stories and things."

"The children's hospital."

Hutch smiles, and stands up. He knows we have to get back inside, too. Even if we're just talking, I feel like we're being watched. Maybe that's just the guilt of my dirty thoughts.

"Good," he says. "The van leaves after breakfast. I should head home."

He carries my tray, and holds the door for me to go back inside. The cafeteria is almost empty, with the exception of a few stragglers.

"Goodnight," I whisper to him, then put as much distance between us as I possibly can. I brush my teeth and get into bed. I'm not hungry, but I do have a terrible ache in my belly.

I'm full of too much want. I know if I'm not careful, I'm going to slip up. As I jump into bed and get comfortable, I feel something under my pillow. It's a tiny book of poetry. I don't remember putting it there. I open the cover, revealing a square cutout in the center. Nestled between Walt Whitman's words are three tiny blue pills.

CHAPTER 20

Because of my neck brace, Vilma and Jermania allow me to sit in the front seat. Vilma puts on my seatbelt for me.

"Your shirt is on backwards," she tells me.

I sigh. "You're lucky I'm *wearing* a shirt."

She snickers, and tries not to laugh at how much of a mess I am in the mornings. Hutch, on the other hand, gives me a look that makes me want to break apart at the seams. It's part adoration and part pity. My hair could double as a bird's nest, and in my haste not to be late, I'm pretty sure I left crud in my eyes. At least my breath is minty fresh. I can't remember if I put on deodorant. I tell myself we're going to be visiting children with actual problems, and petty things like hygiene should be the least of my worries.

"Everyone strapped in?" Hutch says, adjusting his rear-view mirror.

"Yes, sir," Jermania mutters. It's the most I've heard her say.

"So, are you actually volunteering, or did you punch someone, like River?" Vilma asks Jermania.

I wish I could turn around to get a look at Jermania's face. Hutch says, "Vilma."

"I'm just trying to make conversation, you know? It's an *hour-long* drive to Zoo Town."

"What about you, Vilma?" I ask, turning the question back on her. See how she likes it. "Are you actually volunteering?"

"You bet," she says. "I'm not allowed to see my kids until the program is done, except on family day. I feel out of touch sometimes. Like what if I see them again, and I don't know how to talk to anyone anymore? All I do is talk to crazy addicts and counselors. I feel like I'm losing my ability to be a mother."

"I don't think that's something you lose," Hutch says. Then we all stay quiet for a while.

This early in the morning, there are mostly just giant trucks on the road. I put my head back and watch the trees zoom by. Every now and then I feel Hutch's gaze turn toward me. I wish we were alone. Granted, I'm not exactly in the right physical condition to be getting frisky, but I'd like to just be with him.

Gah, who *am* I?

A little under an hour later, we arrive at the hospital. Hutch parks, and we get visitor badges. I hate the way hospitals smell. I realize I maybe didn't think this through. The last time I was in a hospital was to wait for my father to die. I picture him, weak and wrinkled. He'd aged a hundred years in the six months since his diagnosis. I start to breathe really fast. I turn around in place, like I'm doing some sort of bee ritual dance. Really, I'm trying to convince myself not to run out of here. This isn't about me. I mean, it is, because I have to do something good in exchange for having hit Randy. But this is also about the kids that were promised a visit.

Hutch's hand falls on my shoulder. I jerk back.

"It's not you," I blurt out. "Sorry. I just. I just get anxious and I don't like being touched when I'm anxious."

He nods, understanding. "What do you need me to do?"

I sigh. I wish he wasn't so… giving. When you're ready to give all of yourself, it makes it easier for others to take advantage of you. I don't want to take advantage of Hutch, but I don't want anyone else to do it either.

Listen to me, complaining for once that a guy is *too* good. Another first.

"I'll be fine, I promise. I just didn't think I'd have to come to one of these places for a long time. I didn't really think about it until we walked in."

He smiles, and his smile gives me a little bit of courage. He nods in the direction of the pediatric wing. Nurses and doctors walk in the opposite direction. Despite the tired look in their eyes, they still wave and greet us happily.

The room we enter is painted sky blue, with clouds and a

rainbow of balloons. There are six beds lined up together. The kids are already awake and sitting up in their beds. Two of them are hooked to so many tubes they can't go very far. Some of the others dangle their feet from the edges of the beds. They smile shyly. Some wave their arms over their heads, recognizing Hutch and Vilma.

A little girl with tan skin and a bandage around her head stands on her bed. She holds her arms out and waits for Vilma to come over and hug her.

"Who are you?" a little blond boy with big brown eyes asks me.

I don't know why this question, of all things, throws me a little bit. Maybe because I was just wondering this myself. "I'm River Thomas. I'm new here."

He nods, making a funny face, like he accepts this as an answer and will allow me to be here. "I'm Jimmy. What happened to your neck, River Thomas?"

"I fell off my horse."

Jimmy's eyes widen. "Did it hurt?"

"A lot. But I'm okay now. This is just in case."

"In case what?"

I look to Hutch for help. Hutch only laughs and picks the boy up. "Let's take it easy on the new kids, okay, Jimmy?"

"Okay," Jimmy says, shoving his thumb into his mouth.

The kids range from four to eight years old. The nurse comes to check in on us once, her eyes lingering on Hutch when she says, "If you need *anything*, please let me know." She gives the rest of us a pitying look. I'm sure all she sees is a bunch of addicts. I recognize the disapproval in the cock of her eyebrow, and the tightness of her lips. Still, she leaves the room and tells us she'll be back at the end of the hour.

"Let's gather 'round," Hutch tells everyone. Because two kids are bedridden, we sit closer to them. Hutch points to Jermania and me. "We have two new friends with us today. Can you guys say hi?"

The kids all wave.

"Can you tell them your names and something about yourselves?"

Jimmy raises his hands. "I'm Jimmy and I like guitars and horses and my heart beats like a drum."

A little girl shakes her head. She doesn't want to talk.

"Its okay Daisy," Hutch whispers to her.

She wears a crocheted cap to cover up her bald head. The girl that's attached to Vilma is named Hannah and she likes super heroes and cupcakes. Their happiness is a marvel to me. I haven't been around kids in a long time. They're precocious and lively. They're curious in the most innocent of ways.

"Michael isn't here," Jimmy says. "Michael got a fever and they took him to the bad place."

"What's the bad place?" Hannah asks.

Jimmy shakes his head. "It's where the doctors and nurses take you when you can't wake up."

Vilma and Hutch exchange a sad look. Something in my chest feels too tight. After a period of silence, Hutch goes to the corner of the room and holds up a book in one hand and a guitar in the other.

"What do you guys want to do today? We could read—"

"Sing a song, Hutch!"

"Yeah, sing us a song!"

Hutch sets down the book. "Okay, you guys asked for it."

"I didn't know you played guitar," I say. I realize there's no real reason that I *should* know something like that. Still, Hutch just shrugs.

"Not very well," he says. "I apologize in advance."

Hutch takes a seat on a wooden stool facing the rest of us. The morning light that filters through the white curtains is like a spotlight just for him.

"I want to hear Metallica!" Jimmy says. "My daddy says Metallica is the best in the *world*."

Everyone laughs. "You got to pick last week. It's Hannah's turn."

She hides her face in Vilma's shoulder.

"Do you want to whisper it to me and I'll say it?" Vilma asks.

Hannah nods. She cups her hands around Vilma's ear and tells her the song, like a secret.

"I love that song," Vilma says. This seems to make Hannah happy. "Okay, Hutch Swift. Let's hear Love Song."

"It's Love *Story*," Hannah says in her little voice. When she realizes she's spoken out loud, she covers her mouth with her hands. Jimmy makes a raspberry with his tongue, but everyone else bounces with excitement. One of the little girls with a patch over her eye pumps her little fist into the air in a "yes" motion.

Hutch chuckles. "I don't know all the lyrics, so I'm going to need some help, okay?"

All of their little heads nod as Hutch adjusts the tuning and strums.

"River?"

"Hutch?"

"Come on, girl." He adds a twang to his words.

"I don't know the words."

"Everyone knows the words. Plus, this song isn't in my key."

"I don't sing," I say, trying to maintain a pleasant smile while widening my eyes at him. That's a lie—I do like to sing. Before I dropped out of high school I was in the school choir. It was the only club I regularly went to even if I was cutting class.

"Come on," he says again.

"Yeah, River," Vilma says. "We all hear you when you're walking around by yourself."

"Come on, River Thomas," Jimmy says.

He shakes his head in my direction, and I realize I have no choice. I take a deep breath and walk over to Hutch. My face feels like it's on fire, and my cheeks hurt from smiling.

Hutch starts playing the intro, lowering the key for my voice. Of course I know the lyrics. Working at bars, I know all the lyrics to every hit song and one-hit wonder to hit the airwaves. It's my guilty pleasure. I turn my body toward Hutch. He hums along with me, strumming.

When I get to the lyric, "'Cause you were Romeo, I was a scarlet letter" I can't help but catch his eyes. I wave my fingers at the kids, inviting them to sing along. Hutch's deep voice adds a nice bass to the whole thing. I can feel my heart doing summersaults as he brings his guitar closer to me and sings,

"Baby, just say yes."

I step forward and grab a little girl singing at the top of her lungs. She raises her hands, twirling her wrists like she can wrap the notes around her. Together, we all end off-key, but it still sounds amazing.

I do a slight Texas dip, then clap in Hutch's direction. One by one, the kids pick different songs. Mostly pop songs, and one request for Clementine. The whole time Vilma comes out of her shell more and more. Even Jermania sings along, with a voice that would put Christina Aguilera out of business.

When the nurse comes back in, the kids all make disappointed noises. We kiss their foreheads and bask in their hugs. I feel my heart fill up in a way I never thought was possible. I've never done something like this before, and it feels good to bring happiness to others in a selfless way.

As we make our way out of the hospital, Jermania and Vilma's hums echo down the hospital hall. I turn around to find Hutch. The nurse has barricaded his way. She hands him a folded up piece of paper and pets his bicep. Hutch pockets the paper. I whip around, and act like I didn't see anything, but Vilma and Jermania have already seen. They hoot and holler as he follows us out the front door.

"My boy got himself a number," Vilma says.

I don't know where I'm walking, so I just pick the direction of the parking lot.

"River," Vilma shouts. "Come back! We're getting lunch."

I've never been the jealous type. Even when I knew the guys I dated were less than faithful. Even when I was less than faithful myself. That's why I've always made it a point to have no-strings-attached lovers and hookups.

I put on a happy face, and follow my fellow patients into a cafe called The Liquid Planet. Vilma and Jermania grab seats at the front and give us their order.

Hutch stands directly behind me. I can feel the heat radiating from him. Or am I doing the radiating? Either way, it's hot in here.

"Hi," I say, speaking faster than usual. "Can we get three

hot cocoas, a lemonade, two tuna salad sandwiches, one ham and cheese, and a BLT? Please."

I step to the side and let Hutch pay.

"River," he says, playfully.

"*Hutch*." I say his name the way I would normally say "leprosy."

"I love the way you sing."

I flick my eyes in his direction. *Don't smile. Don't smile. Stop it. Stop smiling this instant.* We head back to our seats to wait for our food. When we reach the table, Vilma is crying.

"Hey, what's wrong?" I ask.

Vilma shakes her head. "It's nothing. Happens every week."

Jermania presses her lips together in concern. "Then why do you do it to yourself?"

"Because I have to remember what it's like to be a mother. You girls are too young. You don't understand what it's like yet."

"I never will," Jermania says. "I had cervical cancer when I was nineteen. I can't have kids."

Vilma reaches out her hand and pets Jermania's arm. "Poor girl."

Jermania shrugs. "I didn't deal with it well before. I didn't know how badly I wanted it until it was definite that I never could. What about you, River? Do you see kids in your future?"

I shake my head. "God no. This cycle of jerks stops with me."

I regret saying it when I see Vilma's face.

"I'm sorry, Vilma. I didn't mean anything by it. I'm just not the nurturing type. I never had a normal childhood. I wouldn't even know where to start."

The waitress brings over our food and drinks. Even though I didn't eat much yesterday, I'm still not hungry. I force myself to take a few bites of my BLT.

"I don't think you should worry so much," I tell Vilma. "You love your kids, and you're getting help to be with them again. There are people who wouldn't even bother. My mom would never in a million years choose me over partying. It's not because she forgot how to be a parent; it's because she never wanted to be one. That's what makes you different."

Vilma stares at me with wide eyes. They glisten with tears. "Thank you, River."

"What about you?" Jermania asks Hutch. "You going to call that cute little nurse? Baby-making takes practice, but you look like you'll be a pro."

"Hutch claims to be single." Vilma cackles, suddenly in a way better mood now that the conversation's picked up and become about Hutch and his love life.

"I mean," Jermania says mid-bite, "You're too much of a jock for my taste, but you're hot as hell. Anyone would be lucky to have you."

Hutch's eyes flick in my direction, and I look at the steam rising from my hot chocolate. "Would it make this conversation end if I said yes?" he asks.

"Uhm, no," Vilma says. "I want to know what's wrong with you. You're handsome. You have a good job. You sing Taylor fucking Swift songs. You're like this dream guy that people only write about in romance novels. I'm just trying to understand why you're single."

"Oh man," Jermania says. "Are you one of those guys married to his job? Because we're really not worth it. Give me the nurse's number. I'll set up a date for you two."

Jermania reaches into his shirt pocket and pulls out the slip of paper. Hutch tries to grab it back, but Jermania holds it close to her chest.

"Relax, Hutch," I say. "We don't have cellphones to call her."

"Just tell us the truth."

"First of all," Hutch says. "You are all worth it. And I do manage to have a life outside of HCRC. I've gone on six dates in the past year."

"Please tell me that means you've had sex at least six times this year," Vilma says. "If only because otherwise all of this—" she waves her hand at Hutch's frame— "is a total waste."

Hutch bites his tongue, and smiles from ear to ear. "Do you really want to know how many times I've had sex this year? And if I hear a word about this back home, I will switch your volunteer sessions to shoveling manure with Simmons."

Vilma and Jermania mime locking their mouths and throwing away the keys. I just sit back and pretend like my insides aren't exploding. I mean, I know how many times *I've* had sex this year. But I don't want to know Hutch's number.

"Once."

"I don't believe you." Vilma takes a huge bite from her sandwich.

"Believe it or not," Hutch says, making sure he looks at me. "It's true."

It feels weird divulging these things to each other in a conversation with other people. It's something I wouldn't even ask Hutch because I'd be afraid he'd ask me back. Romeo and the Scarlet Letter is right.

"One time with one person?" Jermania asks skeptically. "Multiple times with one person?"

Hutch's dark eyes glance at me. "One night with one person. It was a while ago. She wouldn't even tell me her name. The next morning, she was just gone. Left me high and dry."

"What a bitch," Vilma says. "You deserve way better than that."

"Yeah," Jermania says. "You deserve at least a second roll in the sheets."

I laugh. "They're right. She's a dick."

Hutch leans back in his chair and looks into the black coffee that matches the darkness of his eyes. Then he adds, "It's too bad I don't know where to find her."

The girls are quiet. Vilma looks between Hutch and me for a second. Her forehead wrinkles. I watch the realization dawn on her slowly. Then doubt. She could never imagine Hutch breaking the rules like that. Me? Sure, why not. Not Hutch. I watch her trying to convince herself that she's imagining things, that the girl Hutch is talking about could be anyone.

"You should call the nurse," I tell Hutch.

Hutch makes a face, but takes the piece of paper back from Jermania. He folds it back into his chest pocket. We finish our food in a friendly silence and drive back to HCRC. I avoid

Vilma's eyes and Hutch's the whole time, just sit with my arms crossed over my chest.

Maybe I imagined the look on Vilma's face. Maybe it's my own guilt surfacing. As we head into the ranch, I head straight for my room. Vilma catches up with me on the steps. She grabs my arm and pulls to turn me toward her.

She's smirking, like we're in on a big secret together. "I smell something funky."

"Maybe you stepped in horse shit on the way in," I tell her. I smile, poker face on.

"Don't bullshit me, River. It all makes sense. The way he looks at you, the reason they switched your counselors. You two are bumping uglies! How big is it? I won't tell anyone, I swear."

I laugh in her face and place my hands on her shoulders. "You're crazy. They switched my counselors because Hutch had too much on his plate. Besides, he's too vanilla for my taste. I've already got my eye on a prize."

Vilma places her hand on her hips. "Yeah? Who?"

I shrug one shoulder innocently. It's astounding how easily a lie comes to my lips. The most believable lies come from some form of truth. "Why do you think they had to separate Randy and me?"

People will believe what you want them to if you leave enough blanks. Life is just a big game of Mad Libs. I hate that Randy was the first person to come to mind, but I'm really reaching into blank space. From now on, Hutch and I need to be more careful. No more duets. No more staring at me like smoke slipping through his fingers. No more.

I have to throw Vilma off our scent. I don't care what happens to me. I don't want Hutch to lose his job. I know what I have to do, even if it means hurting him along the way.

CHAPTER 21

I stare at the little blue pill for hours before I go to bed. Part of me wants to place it on my tongue and let the chemicals work their magic. But the part of me that spent an afternoon singing to sick kids tells me to flush it down the toilet. I place the pill back in its secret compartment, and shove the book under my mattress. I tell myself that it's evidence for later. I'm not going to take it. I've been doing so well, even getting up to six hours of sleep a night.

Two days later, I still ache everywhere. I can feel the pills under my mattress, like they're a pea and I'm the princess of the Kingdom of Addicts. I brush my teeth and wash the sleep off my face. I race down to the nurse's office. If I had a tail, it would wag.

"Someone's happy," Nurse Jean says.

"Someone's neck brace is coming off."

She gets her supplies and has me sit down. I see Taylor pushing his mop down the hall. He winks in my direction, and it takes all of me to not give him the bird. I give him a fake smile, and he keeps walking. He's like a vulture, the way he hangs around doors.

"If you feel any pain," Nurse Jean says, "we're putting it back on, you understand?"

"It doesn't really hurt," I say. "It just feels stiff. When can I ride again?"

"I wouldn't recommend it for another week."

I pout, but promise her I'll be careful. When she takes the brace off, I feel like a whole new person. I stretch slightly from side to side.

"How do you feel?"

I take a deep breath. "Free."

Back in my room, I dab on pink lip gloss and fluff my curls out. I find a bright blue, long-sleeved shirt with a deep neckline that accentuates my small boobs. It's too cold for shorts, but my jeans fit like a glove. I head down to the cafeteria and pile eggs and bacon on a plate. I can feel heads turn in my direction as I look for my mark. The girls wave at me, but Randy, whose eyes linger on my cleavage, sticks a foot out to block my passing.

Rumors catch like wildfire. I know this from way back in high school. My reputation clung to me like cigarette smoke, and I did nothing to dissuade the whispers that carried my name. Most of the time, I took silent bets on the things people said about me. Who was River Thomas going to blow on prom night? Who was River Thomas going to make out with in the boy's locker room? It didn't matter that I didn't date boys in high school, and I didn't go to my prom because I dropped out of school beforehand. I just had a "look" about me. That's the way people are, and here at rehab it's no exception.

All they have to do is assume I'm "that kind of girl" and see me talk with a handsome guy, and the assumptions are all theirs to make. I wonder how long it'll take before someone "sees" us fooling around in the elevator or by the stables.

"Where you going so fast, babycakes?" Randy asks.

"Are you going to offer me a seat, or what?"

Randy pats his lap. I take the seat beside him. When I look over my shoulder, Maddie, Vilma, Fran, and Julie are leaning in conspiratorially.

"How was your volunteering?" I ask.

"Who cares? I'm just glad it was a one-and-done thing. I think I might've caught something from those old geezers."

"Charming."

Randy is incredibly attractive. His hair is like polished gold, and his eyes are a darker blue than mine. He's got a smile that would be certified in panty dropping, and he's not shy about pulling up his shirt and showing off his tight abs. Still, he doesn't do it for me. I'm more sexually attracted to my breakfast than I am to Randy. Still, I have to put on a show to keep the heat off Hutch and me. This rumor won't ruin someone's life, just my reputation, and I don't care about that.

"So," he says. "You want to take me up on my offer?"

"What do you have in mind?"

"Just a night you'll never forget." He traces my cheekbone with his finger.

I stop myself from laughing. I hate when guys try so hard. Is it terrible that I almost feel sorry for him?

When I look up, Hutch is walking across the cafeteria with his breakfast. He's looking at us. He picks the first table in front of him and sits down, glancing in our direction every now and then. I take a deep breath.

"Aren't you in here for sex addiction?" I ask.

He shrugs. "I'm in here for a lot of things."

"You're not still mad I punched you?"

"Nah," he says, smiling. For a moment, his facade falls. He's just a cute guy trying to flirt. "I deserved it. How about it? Let me make it up to you. I've been told I have an excellent tongue."

He leans into my shoulder, which makes someone whistle across the room. I try not to pay attention to the heads that are turning in our direction. I try not to pay attention to Hutch staring at us.

"Tomorrow night?"

"3F?" I ask. Suddenly, I want to abort this plan. My heart hammers in my throat and my legs start to shake.

Randy smiles. I kiss his cheek, and take my tray to the garbage. Then I head out to the courtyard and breathe deeply, trying to draw strength from the clean mountain air.

• • •

I know I have to explain to Hutch what my plan is. I also need him to get some things for the Halloween party. He wasn't at the cafeteria for lunch or playing basketball with Simmons. I find him reading a book in his office.

The halls are clear, so I walk right in and shut the door

behind me. He glances in my direction and then goes back to some Dennis Lehane novel that looks well-loved and worn. I sit in a plush leather chair across from him. We don't speak. I can practically feel his mind racing with questions.

There's a giant clock on the wall. I can hear it *tick tick ticking* the minutes away. I alternate between looking at the floor, Hutch's jeans, the clock, the door, the turning pages, and Hutch's lips. No, look at the clock again.

I decide to break the silence. I grab the book from his hands and toss it to the side. "Are you going to talk or are you going to sulk until I go away?"

His features are controlled. He's reaching for whatever shrink training he might've had, but failing. "Okay, let's talk. What was that this morning?"

I wrinkle my brow. "What are you talking about?"

"I'm talking about the show you were putting on with Randy."

"First of all, we didn't put on a show. He was just getting too close. Second of all, what I do isn't your business."

"All the counselors saw you." He says it with disdain. I can hear the pain in his words, and I wish I could retrace my steps this morning. "Relationships between patients are against the rules."

"So are relationships between counselors and patients."

"That's not fair. You know how I feel about you." He shakes his head, tapping his pen on his blank notepad. "Do you know that it only took seconds for people to start talking about you and *Randy?*"

I wish I could smile at his jealousy. "Isn't it better if people talk about me and Randy than if they talk about me and you?"

He looks up. His pen is still. "What do you mean?"

"Yesterday. Vilma basically told me that the girl you were talking about during lunch was me. Really smooth, Hutch. The day I fell off the horse, Taylor tried to help me off my saddle. I didn't want his help, but he made it seem like I was waiting for you. I'm not trying to hurt you, but I also know how important your job is to you. What would happen if you got fired because of me?"

"I'd find another job."

"Not as a counselor. Not if anything about us got on your record. You *know* no one can find out about this."

"Are you sure you're trying to protect me and not you?"

"What's that supposed to mean?"

He sighs. Sets his notepad to the side. He clenches his jaw so tight, the muscles there ripple. "I mean you're afraid of the things I said the other day. You're afraid of letting me too close. You said so yourself. I don't want the answer to be jumping into—"

"Randy's bed? You can't be my boyfriend, Hutch. You're not allowed to be."

"Don't sabotage this."

"You think I'm afraid because you said I was the only girl you've fucked this year?" I scoff. "I'm trying to do what's best here."

"For who? And how? By sleeping with Randy?"

My nostrils flare. "I'm not going to sleep with Randy."

"River, please. Don't do me any favors."

"I have to. I owe you. You saved my life up on that cliff. You carried me to the hospital when I fell off my horse. I owe you for so much, I can't even begin to pay you back."

"I'm not keeping a running tab for you. I'm doing these things because I care about you, River. Why is it so hard for you to let me care about you?"

"Because!" I stand up, pushing the chair back. I pace back and forth.

"That's not an answer. You and I keep going back and forth—I try to protect you; you try to protect me. We're going around in circles, and the only thing we've accomplished so far is more distance."

He stands and closes the space between us so quickly, I gasp. His hands hover over my shoulders. He's afraid to touch me. He should be. I'm a wildfire. I burn everything in my path. But I see the decision in his earth-brown eyes. He decides to hold me.

I close my eyes and breathe in his scent—leather and grass

and coffee. His hands trail down my arms, holding my wrists with his palms. He brings my hands to his lips and kisses each one. He turns them over, kisses the inside of my wrists. I feel like I'm being stretched too thin. I don't know what's right or wrong anymore. I never used to care, but I care now.

I open my eyes. His stare is too much for me. I try to look away, but he cups my face with his hands. His touch is firm, but tender.

"Why are you afraid to look at me?" he whispers.

I glance at the closed door behind us. If someone were to come in, it would be over. Yet, I can't pull away. I hold him tighter. I wrap my arms around his waist. Press my hands against the hard muscles of his back.

"Because I've never felt this way about anyone before. It's freaking me out."

He smirks. He thumbs my jawline, sending shivers down my skin. "You don't have to freak out alone. You don't have to protect us alone."

I pull back. "Now you know how I felt seeing you with the nurse."

He graces me with his brilliant smile. "I wouldn't take you for the jealous type."

"I'm not. Mostly because I've never cared before." I trace my fingers down his spine.

"Jealousy is normal," he says. "But it's not healthy. I don't like to lose my cool that way."

"Relax, Dr. Shrink. Just be yourself."

"I am being myself."

"I mean you don't have to be a counselor with me." That's the magic word. It pulls us back to the wrongness, the reality of this. We let go and unhook ourselves from each other. He's two feet away, but it feels like miles.

He sits back, gripping the arms of his chair tightly. "Fine. I've wanted to smash Randy's brains in ever since you made his nose bleed. I hate that you kissed him."

"His cheek."

"I don't care where. I hate it. I hated seeing you with him."

"You're not my boyfriend, Hutch."

"But I want to be." His stare is unwavering. I force myself to hold on. "I've never felt this way about another woman. The more I get to know you, the less I care about losing everything."

I feel dizzy. My mouth is dry. "Don't be reckless. We have to be smart about this. We can have it all. You just have to trust me. Can you do that?"

He clears his throat. He leans forward. "Yes. I can. I will. What do you want me to do?"

"I'm going to go to Randy tomorrow night."

He shuts his eyes and looks down. "Absolutely not."

"I just need people to see me going down the corridor. I'm not going to do anything with him. I'll stand him up. But I know guys like him. He's going to save face. He's going to make up all kinds of things about me."

"I don't like this."

"You haven't even heard about what you're going to do."

His eyes widen. He licks his lips. "What am I going to do?"

"You're going to leave here and go on a date."

"No, I'm not."

"Yes, you are. Or at least *tell* people you are. You know who the gossip mills are. You also have to stay away from me for a little while. I mean it, Hutch. You're always there when I need help. It'll get noticeable."

"This is either a really smart plan," he says, "or the most elaborate ruse to blow me off ever."

I get out of my seat and kiss him hard and fast. I forgot how sensitive my neck still is, but I don't care. I lose track of time as Hutch kisses me back. His lips taste my lips and his tongue finds my tongue. I rest my knees on either side of him, and the armchair groans with our weight. His hands grab my ass and squeeze so hard, I cry out. I'm so wet I could put the Clark Fork River to shame.

I stand back, placing a hand over my heart. I sit back just as someone knocks on the door. One of the temp counselors. Hutch clears his throat, but keeps his notepad over his crotch area.

"Hey, Simmons. We're just wrapping up here. What's up?"

"I just wanted to go over the camping trip. You got a sec?"

"I'll just be going," I say, hoping Simmons doesn't notice the redness on my lips. I pull out a piece of paper from the back of my jeans. "Here's the list of supplies we need."

"River Thomas, right?" Simmons asks. I nod. "I'm Dr. Simmons." He holds his clipboard up. "Have you signed up for the camping trip?"

"I don't really have any camping stuff."

"Oh, we provide it. I can put you down—spaces fill up quickly. Last month Hutch and I did a great campfire medley. I heard about your singing at the Children's hospital."

I hang onto the doorknob. "Sure thing. Sign me up."

I don't even glance at Hutch as I exit the room, and it kills me.

• • •

Not looking at Hutch is harder than I thought. The next day I feel him everywhere. He's there when I go for my walk—as I'm heading out on the trail, he's on his way back. Despite the brisk fall air, he's shirtless and in shorts. Still thinking about our kiss this morning, I'm ready to continue it. But as I start to take a step toward him, Maddie and Julie come jogging up from behind him, followed by Pete. Maddie and Julie burst into giggles as Pete runs past them, shirtless. Hutch just shakes his head and keeps his headphones on.

I break from the path and head into the woods. I'm getting better at orienting myself. Now that I've spent more time in the trees, I can tell the subtle differences between the patterns. I keep a lookout for the doe that likes to hang out here, but no such luck.

I spend lunch sandwiched between Vilma and Jermania, who ask if I'm actually going to hook up with Randy.

"I haven't decided yet," I say. "I mean, he's totally hot. He just talks too much."

Vilma tries to wave Hutch over, but he's sitting with the

other counselors today. "Well, if you do hook up with Randy, be sure to tell us every filthy detail."

I smirk and bite down on an apple. It's brown on the inside, and I end up throwing it out.

After lunch, I find myself being extra quiet during group. Maddie is telling a story about the first time she got blackout drunk. She woke up naked in her basement and didn't remember getting there. She cried a little bit, but my feelings have started to change toward her. What looks like a sad, lost little girl is actually someone incredibly calculating. Someone like me. Perhaps I'm not the best con artist in this whole joint after all.

She stops me after group and nudges me in the ribs. "So, are you feeling better?"

I smile and take the arm she extends, like we're schoolgirls skipping around between classes. "Much, thank you."

"There's more where that came from, you know."

I give her a playful grin. "Really?"

"You didn't… tell anyone?"

"Of course not! I can keep a secret."

"Me too," she says, just to say it. "Speaking of secrets, I heard you're meeting up with Randy tonight."

"From who?" That was fast.

She shrugs. "From Randy. He's telling everyone. Did you know his parents own a burger chain in Iowa? I've never been to Iowa. Anyway, he's rich."

I can practically see the light bulb go on over Maddie's head.

"I'm sure he rolls in his dad's money before bed," I tell her. I let that simmer. If I've read Maddie right, I bet she's going to give Randy an invitation to the barn, even if she doesn't trust me enough to invite me. She changes the subject right away.

"Are you going on the camping expedition next week?"

"I am. And you can't laugh at me. It's going to be my first time."

"Well, let's hope the third time is the charm when it comes to you and the great outdoors."

"Let's hope."

Before dinner, I decide to go to the stables. Jillian is putting the horses away when she spots me.

"I'm so happy you're feeling better," she says. "Did you want to see Apollo?"

She leads me to his stable, and hands me a carrot. "When you're done, just close the door."

"I will." I head inside to grab a brush. "Hey, boy, did you miss me?"

He licks his lips and yawns. I didn't realize horses yawn.

"Of course you didn't. You're a horse." I get into a rhythm brushing his flank. "You know, the only pet I ever had was a goldfish, and that ended with a flush down the toilet. Ever since then, my dad wouldn't let us have pets.

"Even between the two of us, we couldn't keep plants alive. I begged him to buy us a cactus after I did a report on the desert in junior high. The little ones with the tiny flowers. It was dead within the week. I'm less nurturing than the deserts of New Mexico. Isn't that something? You don't seem to mind me though." I rub the spot between Apollo's eyes, and he makes a funny noise. I give him his carrot, and he munches away.

"So this is where you like to hide," Randy says, wrapping his arms around me from behind.

I jump. "I'm not hiding."

He holds his arms up, like he means no harm. He leans against the frame of Apollo's stall. He shuts his eyes and looks like he's trying to find the square root of pi. He mutters something that sounds like, "trust fund."

Then he drops his pants. He's commando, and semi-hard. As if thoroughly offended, Apollo kicks his forelegs up.

"Put that thing away," I hiss at Randy. I'm trying not to laugh at how stupid he looks, pantless in a horse stable.

"I thought… You said…" He backs away and looks around, panicked.

I scoff. "Dude, seriously. You think I'm going to have sex with you in front of all these horses?"

He looks up at the roof and curses. His blue eyes glimmer in the gaslight. He looks even more mortified when he looks down at his crotch.

Apollo and I exchange a long look, and I swear even the horse is embarrassed.

"Hold on a second," Randy says. "This never happens."

"Mmhmm." I continue brushing Apollo's mane. I wish I could say this is the strangest thing that's happened to me, but I worked in a village dungeon for a stint.

"This almost never happens." He spits on his hand and I'm forced to listen to the terrible sound of him trying to get it up. I just feel sorry for the horses.

"Randy," I say. "Stop. You don't have to do this."

"You don't understand!" He starts to cry. He pulls up his pants. "You don't know. I think I just stole too many of my dad's Viagra as a kid. Now I can't get an erection without them."

His hands are trembling. He turns around and looks at me with the most pathetic face. "I'm sorry. Please don't punch me in the face again. You won't tell anyone, will you?"

I sigh. This is your life, River Thomas. "Fine. But you have to do me a favor."

"Anything."

I tell him what I want him to say and he looks surprised.

"Are you sure you want that? Why?"

"You're really not in a position to ask me questions."

He smiles, and for a moment he almost looks like a good guy. He starts to approach me for a hug, but I put my arms way up to stop him.

"You're okay, River."

"I wish I could say the same for you."

Randy leaves first, and I follow fifteen minutes later, locking the barn doors behind me. When I walk into the cafeteria all eyes are on me. It feels like high school all over again. Randy is sitting with a bunch of guys, whispering something and grinning from ear to ear. I wonder how much damage can be done in fifteen minutes. From the looks I'm getting, the answer is "a lot."

I sit with the girls. I should be glad that my plan actually worked, but I'm not. I stab at my cold food and sulk. I don't notice something is wrong until Vilma elbows me. Julie has her head in her arms and is sobbing.

"What's the matter?" I pat her head.

Vilma and Maddie look at each other. They press their fingers to their lips and thumb in the direction of the counselor table. Hutch is missing. I feel his absence like a hole in my chest. I know where he is without even asking.

Julie sits up. She wipes her snotty tears from her face. She tries to speak, but her sobs shake her too hard.

"Hutch went out on a date tonight," Fran says. "I heard him telling Simmons. Some nurse he met in Missoula. I bet he won't be coming home tonight. She picked him up and everything."

I feel myself start. Heat flashes across my skin. I press my hands on the table. *Don't cry. You told him to do this. This was your fucking plan in the first place. You are not allowed to get mad.*

And I'm not mad.

It's even worse than I imagined. I'm *hurt*. I'm hurt because the man I want did exactly as I asked him to. I'm not allowed to feel this way. I'm not allowed to show it.

"Good," I say, pressing one hand on top of the other. "Maybe he'll loosen up a little. Isn't he so uptight?"

"River," Maddie says, pointing her thumb at Julie.

"Sorry," I mutter.

"It's okay," Julie says. Her shoulders slump towards the ground. Her eyes are red. She looks the way I feel inside. "I never really thought we could be together. I just love him so much, you know?"

I freeze when I hear how easily her proclamation comes out. Here I can barely say the word without flinching.

"Let's have a happy story," Maddie says, turning to me. "I heard you blew Randy in the stables. Details please?"

I was wrong. Fifteen minutes. That's all it took to break a handful of hearts.

CHAPTER 22

FORTY DAYS SOBER

Helen calls me to her office first thing in the morning. I go through ten thousand scenarios of why she wants to see me. Hutch? No. Randy. Did Taylor say something? Does she think I'm not working hard enough on the party?

"I didn't go down on Randy last night," I blurt out as soon as I get through the door.

I realize too late that Hutch, Simmons, and Ransom are also in the office. Helen raises a stern eyebrow. She looks from me to the other counselors in the room. I want to die. I usually have a high threshold for humiliation. Hell, after everything I've put my friends through over the course of drunken nights out, I am the queen of morning regret. But here, with Hutch trying to mask the same hurt I feel, I can't take it.

My plan has spectacularly spiraled out of control. This was my doing. But the awkward faces of the people in front of me are getting to be a little too much.

"Thank you for that, River," Helen says, "but that's not the reason I called you here. Although I am happy you've resisted Mr. Rider's charms."

"Oh," I say, wishing I could press myself so hard against the wall that I'd go right through it. "Okay. What's up?"

"I wanted to go over your file a little bit," Helen says. "I got a strange inquiry about you, and I wanted to verify it with you."

I swallow the lump in my throat. I nod.

"Someone claiming to be your uncle asked if you were staying here."

"My parents were only children," I say. "My only family are the two people listed."

"Sky Lopez and Leti Delgado?"

"Yeah."

They look concerned. I should tell them about the strange e-mail I received. I should tell them about the anonymous note someone left for me at the hospital. I should tell them about the text message. I know who's looking for me. The fact that he's found me shakes me to my very bone. I need to get out of here. Right now.

"What did you tell him?"

"I want you to know that everyone in this facility is on your side. If there's someone who could pose a threat to you, someone you're avoiding or afraid of, please tell us."

"What did you *tell* him?"

"I said there was no one here named River Thomas, and that perhaps there was a mistake."

"Could I talk to you alone for a second?"

Helen looks at the counselors, and they head out the door. I don't have to turn around to see that Hutch lingers. Finally, he leaves. All of last night's events feel like they happened to someone else. They feel so insignificant and far away.

"River, who is looking for you?"

I start to pace around the room. "After my dad died, I got into the most volatile relationship of my life. He was a poker player too. We met at a game one night, and a month later we were still together. It was one of those downward spirals that you don't feel until you're lying in an alley somewhere."

Helen presses her hand to her lips. "Oh, River."

"It's not what you think. I mean, it could have been worse. He just pushed me through a glass window. It sounds terrible when I say it out loud, actually. I slashed his face in self-defense. Someone saw us fighting and called the cops. I tried to get a restraining order, but his damage was worse than mine, I was the one who was seen as the attacker.

"I didn't hear from him again until this summer, after a family wedding. He'd been looking for me. When I was on my way here, I got a text from an unknown number. I turned my phone off and gave it to you to lock up. Then I got a weird e-mail. I know it's him. I didn't think he would find me. Then there's the note…"

"What?"

I tell her about the note that was slipped among my other hospital cards.

"I wish you'd come to me sooner. Brought me the note."

"I didn't think he'd find me here. I'm sorry, Helen. But I have to go."

I turn around and leave her office. Hutch is hovering outside in the hall. When he sees me, he starts to grab me and ask me what's wrong, but I duck out of his hold. I can hear Helen's steps right behind me. My hands are shaking. When I reach my room, I grab my duffle bag. I pull all of my clothes out of their drawers and throw them on the bed. I go to the bathroom. All I have there is a handful of toiletries. I don't know where I'll even go. I just know that I can't stay here.

"River!" Helen and Hutch are at my door. They close the door behind them.

"You can't keep me here, okay?" I say.

"Where are you going to run off to?" Helen asks.

I shove my clothes into my bag. "Anywhere. Canada. Alaska. Does it really matter, in the end? I chose this place because it was in the middle of nowhere and he still found me. What does it matter where I go? He'll still find me."

I feel like I can't breathe. I feel like there isn't enough air in this room, in this building in the middle of the mountains. I pace back and forth. Then I remember the book under my bed. It'll calm me down. I just need a little blue pill to bring me back down to earth. I lift my mattress and reach for the book.

"River!" Hutch says. "What are you doing?"

I come up empty. The book isn't there. Someone was in my room.

I turn to Helen and Hutch. "I just want to go!"

Helen comes around and wraps her arms around me. "I will do everything I can to make sure no one can hurt you. If you run now you're going to run for the rest of your life. I've already alerted the staff. If anyone inquires about you at all, they are to say that there is no one here by that name. Then we'll forward that information to the police to establish a paper trail."

I look at Helen with a little bit of shock. Whatever bet I had on her, I lost. I was wrong. I underestimated her. "You used to be a cop."

She nods. "That's another story. In the meantime, we're going to move your room to the ground floor."

I keep packing my things. I realize that, besides some clothes and books, I don't have much with me. Hutch insists on shouldering my bag for me.

As I follow Helen and Hutch out of my room, other patients stand at their doors and in the halls to watch us. They whisper about my fate, what I've done wrong. Even Randy looks guilty, assuming I'm in trouble because of him. I don't know how, but in my gut I know that Taylor has something to do with this. I've thrown myself into a game I don't think I can win. It might be too late to back out now.

・・・

I stay in my new room the rest of the day. At some point, Helen knocks on my door to bring me food. She tries to tell me that I'm safe, and everything is going to be okay. I even pretend I believe her. She's trying so hard; the least I can do is make her feel good about it.

This room actually locks. I bask in my newfound privacy. Other than that, my room is the same as before, only a little bigger. This one has a desk with a reading lamp. I set up my books there. I handwrite a letter to Sky.

Dear Sky,
Things are bad. Like, really bad. I never told you the whole truth about Kiernan. You only met him once. I know that you think I started partying extra hard because I

was sad about my dad. That's not wrong, but it's not the whole story. I was trying to make myself forget about Kiernan. No one ever treated me that way before, and I was so lost in my grief that I let him. You know me, Sky. You know I know better. I was just lonely, and he was the first guy that I'd liked in a long time. I wasn't in love, but I found myself unable to let go of that. I was needy. I should've gone to you or to Leti. I was just afraid.

Now he's back, and he's probably looking to scare me. The thing is, he was never that violent before, only verbally abusive. I'm not the kind of girl to let myself get talked down to, but we were fucked up for 90 percent of our relationship. I'm telling you this now because he knows I'm here. There are some weird things going on. I still haven't gone back to the barn because of my accident.

The pills I got a girl to give me vanished from under my bed. The director moved me to a new room with a lock. So, win? I love you and miss you. Despite all the bad feelings that come with K, I realize I really don't want to leave here. I think I love this place. Not being an addict at a recovery center, but the sound of trees and the big Montana sky. Plus... there's Hutch.

Call me crazy. And please just call me.

Love,
Riv

I fold the letter, seal it, and take it to Hutch's office. I know he's in there with another patient. I wait down the hall until the hour is up and Maddie exits the office.

She gives me a smile. "We're not neighbors anymore! What happened?"

"Helen wants to keep an eye on me," I tell her. "Thinks I'm bad news."

Maddie shoves her hands in her pockets. "Because of Randy? That's stupid. Other patients have gotten caught having sex all over the place and they're still here."

I give her an innocent face. "Beats me. Anyway, at least I have a lock on my door so no one can go through my stuff."

Her eyes widen, and she looks away. "Okay."

I'm irrationally angry with her. Why would she go into my room? How would she know where the pills were or that I didn't take them? I should know better than to expect more from someone like Maddie. Is this what Sky and Leti feel like when I let them down? Because it feels shitty as hell.

"River," Maddie says. "I'm sorry. Things will get better."

I wave goodbye to her and head into Hutch's office.

"You got some free time?" I ask him.

"Of course." He looks around the room and shuffles papers on his desk. "Are you okay?"

"Yeah, I'm liking my new digs. Can you do me a favor?"

"Anything."

"You should be careful about giving people blank favors."

"You're not just any person, River."

That brings a smile to my face, at least. "I need you to send this letter out. It's to my friend Sky. I don't trust anyone else to do it. Take it with you when you go home tonight."

"That's kind of a problem. I won't be going home tonight."

"Why not?"

He shrugs. "I'm staying here. Helen thinks we need more people for security."

"And you volunteered your muscles?"

He smirks. "Something like that. I'll be sure to make a post office run tomorrow."

"Thank you."

"What else can I do?" He looks as helpless as I feel.

"Can we nap? I'm suddenly really tired."

He brings me into a hug. I feel so secure in his arms. It's a strange feeling to have. He kisses the top of my head. I wish I could stay in this moment. But when someone knocks on the door to his office, I'm forced to jump out of his arms and into the patient's seat while he opens the door.

It's Julie. When she sees me, she's surprised. "Hey River!"

"Hey Julie," Hutch says, opening the door wide to let her in. He might as well be saying, "Nothing's going on here! Come in!"

She pulls her long sleeves around her hands and covers her mouth. "I just wanted to sign up for the camping trip."

"Oh, well, Dr. Simmons is handling the sign ups. But I'll make sure to put your name down."

Julie smiles like Hutch is the sun shining down on her. It's painful to watch, really. That reminds me about last night. It feels like so long ago. Every time I turn around, something is changing, and I'm not sure I can keep up.

"Oh, okay. It's okay. See you guys at dinner."

When Julie leaves, I fill Hutch in on everything that happened. Julie and her waterworks, Randy and the stables. To my surprise, Hutch is laughing.

"It's not funny!" I stomp around the office. I pull a book on nature photography from the shelf and sit on his desk. I'm making myself quite comfortable, and he's letting me. "It was terrible watching him trying to get a hard-on."

Hutch is almost doubled over. "At least I know I've got nothing to worry about."

"Really? Like you were worried before? How was your *date*?"

His laugh gets cut short. I flip through the colorful pages of lakes and rivers and mountaintops. I try not to let myself look too disappointed. It seems petty after everything that's been happening.

"It wasn't a date, River." He walks over to me and takes my face in his hands. How did I ever function before his embrace? I turn my face away, but grab onto him by the waist of his jeans. His belt buckle is cold, but the skin of his abdomen is hot where I touch it. "I thought it would be more believable if people saw her pick me up. We met other nurses and went to a bar in Hamilton. That's it."

I shrug.

"Don't get pouty. I was doing exactly as you asked."

"I just wasn't prepared for it. Besides, you should have seen

Julie crying over you last night. I think that's going to be trouble if you don't put a stop to it. You have to keep up the act. I told Maddie I was in trouble over the Randy thing."

"I'm afraid of all this lying," he says. "Someone's going to get hurt."

"It's a little late for that. Now, I'd better go and make my rounds. Stay away from me if you know what's good for you."

He presses a swift kiss to my lips, and I feel the promise of more in his kiss. "I officially can't do that. We are neighbors now, after all."

"What do you mean?" I turn around before letting myself out of the office.

"I mean you're in the staff wing. My room is directly across from yours."

CHAPTER 23

I've become sort of a legend overnight. Rumors fly all over the facility as to why I've had my room changed. I sit with Vilma, Fran, Jermania, and Julie during dinner. It's taco night, and they fire questions at me faster than I can answer them.

How did Helen find out?
What did she say to you?
Is Randy's dick really eleven inches long?
What's it like on the staff floor?

"I guess Randy was running his mouth. She told me I was under watch. It's not eleven inches long. And the rooms are basically the same as the rest, just with different lamps." I don't tell them that there are locks. I don't tell them that Hutch is right across from me. I don't tell them that I'm basically under protection.

"I don't know what the big deal is," Julie says. "Maddie says that people have gotten caught doing worse before. Why are they punishing you so much?"

"It doesn't matter," I say. "They might switch me back if I keep my head out of trouble."

"I don't know you well," Jermania says, "but you look like your middle name is Trouble."

I laugh, and we toast with our juice boxes. On the other side of the cafeteria, Randy is trying to hit on the brand new patient. Poor girl. When he catches me watching him, he turns red, picks up his tray, and runs out into the courtyard.

I go to bed early with the excuse of a headache. On the way there, I bump into Maddie. She looks disoriented.

"River!" she shouts. "You're so pretty. I hate that you're so pretty."

"Hey, are you okay?" I take her face into my hands. Her pupils are like pinpricks.

She brushes me away. "I'm fine. Leave me alone."

"As you wish." I keep walking and lock myself in my room. I feel antsy, knowing that Hutch's room is across the hall from mine. It brings a buzz to my skin. Is he going to visit me in the middle of the night? That would be really stupid, considering the other counselors are just down the hall from us.

I wake up at two in the morning. So much for being able to sleep through the night now that I have a lock on the door.

I sit up in my bed and flip the lock. I slowly turn the knob and look up and down the hall. The facility is completely quiet, except for the sounds of bugs and night critters outside. I walk the four paces it takes to get to Hutch's door. I press my hand to it. Should I knock? I shake my head and turn right back around.

Light floods behind me. My heart jumps to my throat when I see him standing in his open doorway. He's just roused from bed. He's in a pair of boxers and nothing else.

I step back into my room. He looks up and down the hall, quietly closes his door, and follows me in.

I close the door, careful of making even the slightest sound. Even the springs of my mattress sounds extra loud in this silence. We speak in the softest whispers.

"Hey," he says, standing close to the door. He turns off the ceiling light, but leaves on the desk lamp.

"Hi."

I watch him stand in front of me. He's the most perfect man I've ever seen. He takes a step closer, within reach. I press my hands to his lower abs. They make a perfect V, and I run my hand up his stomach, feeling every ripple of muscles beneath his skin. I rub his chest, then his arms. I wrap my hands around his neck and kiss him. We fall back onto the mattress.

Neither of us moves. We just keep our lips pressed together. My heart fills with the feeling of Hutch against me. Kissing him is like breathing after holding my breath underwater for far too long. He's the first to move his lips. He searches for more, and more, biting softly on my bottom lip. I'm so dizzy I fear

I might be dreaming.

"I've missed you so much," I find myself saying.

He holds my face in his hands. Presses himself against me so our best parts are lined up. He whispers my name, and I wonder if I'll ever get used to the way he looks at me. He brushes my hair back and presses a kiss to my cheek. Then he bites it.

"I'm right here," he says.

"You know what I mean." I rake my fingernails down his strong arms.

He sets his mouth on mine and nips at the bottom lip. "I do. I want you to know that I'm not going anywhere."

"Montana forever," I say, my laugh almost a shudder as we kiss.

"Shhh," he whispers.

He runs his hands through my hair, then starts moving down. I try to pull him up on top of me, but he answers with a wicked smile.

I watch him bend down and push my knees apart, and the thrill that runs through my body tells me I'm wide awake. He looks up at me. The muscles of his back ripple as he bends down to taste me between my legs. He pushes my lips apart with his tongue. I take my pillow and press it over my face. Hutch grabs me by my hips and pulls me against his face.

A little cry escapes my mouth when he pushes his finger inside me. He moves it around in a way that makes me want to scream some more. I can feel all of the tightness unwind from my body and concentrate in the pit of my stomach. I pull on his shoulders, trying to tell him to stand up, but he keeps his lips around my clit, licking delicious circles. I squeeze my legs around his head, and tug on his thick, beautiful hair. I can feel the walls inside me tighten as I come on his mouth. I bite down on the pillow until the waves of pleasure stop, and then I lie perfectly still.

I sit up and move over on the bed. Hutch climbs in beside me, and we lie down facing each other. He leans in and nuzzles my ear.

"You taste delicious," he whispers.

I smile, already feeling sleep blanket me. I reach out and rub his hardness. "Your turn. You don't have any condoms in these boxers do you?"

He shakes his head. "Not tonight."

"Why?" It comes out more like a whine.

He brushes my hair back. "Tonight is about you."

He pulls me against his chest, and I go willingly. I bury my face against him. I memorize the way his heart beats under my fingertips. I tap them out like a Morse code meant just for me.

"How long will you stay?" I ask. The clock says it's three a.m.

"For as long as I can." He kisses my forehead. I can't remember the last time I felt this warm and safe with someone. I can't remember wanting someone the way I want Hutch. Even this close to him, I feel like I'm too far away. I wrap my arm around him and throw my leg over his side. I feel his chuckle vibrate through my skin.

"Forever," I say.

"Forever."

I tilt my face up and kiss him luxuriously, lazily. I could kiss him until our lips are dry and raw and numb, and even then I'd want to keep going.

At some point I fall asleep. I wake up alone. My heart sinks with disappointment. Is this what he felt like when I ran out on him? I look around the small room, but there really isn't anywhere for him to have gone other than back to his own room.

The only thing that's different than when I left him is that Hutch has left me a note.

"I'm going to dream of tasting you." I pull the cover over my head, and dream of him, too.

CHAPTER 24

Hutch doesn't come back the next night. He goes somewhere with Simmons to get the rest of our camping supplies, and I'm out cold before they come back. But it's okay, because our party-planning sessions are filled with plenty of making out. We're too nervous to actually try to have sex, considering how often people knock on his door. It's easier to pull our lips apart than our other appendages.

It makes me all the more anxious to go on the camping trip. Throughout the day, I busy myself creating different scenarios for us to get together. All together we have a group of sixteen, plus two counselors and Jillian. Of the patients, the only people I know are Randy, Julie, Jermania, and Pete.

Everyone is in charge of their own tent, sleeping bag, and food supply. It's supposed to teach us about independence, and self-reliance. I've never pitched a tent, and I've never slept in a sleeping bag before. Though the prospect of trying to fit inside one with Hutch is pretty spectacular.

The morning of the trip, we pile into the van at the ass crack of dawn and drive up to Flathead Lake.

Simmons tells Jillian about the Flathead Lake monster, which is supposed to be a cousin of sorts to the Loch Ness monster.

"Can I stick my head out the sun roof?" I ask.

"For a minute," Simmons tells me. He's by far the most chill of all the counselors.

I wonder how Hutch is faring in the other van. We decided to separate from each other to keep up the ruse that there's nothing between us, though other than Vilma there haven't been anymore hints, and she's not even here. Still, I feel extra guilty and want to be more cautious. I pull back the sunroof and stand on the seat so that half of my torso is out. I raise my hands in the air like I'm on a rollercoaster. I shout into the massive Montana sky, the trees, and the snowcapped mountains.

The van behind us honks. I turn around for a second to see Hutch's panicked expression. Jillian tugs at my pant legs, and I come back inside.

"It's amazing. It's not even cold yet."

"Camping is even better when it's warm out," Jillian says. "Though we don't go camping much in Spain."

"I think I'd like it better there, eating tapas and drinking wine," Simmons tells her.

Jermania and I look at each other. She smirks, and I know she's thinking the same thing. Simmons is trying to flirt.

The ride is extra long, since one of the grouchy older campers calls out for music, and we end up listening to old-man country songs for the remaining hour. When we get to Flathead Lake and park in the campground, I'm stunned at how beautiful it is out here. There aren't many tourists, but there are still local campers who are taking advantage of the unseasonable warmth.

The second van, led by Hutch, arrives five minutes after we do. Hutch gives me a look that tells me he does not approve of my sunroof antics, but I simply smile and shoulder the weight of my gear.

"I'll go rent the kayaks," Simmons says.

"Kayaks? This isn't the camping area?"

"It's *a* camping area," Hutch tells me. "We kayak to one of the smaller islands inside the lake. They look tiny from far away, but they're pretty big."

"We get a whole island all to ourselves?"

He smiles. He looks devilishly rugged in his faded jeans and thick boots. He's got a lightweight sweater with all kinds of pockets. I notice the knife strapped to his hip.

"Planning on cutting down some trees?" I point to the weapon.

"That's just in case."

"Is anyone else packing?"

"Simmons has his riffle. Just to scare away any bears. And

we have flares for emergencies."

I widen my eyes and freeze, just as Hutch breaks into a laugh. I punch his arm, and he ducks. He's extra playful, which is hard to resist. Everyone is in a good mood out here.

"Two people per kayak," Jillian informs us. "Raise your hand if this is your first time in a kayak."

I raise my hand and so do six others.

"Buddy up with one of the more experienced campers," Simmons tells us.

Randy slides up beside me and winks. Someone behind me (Julie probably) giggles. I shake my head, but it's already decided.

"Don't worry, Sweetheart. I know CPR. I won't let you drown."

"Please, do." I roll my eyes in his direction.

At the lake, I walk to the waterline and stare out at the pristine blue. The water is cold. It ripples, and has a silver sheen. The trees are a deep, dark green. It's something I've only ever seen in photos. Now that I'm here, I commit it to memory. I never want to forget this view. It feels endless, like I'm the smallest thing in the world. It's thrilling and scary—just like my feelings for Hutch.

"River," Randy calls out. "You ready?"

Randy is already in our tandem kayak. He takes point. Hutch helps me with my things, and tightens the life vest around my chest. I'm supposed to pull on it to inflate if I fall overboard, which does exactly zero to calm my nerves.

"Keep your strokes in time with Randy, okay?"

"Don't worry," Randy says. "She knows how I like my strokes."

I snicker, and Hutch settles a disapproving glare at Randy. "I'm just fucking around, man," Randy says. "Relax."

Hutch's jaw ripples from the tension as he walks away, a hand on his knife.

Men are dumb. I inhale deeply to calm my nerves. Then I realize I'm at Randy's mercy to get across the water and onto the island in the distance. As we push off, I paddle tentatively, hitting Randy's oar by accident.

He turns around, losing all the sass and annoyance that he displays in front of others. He's got two-face syndrome. I don't think that's a real thing, but it's something I notice with a lot of people. They act one way in front of a crowd and way differently when they're one-on-one.

"Relax, River," he says.

"I hate when people tell me to relax. It makes me less relaxed. I've never been in the middle of a river. How deep is this thing, anyway?"

He chuckles. "I'm not sure. Don't think about that. I'll start counting, okay? Start with the left. Right. Left. Right."

We fall into an easy rhythm. After a few minutes my arms are burning. I should've listened to Ransom and joined his morning kickboxing class. It's too late for that now. Our yellow kayaks cut across the water, and I shout. Others answer my shout with even more hooting and hollering.

"It's really hard for you, isn't it?" Randy asks.

"What's hard?" I shout. "And if you're trying to be a perv, I swear to God I will murder you."

"I mean *trusting* someone else."

I don't answer, but the truth is yes. I do have a hard time putting my trust in someone, even with something as small as paddling across a lake. We paddle in silence, our grunts getting more and more labored the closer we get.

"Why are you like this?" I ask him.

"Like what?"

"I mean, you're cool when it's just us. But when you're in front of other people, you're a huge dick."

"I am what I am."

"Don't forget, I've seen your dick."

He barks a laugh. "Oh, right. Thanks for not telling people, by the way. I don't know, I guess I just act out. I don't know why I say or do things, but when I do, it's almost impossible to take back. I think in the scheme of things, I'm way less fucked up than the rest of my family."

"Yeah?"

"One time I told my mother about my dad's affairs. I had no

idea that they had already agreed to sleep with other people. My dad practically has a whole other family in Seattle, how fucked up is that? Shit, all they do is tell me how to live my life, and who I can date, and what to do with my money. Fucking hypocrites. My dad said I couldn't have my trust fund until I finished rehab and started a family. So here I am."

I feel like I've been hit with cold water. I've never heard him talk this much about himself. "So here you are, with your pill addiction."

"You know, I can't get a hard-on for more than a minute unless I'm popping pills? I think I did something to my dick. The doctors tell me that's not possible, but of course they would. They get paid by the drug companies. It's all a fucking scam. And who gets fucked?"

"Everyone, unless it's by you."

He splashes me with cold water. Then he asks, "Are you going to tell me why you *wanted* people to think we hooked up?"

"I have my reasons." That's something my dad always used to say when he didn't want to explain things. Like why he kept giving my mother money even after she left us. Why he didn't tell me he was sick until it was too late. *I have my reasons.*

"Well, whatever they are. You're okay, River Thomas."

"You're... tolerable, Randall Rider."

"I hate my name. I think I might change it, after I get my trust fund."

"Must be nice."

"It's the only good thing about being my father's son."

• • •

We get to land, and Randy hops out of the kayak. He pulls it halfway from the water so it doesn't get carried back out with the tide. I get out and pull it the rest of the way. My arms are *killing* me, but I can't stop now. We spend half the day setting up camp and building a fire.

Simmons has it down to a science. He's got oil and a lighter, but he wants to show off and impress Jillian. Her cheeks are red from kayaking, but she still sits near him and smiles. He pushes up his glasses after he blows on the little spark that comes from rubbing sticks together.

Others help collect wood, and we keep it under a tarp. There's a 30 percent chance of rain tomorrow.

"I have to go to the bathroom," Julie announces.

Simmons hands her a shovel and a roll of toilet paper. Her jaw falls down to her chin with embarrassment. She grabs both and scurries to the other side of the island.

"Do you need help with your tent?" Hutch asks me.

"Where's yours?"

He points to a tree. "We've got the whole island to ourselves, so everyone can spread out."

Then I have a thought. "Simmons," I shout. "Be straight with me. Are there any bears?"

Simmons pokes the fire with a stick and grins. "Maybe just a few lynxes."

"What the hell is that?"

"Stop scaring her," Jillian says, poking him in the stomach. "This is my second trip, and I can tell you I've never seen a bear here. Or the monster they keep promising."

As it gets dark, we huddle in a circle and cook beans and the chicken from the coolers. Over the next couple of days, we're supposed to fish for our food. I've never had to go further than my delivery app for my dinner.

Because everyone is so tired, they turn in early. The problem with tents is that you can hear everyone else's snores and farts and sleep talk. Later that night I hear a zipper, and sit up to realize it's mine. In here, Hutch and I can't even talk because we'd be heard. He closes a little latch I didn't even know existed from the inside.

I let him into my sleeping bag, and fall asleep to the sound of his heart, the steady feeling of his body pressed against mine.

CHAPTER 25

I've decided I hate waking up to find Hutch missing. This time there isn't a note, just a faded green leaf shaped like a spade. I grab my toiletry bag and head out to get some water to brush my teeth.

What I don't expect to see is Jillian emerging from Simmons's tent. She looks like a deer in headlights. She grabs my hands, and I shake my head—I feel like I'm trapped in a silent film. I pull her with me and we walk fifteen minutes to the other side of the island, where we can finally talk without being heard.

"I won't say anything," I say first.

"River, this is important. It isn't against the rules for us to be together, but Helen frowns upon staff dating staff."

"I'm a steel trap," I tell her. "I won't spread it around. Just, be more careful. You saw what happened with Randy and me. And we didn't even *do* anything."

She looks nervous and scared. I wish I could tell her that I know how she feels, but our situations are way different, even if they both include sneaking around.

Once she's calmed down a bit, she goes back to the camp. I brush my teeth while sitting on a log. It's a long way from bartending on the Lower East Side, but I feel a lot happier doing this. I still feel like I'm missing a nice whiskey to warm me up, and maybe some beers. The only thing I don't miss is harder drugs. I've been feeling a different kind of high lately, and it has everything to do with Hutch. I wonder if I'm just replacing a deck of cards with Hutch.

I spit my toothpaste on the ground, and wash my face with cold water. It wakes me up faster than any coffee in the world.

"What's on the agenda for today?" I ask back at camp, after

I've changed into leggings, sweat pants, and a flannel shirt.

Hutch has already gotten the fire started. He looks rumpled and adorably rugged with a day's worth of facial hair. I assume no one's shaving anything in the week we'll be out here.

"A hearty breakfast of beans and bacon."

I make a face. "We're going to stink up the whole island by the time we're done with this."

"How do your arms feel?" Hutch asks. "You up for some kayaking down the river, River?"

I sit on the log and smile at the flames. "You think you're clever, don't you?"

"Sometimes. It's usually purely accidental."

"I wanted to go kayaking, too," Julie says, emerging from her tent.

"Great," Hutch says, and I'm slightly disappointed it won't just be the two of us.

I think of Jillian and Simmons, who are also trying to keep their romance a secret. They aren't doing a very good job—it's day one and I've already caught them. I know Hutch and I have higher stakes. I feel like I'm gambling, even though I haven't been at a table in months. But I'm gambling with something more valuable than money—Hutch's future, and my own heart.

After breakfast, Simmons takes a group of six out fishing. Jillian and three others stay at the campsite to "meditate." Meditating is a pretty flimsy way of saying they're too tired to do anything but hang around. Still, everyone seems to need this break.

That leaves Hutch, Julie, Pete, and myself, who are going kayaking. I see Julie standing by Hutch's kayak. She holds the life vest against her chest and squeezes it like a stress ball. It's disturbing how much she watches him. I'm trying not to let it bother me, but it's difficult. It's a crush that's going very, very wrong.

"Come on, Julie," Pete tells her. He's been growing out a beard for a couple of days. It makes him look more grown-up and serious. He prods her in the back with his oar. "River should go with someone more experienced than me, because she's the newbiest."

Julie looks disappointed, but drops the vest back on the kayak and goes with Pete, muttering, "That's not a real word."

I pick up the life vest and strap myself in. Hutch and I take off in the same direction as Pete and Julie, but keep a healthy distance between the two kayaks. The wind is strong, and the current gets rougher the further out we get. At least the morning sun is shining.

"You okay?" Hutch asks every now and then.

My arms are tired, but we're paddling slowly. The way the kayak rocks makes my stomach queasy. Hutch comes to a stop, smack in the middle of the lake.

"If you're tired, you only have to say so," he tells me.

He stands, and I freak, fearing we're going to flip over. But he's perfectly balanced, like a surfing lumberjack. He turns himself around so we face each other. I like the view ten times better now that I can see his face.

"Did you see anything weird this morning?" I ask.

"Weird like how?" Hutch normally looks to the right, but he's looking to the left, like he's searching for an answer. I have the feeling he's lying to me.

"You should never play poker." I laugh, and splash him.

"Why not?"

"You're obviously hiding something. Your nose twitched a little. It never does that."

"You're too good for your own well-being."

"So, what did you see?"

He shrugs. "Same thing as you, I guess. Simmons saw me leave from your tent."

"What?" I clap my hand over my mouth. My voice echoes in the valley. "Don't you think it's something you should've told me earlier?"

"When?" he says. "In front of the whole camp?"

"Ugh. This whole time I was telling Jillian to be more careful."

"Simmons and Jillian. Wow. No wonder he was so understanding and offered to keep my secret. I've never done anything like this before."

"Do you want a prize?" I ask, too sassy for my own good. "Neither have I."

After a little bit of silence, we start to laugh.

"It's not funny," I tell him.

"You're the one cackling."

"I do not cackle."

"Well, I've got to tell you, I feel a little relieved that someone else knows. I felt like the heart under the floorboards in *The Tell Tale Heart*."

"I felt like Hester in *The Scarlet Letter*."

He holds his oar across his lap to steady himself. Julie and Pete are paddling nearby, but not within hearing distance. He reaches out and tucks a stray curl back over my ear.

"You have nothing to be ashamed about. Unless you're ashamed of me."

"I'm not."

"The Scarlet Letter is about shame."

"Well, I'm a high school dropout; you can't expect me to get all the facts right."

He sighs, stretching his arms out against the breeze. The wind is getting stronger, and clouds appear from behind the mountains.

"Are you ashamed?" I ask, looking off to the side to avoid the intensity of his eyes.

"River," he says my name in that way of his, like I'm important, like he *needs* to say it. "If I'm ashamed of anything it's that—"

He looks away.

"Of what?"

"That I'm taking advantage of you."

I shake my head, confused. "How? We're both adults. Sure you're three years older than me, but it's not like anyone can accuse me of having daddy issues. If that were so, I'd date guys twice my age, and that's just gross."

"I'm glad you don't think being with me is gross," he says, searching the dark clouds for something. "I'm just—at the end of the day, I'm still a counselor. No matter that we met beforehand. You're someone searching for help and recovery, and instead of giving that to you, I'm thinking about ways to get into your bed every single night. I'm thinking about kissing you every moment I find. I'm thinking about never letting you go. That I care for you more than I do for my own future. I want you to be my future."

I want to say something. I want to tell him that I feel the same way. Except, I want to take the brunt of the hurt if something goes wrong. I want to protect his future, because sometimes I don't feel like I have one myself. He's too good to bet everything on me.

But I can't find the words.

"All I want to do is be with you and keep you safe," Hutch tells me. "I want to hold your hand and kiss you in the middle of the day, not just in the dark. Right now, we can't have that."

I try to process his words as it starts to drizzle. "Hutch, I make my decisions for me. If you think that you're taking advantage of me, you're wrong. I picked you, okay? From the moment I saw you at the bar, I had to know you, even if it was just for one night. I wanted you then, and I still want you now. Maybe you're the one who's too fucking good for their own well-being. Maybe I'm the bad one, and I'm ruining your life just by being near you."

I can tell he wants to kiss me, but just then, Julie and Pete paddle over to us. "We're heading back! It's getting too windy!"

Hutch stands on the kayak to position himself forward. The current makes him wobble, and I'm afraid he's going to fall. He sits and we paddle forward. The clouds darken overhead, and it starts to pour. I can't see anything ahead of us, except a little yellow kayak ahead. Water splashes all around, like hands pushing our kayak from side to side. I start to panic, and I lose my rhythm.

"Hutch!"

"Let me—"

"What?" The kayak is rocking too much.

Then it flips, and we're underwater, and I don't have time to hold my breath. The water is freezing and dark, and I breathe it into my lungs. I force myself to reach for the surface, but I don't know which way is up or down. I gasp as I break the surface, but I feel the current pushing me away from the kayak. My lungs burn and my throat is raw from coughing up water.

Pull the string! I tell myself.

But my fingers are freezing, and it takes me a few long moments to find it. When I do pull it, nothing happens, and I start sinking. I feel something brush against my leg, and in my panic, I scream. I start kicking my legs just as arms wrap around me. I'm choking.

I can't breathe.

I open my eyes to darkness.

Darker clouds and darker water.

CHAPTER 26

Hutch is shouting my name. "River! River. Oh God, River please. Come back to me. River!"

His voice is far away. Like we're on opposite ends of a tunnel. A fist punches me in my solar plexus just as I open my eyes. I feel cold water coming up and turn over to retch. I sit up, gasping for breath.

I close my eyes again, but someone is asking me to stay awake. It sounds like Jillian. Then Randy. Randy, of all people.

Hutch wraps his arms around me. He's trembling from head to toe. His lips are nearly blue from cold. The other campers are standing and crouching around us. The rain has stopped and given way to a cloudless sky.

"Thank God you're okay," Jillian says.

Hutch lets go of me. He's breathing hard and fast. He runs his hands through his wet hair, then takes off. Meanwhile, I sit up and keep coughing. Jillian wraps a blanket over my shoulders.

They all start shouting things at me. At least, it sounds like shouting. My head is aching, and I breathe in small gasps. It hurts where Hutch punched me in my chest. No, not punched—where he did chest compressions for CPR.

When I feel well enough to stand, I take stock of the camp. Most of our supplies and dry firewood were shoved under a makeshift tent of kayaks. The actual tents sag where water has collected. Everyone goes to theirs and shakes the water off, and they bounce right back. All except for mine. A branch fell off a tree and punched a hole right through it, wetting all of my clothes inside.

"Come," Jillian tells me.

Simmons gives everyone else tasks to clean up our camp

area. I follow Jillian into her tent, shivering down to the bone. She gives me dry clothes and a towel.

"I'd... kill... for... some... whiskey." It's hard to get a whole sentence out when your teeth are chattering.

"Take this for now." She opens a packet of hand warmers. I want to rub them all over my skin. But between them and the borrowed clothes, I soon feel loads better. "That was really scary."

"You're telling me."

"I've never seen Hutch react that way," she whispers. "He was screaming your name. Randy tried to get him off you because he was pressing your chest too hard. He was afraid he'd break your ribs, but Hutch just shoved him away."

"Then why isn't he here?" I feel something well up in my chest. If my tear ducts didn't feel frozen, I'd probably cry. Hutch saved my life, again. And then he walked away from me. After all the things he said to me in the middle of the lake. He just walked away.

Jillian places a hand on my shoulder. "He'll be back. He was scared. He really cares about you."

I nod my head and wrap myself in the blanket. "So do I."

"I think we can help each other out," Jillian says.

"How?"

"You need a tent. We can say you're staying in mine. But it might make sense if you sleep next to someone bigger. For body heat. We can switch after everyone's gone to sleep."

"Let me go find him."

I leave the tent and the other campers descend on me. They tell me how Hutch dragged me to the shore and started CPR. How my whole face turned blue, and everyone thought I was dead.

I didn't feel dead. I just felt heavy and cold. Like a stone, dropping down into the water. My chest still hurts, and I feel disoriented from everyone's attention. I see Julie scowling on a log with her arms wrapped around her chest. There's something dark in the way she looks at me, but I push it away because I need to find Hutch.

LIFE ON THE LEVEL

It's a terribly beautiful afternoon, now that the morning storm is gone. I walk along the water's edge, over the broken branches and piles of leaves. It's like the hand of God raked over our tiny little island just long enough to try to drown me. That's a really terrible thing to think. Maybe I've just infuriated the big bopper long enough, and that was my comeuppance.

When I see Hutch, he's standing with his feet in the water. His arm is resting on a low branch. His wet shirt clings to his muscles, and as I get closer I can see little rivulets of water trickling from his dark curls. He turns around when my foot snaps a branch in half. He doesn't say anything, but he stares at me.

I'm used to Hutch being all smiles and sexy smirks. This is the first time I've ever seen him lost. He breathes hard, like he was the one who almost drowned. Like he's struggling against a current I can't see. His eyes glisten. They furrow angrily as he grips me and pulls me against his chest. He burrows his face into my neck, and then this terribly beautiful, sweet man trembles. I can feel his body shudder, and he grips me so tightly it hurts.

I don't feel cold anymore. Something in my heart is melting right into Hutch's arms. He's as solid as the great big trees that surround us. He's as strong as the earth beneath my feet. His emotion is almost too much for me to bear, but I tell myself I need this. I tell myself I deserve someone like this. Don't I?

"You scared me half to death," he says, getting down on his knees and pressing his face against my belly. "I thought—for a very real moment, I couldn't hear your heart beating, River. You were gone."

I rest my cold, wet hands on his cheekbones. I could stare at him all day. If I were to drown, I would take the image of his face with me to the bottom of that lake. I bend down and press my mouth to his. My heart skips a beat, and then skips a handful more at the thought of someone coming to look for us. But right now, I don't care. My heart hurts from this thaw. My heart hurts from Hutch showing me this kind of emotion.

"I'm right here," I say.

I press my hand on his chest as he stands back up. He keeps

my hand pressed there. I wish I could leave my body and look at us, standing on the shore of an island in the middle of a lake, in the middle of nowhere. I press his hand against my face.

"I think you scared everyone," I tell him.

He nods slowly, focusing on my face. "Shit. I think I gave Randy a black eye."

"Oh, don't worry. It's still in the green phase right now. Probably won't be purple until tomorrow."

He shakes his head solemnly. He hasn't come back to me 100 percent. I'm not used to someone caring about me like this.

"Hutch, why did you walk away from me when I woke up?"

He turns away from me. "I guess I scared myself into thinking that I had lost you. When you opened your eyes, I can't even explain what I felt. It was like little pieces that were starting to break apart inside me came back together. You were *breathing*. And there they were, everyone looking down at us, when all I wanted to do was kiss the warmth back into you."

"Thank you," I tell him. "For saving my life again. I have nothing to give you back, you know. It's getting pretty annoying."

"I haven't been shaken up like that in a long time. I'm starting to realize—" His midnight eyes are too intense. I feel myself getting lost in them. Screw it, I'm already lost in this man, and I don't think I can find my way back. "I'd go crazy without you."

"Careful with that kind of talk." I tug on his chin. "They might throw you in psych."

"Come here." He pulls me into a hug. I want to do away with these wet clothes and create some body heat. I tell him about Jillian and our plan with the tents for tonight. "I don't know about bringing Jillian and Simmons into this."

"It's already done, Hutch."

Hutch doesn't seem to want to let my hand go as we approach our camp. The look he gives me scares me a little bit, because no one has ever looked at me like that. It's like he's afraid I'll float away if he doesn't hold on. To be honest, I'm afraid I'll do just that.

Back at camp, everything is back to normal, if a little damp. The fire's going again, and I'm told there will be trout for dinner.

I sleep for most of the day, which is going to throw off my internal clock completely. I dream of water closing over my head, Maddie's dilated pupils, and Hutch screaming my name. Even though there's no way I could remember this, I see him hitting my chest, and when I sit up I gasp for air like I'm right back underwater.

"What are you doing here?" I ask Julie. She's unzipping the door of my tent.

She has a bag of beef jerky and water for me. "Simmons told me to bring this to you. Everyone's out looking for more dry firewood."

I rub the grogginess out of my eyes and take the bag. I chew a piece of jerky while Julie sits there gnawing on her thumb.

"So, what was it like?" she asks.

"Drowning?" I shrug. "Like falling asleep in really cold water."

"No," she snorts. "What was kissing Hutch like?"

I nearly choke on my jerky. Choking on food is a far less badass way to go than drowning in Flathead Lake. Still, I'm trying to figure out if Julie followed Hutch and me. Did she really see us kiss? Or does she mean…

"I wouldn't call CPR a kiss."

She makes a sour face, like she ate a handful of Warheads and is refusing to spit them out. "A mouth on a mouth is a kiss. I should throw myself into the lake, if that's what it takes."

"Don't be stupid," I snap. "You can't hurt yourself just to get a boy's attention. This isn't right, Julie. You're fixating on someone you just can't have."

It's like telling a baby she can't have ice cream for dinner. She pouts and sucks her teeth.

"You don't know what you're talking about, River. You know, everything was fine with Hutch before you came along. Now all he does is try to make sure you aren't jumping off cliffs, and taking care of you because of your stupid accidents. Who's the one doing stupid things to get a guy's attention now? I was supposed to be the one in that kayak, not *you*. That was supposed to be my kiss, not *yours*."

I grind my teeth as a suspicion forms. I dig my finger into her chest. "Listen to me, Julie. If you pull a stunt like that again, I'll make sure Helen throws you out faster than you can say 'my name is Julie and I'm a psychopath.' Do you understand me?"

Julie's eyes go wide with fright. She scrambles to her feet. That was probably a really stupid thing to do. Still, it makes me wonder. I run out to the kayak—in all the excitement, it was left right where it was pulled up onto the sand. My uninflated life vest is still on the ground. I pull the cord, and nothing happens—it's been tampered with.

CHAPTER 27

I'm in a foul mood for the rest of the day. Simmons gives me one of his extra sweaters, from the Seattle Seahawks, which draws the ire of some of the California people. My clothes are still hanging out to dry, and I look at my Mets sweatshirt with loving and longing eyes.

Julie keeps her distance, though I admit I have a newfound fear of her. A girl who would tamper with her own life vest to get rescued by the man of her dreams is some next-level shit. I won't have a quiet moment with Hutch soon, so I have to keep this information to myself for now.

I could rat her out right here and now, but I grew up seeing what people did to rats. Even though I'm no longer in some dive bar with Queens' worst barflies and bookmakers, old habits die hard. Besides, information is a powerful thing. That's true from here all the way to New York.

Because we're still a rehab center, we spend the night's campfire like it's an extra-special, extra-big group session. Hutch is more brooding than I've ever seen him before. His dark eyes watch the crackling flames like he's trying to figure out how to hold them in his hands. It's the same way he looks at me.

Simmons is the one who gets the group going tonight. He's got an adorable outdoorsy look that really works for him. It's like the legit version of all those guys in Williamsburg who wear plaid and have beards and want to look like loggers.

"All right everyone," he says in his slightly nervous voice. He doesn't have the same coolness as Hutch, or Ransom's fatherly tone. I think this works for him. "We've had a really intense day, what with the rain and River's accident. How're you holding up?"

"Like a whole new girl," I say.

"Did your life flash before your eyes?" Jermania asks.

"Did you see the Flathead Lake monster?" one of the younger campers wants to know.

I smile at the ground, then can't help but look at Hutch. "Actually, for a moment, I did think I was being pulled under by some hideous sea creature or long-lost dinosaur. It turns out that it was just Hutch, trying to pull me out of the water. I wasn't really thinking straight or I would have panicked less."

Julie looks miserable as I tell my story, but I refuse to feel sorry for her. She could have gotten herself killed. She could have gotten me killed, if Hutch had been slower, or the current had been stronger. I shudder, and hold my hands out to the flames.

"That's what I wanted to touch on," Simmons says. "One of the things that we come face-to-face with during rehabilitation is fear. Fear of life beyond the program. Fear of facing addiction. Fear of the unknown. Fear of the past, or dying, or of ourselves. When I was in my teens, I thought of myself as an adrenaline junkie. I didn't fear anything. I thought I was invincible. Except my high was racing. Rollercoasters, all kinds of skateboarding. I sought out things to get my blood pumping until I felt invincible. It wasn't until my first car accident that I realized I had to slow down. I remember a long period of the darkest sleep. This feeling that something was pressing down on my chest. That was my coma. I didn't wake up for three weeks. I was lucky, I guess. Unlike the kids driving drunk who crashed into me.

"I started to realize that even though I thought I had everything under control—my life, my high, my speed—I wasn't ready for what was coming out of the next lane. And if you take away the fast cars, that's just life. You never know what's going to crash into you or miss you by a hair's breadth. Even though I'm not looking for that rush anymore, I think about it all the time. That feeling doesn't go away."

There's a lot of nodding going around the campfire. For a moment I think of Hutch and myself as two cars speeding on a long, dark road. What if I go one way and he goes another and we never see each other again? What if turning into each other means a head-on collision? What if this relationship is doomed no matter what we want?

Did I just call it a relationship?

"What about all of you?" Simmons asks, prodding the fire. The wood hisses and pops. Cinders and ash rise up in the cool air. "When was the last time you faced your fear?"

Jermania raises her hand and stands. She wipes the back of her jeans, then shoves her hands into her back pockets and shrugs. "Hey everyone. I'm Jermania and I'm... an alcoholic... and previously anorexic. I don't really know the last time that I wasn't afraid, you know? I was adopted when I was ten. Before that, I was in an orphanage in Utah.

"Anyway, I was always afraid of the dark, because I didn't really like silence and I *hated* being alone. There's something inside my head that terrifies me. I can't really figure out what it is. Sometimes I feel like my life is just one long stretch of fear of the people around me, the words they say, the way men and women look at me. And the only way I can drown it is by drinking myself into a stupor."

Simmons shuts his eyes. "How do you feel when you're sober?"

"I feel weird. Like my life is an out-of-body experience. I'm just trying to get used to my body the way it is now."

I listen to all of their words. It's strange, but I don't really miss alcohol. I mean, I like the idea of it now that it's cold. But there are other ways to warm up. There's the fire, and then there's Hutch. I wonder if I'm just trading one vice for another.

"I had a near-death experience," Randy says. He cracks his long, knobby fingers. "I wanted to see how many times I could jack off in a single day, and I dehydrated myself so much that I passed out."

There's a round of *ewwwws*.

"I think you're derailing the conversation," Simmons tells Randy.

"I'm just doing what you've all been saying to do this whole time. Telling you my feelings. What about Mr. TKO over here? Come on, Hutch. Counselors have to share, too. You guys are like our role models."

Hutch stands. The fire casts his shadow to the tops of the trees. He's the king of the woods. He's fierce and bold, and I catch myself drooling a bit as he rests one of his legs on the log, stretching his jeans over that fine ass.

"I've never had a near-death experience," he says. "But I've lost a few people. I never had a good relationship with my father. I thought the day he died would be just an ordinary day. No one was more surprised than I was when I heard the news and broke down. It was like part of me was gone. Well, because part of me *was* gone, and there was nothing I could do to get it back or make amends or figure out if I could have done something, anything, to get it back. Then I lost my mother to liver failure. I loved my mother more than anything, but I was never quite convinced that she loved me back."

The way he says that brings a chill to my bones. What I wouldn't give to jump right over this fire and pull Hutch into my arms and tell him that he's not alone. That maybe I'm falling in love with him with every single moment. That there is someone here for him.

"A few months ago, I lost a friend. I was the one who found her. I think the worst part was knowing that I was a few feet away. That maybe her life could have been saved if I had checked on her sooner, if anyone had checked on her sooner. I'd say that my biggest fear is letting people down."

"Damn," Randy says. "I'm sorry, man."

They go around the circle some more. Julie talks about her bulimia and use of pain medications. The thing that brought her to HCRC was her mother finding her in a pool of her own vomit after nearly overdosing.

Listening to all these close calls makes me want to retreat into my tent. But Simmons won't allow everyone to go to sleep with such dark thoughts, so he brings out his guitar. He's great at fingerpicking, which doesn't go unnoticed by Jillian. Simmons and Hutch switch back and forth. Hutch is all classic rock and Van Morrison. Simmons is '90s alternative. We finish the night with a terribly off-key rendition of Wonderwall. I mean, we have to scare the bears away somehow.

During all of this, I feel happiness flooding my body down to my toes. I feel my eyes flutter as the campfire dies, and everyone scurries away into their tents. Hutch, Jillian, Simmons, and I linger conspiratorially. When the fire is put out and the only light is the sliver of moon in the expansive midnight sky, we split up into couples.

Before I can even fully zip up the tent, Hutch's massive hands close around my waist. He pulls me against his chest and onto his lap. I've always thought of myself as pretty tall, or at least taller than most girls. Hutch is the only man that's ever made me feel petite. I sit across his lap and relax into the easiness of being with him.

Since we're not allowed to talk (it's so painful not to), or use any lights at all lest we create a shadow puppet show, we sink into a different kind of intimacy. We let our hands do the talking and exploring for us. I lean back onto the bedroll, pulling him on top of me. He lines up our noses and brushes his lips across mine. It's like being brushed across the skin with the softest feather. His hands find their way under my shirt. After stripping down, I had to put my underwear out to dry as well. It's a little weird being in Simmons's clothes, but it's all part of our charade.

He squeezes my breast with one hand and brushes my hair back with the other. When he stops, I can hear the rustle of the wind in the trees and the hooting of owls. I can hear the whistles and snores of sleeping campers. If Jillian and Simmons are getting it on, I can't hear that at all.

I lift up my head to pull Hutch back to me. I fear he's too hung up on my almost drowning. I want to show him that I'm perfectly okay. I want to show him how much I appreciate him. Sex has always been something fun. Something to do. I can't count the number of times I've been in love because I don't think I ever truly have. I'm not exactly a romantic, but I think love is a one-shot thing. How do I know if I'm falling in love with Hutch if I've never felt this way for a guy before?

It feels like I'm burning from the inside out. It feels like all of my hard edges are melting and chipping away, revealing a girl

I didn't know I could be. A good, sweet girl who doesn't party and doesn't drink or gamble. A girl who sucks at nature things, but loves getting lost in the wild of the trees. A girl who isn't afraid of being someone new.

Hutch and I already had sex once.

This is different. This is hunger. Reckless hunger, grasping for heat and naked skin. As my eyes adjust to the dark, I trace the lines of his face. I kiss his lashes, and he edges the waistband of my sweatpants down and his sure fingers find my wetness. He inserts them, and I press my head back as he sides his fingers deeper and deeper in. I raise my legs and kick his boxers down with my heels. His erection presses hotly between us.

I feel restless and I wriggle against him, impatient to get him inside me. He lowers his lips to mine and I can tell he's smiling. He whispers the tiniest "Shhh." My blood is pulsing in my throat, my ears, and my center. He's a match, striking against me, setting both of us aflame.

I grab him by the neck and keep his lips pressed to mine. He reaches for something under the pillow. I hear the foil of a condom tear. I part my legs, press my hand on the firm muscle of his ass, and in one jab he's inside me.

I could die from the torture of keeping the scream at bay. He doesn't pull out, but pushes further in, reaching parts of me that have never been touched before. I wrap my legs around him and move my hips against his hard muscles.

He inhales and digs his face into my neck. I can feel the tension in his body, the scream trapped in his chest. He releases some of it by biting my shoulder. It's incredibly unfair to ask me to be quiet during all of this.

Slowly, torturously, he pulls out halfway before thrusting back inside me. He holds my face in both his hands. Despite the chill in the air, our bodies are hot. Sweat drips from the tip of his nose, and I bend up and lick it. I see the pearly whiteness of his teeth, and press my lips to his, squeezing my thighs and rubbing our bodies together until I come all over him. My breath hitches once, and he silences me with his open mouth. He holds me tighter, harder, still, as his body shakes to a finish. My name is a whisper in the night. After he collapses, he wastes no time in pulling me against his chest.

I fall asleep with his hands threaded in my hair, a tangle of limbs and lies, not ready for the sun to rise.

CHAPTER 28

"I think I'm going to add camping to the list of things I never thought I could do," I tell Jillian. We're filling up the water bottles. I'm amazed at how pure the water is, even without the purifiers. "Did you know that in New York they tell you the tap water is fine, but that's just because the pipe systems are so old it can't be measured by any kind of new standard?"

"That can't be true," Jillian says. She looks dewy and sweet in her long ponytail. There's definite color to her tanned cheeks. "Is it?"

"I think so. I heard it somewhere."

She decides I must be joking. We walk around the perimeter of our island, holding onto long branches for balance along the water's edge.

"Can I ask you," she says, "how long have you and Hutch… you know."

I give her my most discerning look. Jillian is quiet and sweet. She never really contributes to conversations, I think because she's afraid to say something wrong in her Spanish accent. I bet she's the kind of girl that likes to tell stories about boys. Even though I haven't known her for very long, I think I can trust her. The horses certainly do, and I like animals a lot more than I like people.

"Since before HCRC."

She gasps, and giggles a little bit. "Did he ask you to, how do you say, get committed?"

I let out a bark of laughter. "I think you mean 'to check in.' And no. I saw him at a bar and I just knew. I had to have him."

"You're very bold. I've worked with Simmons for a year, and only a few weeks ago worked up the courage to ask him for coffee."

"I think it's cute. At least your being together is just *frowned* upon instead of totally against the rules. I understand why it is against the rules, don't get me wrong. I just never thought I'd fall for someone like Hutch. Sometimes I think I should put an end to it to protect him. He loves his job and he loves helping people. I'm a train wreck. I mess up everything in my path and I don't want to hurt him."

Whoa, where did that come from? I've been here too long. The fresh air is making me voluntarily honest.

"Chris is a very smart man. He's kind, and generous with his time. He's patient and honest. I think this is the first time he is doing this kind of thing. The other staff members like to call him Mr. Nice Guy."

"I think this whole thing is crazy. I've never been in a long-term relationship. I don't even think I can call this a relationship. What will happen at the end of November? Do I come visit him and pretend like it was never going on under Helen's nose?" I shake my head and adjust the backpack full of water bottles.

"I like to think it will all work out. Love is not easy to find. I traveled all the way across the world to feel this way. How do you say, it is written in the sky."

"Stars," I tell her. "It's written in the stars."

• • •

That night we do a little stargazing after dinner. It was much warmer in the afternoon, so the cool night is a nice reprieve. We lie on a pebbly shore on the other side of the island. I rest my hands behind my head.

"What's on your mind right now?" Hutch asks beside me. He's at a safe distance, but I've decided that there is no distance safe enough.

"I'm thinking that I can't believe this is the same sky I look at back home. Light pollution is terrible. For the first time in my life, I think I'm actually speechless."

"Isn't that something," Jermania tells me.

I giggle and turn my head toward Hutch. He's drumming his free hand on his chest. "What about you?"

A wicked smile spreads across his moonlit face. "Things."

"I'm thinking we should go skinny dipping," Randy says, sitting up.

Hutch pulls his hand away and points a finger at Randy. His bruise has changed colors like a mood ring. "Please, keep your pants on, man."

"What? You afraid to compare?"

Another head down the line pops up. Pete. "I don't think this is appropriate."

The others giggle. Some people actually stand and flank Randy, who's already lost his shirt.

"River, babycakes, you're not the only one who gets to see the glory that is Randall Rider."

Hutch grumbles.

"I can tell you all that water is 10,000 degrees below zero. Has frat bro life taught you nothing of shrinkage?"

That gets some booming laughs. Randy is making chicken noises in my direction.

"I hope the Flathead Lake monster eats you up!" I shout.

"Simmons! Help me out here, man!" Hutch says.

Simmons is too busy staring into Jillian's dreamy brown eyes to care that this might get back to Helen.

"I think Simmons is off duty," Jermania tells him. "Live a little. This is, hopefully, a one-time deal for some of us. If it makes you feel better, you can close your eyes, or go back to camp."

She's naked in a flash, and Hutch is turning his face away.

"Come on, River!" Randy shouts, putting on a terrible New York accent. "I triple dawg dare ya."

"It is incredibly hard to resist that level of dare."

Hutch tries to grab hold of my hand. I walk to the water's edge where their shrieks pierce the midnight air. Randy's wading into the freezing water, and the others follow him as if he's some pied piper. Hutch stands directly behind me. It's hard to see from the shore. Their dark heads bob in the still water, illuminated by silver moonlight. I stick my foot in the water, and shout, "Nope!"

I'm starting to turn around when I see Hutch, naked down to his toes. It's a startling sight to see him like this in the moonlight, like something out of a Greek myth. His grin is bold, and that dark stare I love so much is on me. I feel the air get knocked out of my lungs. A thrilled scream goes up all around me.

"Come on, River Thomas," he whispers as he walks past me. "You can float on my back."

Then he runs and dives into the water. I look at the stragglers who won't go, either because it's too cold or they don't want to be naked. When I see Julie, with her eyes wide and her jaw on the ground like she's witnessed a miracle, I get the terrible feeling that we didn't think this through. It's funny, because I've always been the person who is down for anything.

"You in, Julie?"

She shakes her head and stares at the water.

"I think she might be in shock," Pete says. "I'll take her back to camp. You guys are going to need a roaring fire to get warm tonight."

I search for Jillian and Simmons, but all I see is a pile of clothes where they used to be. I'm out of my sweats and top in a second, and then I jump into the water. This time, even though it's darker, I'm not afraid. I'm ready for the way the cold knocks the wind out of me. I break the surface and scream.

"Holy *fuck* that's cold."

Jermania floats past me, and all I can think is that I wish my boobs were that big. There's a wonderful smile on her face, like this is the happiest she's ever been. Despite the freezing cold and the fact that I've seen more of some campers than I wish I had, I feel that too. Someone splashes me, and suddenly I feel warmer. Either that or my whole body is frostbitten.

"Where's that glory?" a girl whose name I'm not sure of shouts at Randy.

He swims towards her, and that's my cue to turn away.

I see Hutch staring at me. His face is in shadow, but I know he's searching for me. My blonde head is hard to miss, though it would be a nasty surprise if he mistook Randy's blond head for mine. I throw my head back and allow myself to relax. Tiny fish swim around me, tickling my skin. There's an infinite silence that comes with looking at the night sky this way. When I can't feel my ears anymore, I get out.

"You're on your own!" I shout at everyone.

I grab my clothes and get into them as quickly as possible. I know, without a doubt, that Hutch is a few paces behind me. He doesn't alert them with a goodbye; he just follows me. It's a silent language we've created by sneaking around in the dark. I don't know where I'm going, but I know I need to get warm and I need to be with him.

"Hey," he says in a low voice. Here, we can't hear the campers around the fire, and we're far enough away from the water that I only catch stray hollers.

I shiver, and he drops the clothes in his hands and comes to me. I pull my hoodie over my head and step out of my pants. The pit of my belly tugs as he clamps his hand between my legs, spreading warmth across my cold skin. He picks me up and presses me against a tree. There he keeps my weight up with his body, and uses his hands to brush my wet hair back.

"River—"

"Hutch?" I feel his pause, his need to say something that could change everything.

"I've never seen anyone as beautiful as you are right now."

"Well, I am in the dark."

"Now. Hours ago. Always. Every part of you makes me want to be a better man."

"You're already the best man."

He presses his forehead to mine. I feel the familiar pull toward him. He wastes no time kissing my cold skin, warming me up with long strokes of his tongue. He says my name, over and over, fingering me in the dark. When he pulls his finger out, I feel empty. The feel of his dick between my legs is torture. He hesitates at my opening.

"It's okay," I whisper.

That's all it takes. The head of his cock slides into me and I whimper. Feeling him like this is delicious. He shifts my weight against his pelvis, and that pushes him in deeper.

This time, I don't have to stay as quiet. I moan in his ear, pushing myself tightly against his chest.

"Don't let go of me," I whisper.

"Never," he says, thrusting harder into me. He holds my weight with his hands around my ass. My skin is on fire. I can feel it spread from the pit of my stomach to the tips of my ears. If we keep going this way we're going to set the woods aflame, but I really don't care. Nothing feels as right and as perfect as when he's filling the parts of me I thought were empty. I shudder against him, squeezing my legs around him so he can really feel it.

His heart thunders though his chest, right against mine. He chuckles deeply against my skin. "That's another first for me."

He kisses me, hard and sweet.

"Me too."

"We should head back."

"But I'm not finished." I wrap a fist around his dick, unsurprised that he's ready to go again. I get down on my knees and wrap my mouth around his wet head. I can taste myself on him.

Then there's a snap. I freeze and jump away from him.

"Wait here," Hutch says, stalking off in the direction of the noise.

No, no, no, no. I get back into my damp clothes and hide behind a tree. It's so dark, there's no way someone could have actually seen us properly. I hear faint noises coming from the lake, but nothing that would suggest we've been caught.

The seconds without Hutch feel like hours. When he comes back, I see the shadowy shake of his head. He whispers, "I didn't see anyone. It could've been an animal."

"Do you really think so?"

"Yeah." With the night cloaking his face, I can't see his features, so I don't know if he's telling the truth or not.

"You go back to camp. I'll be there in a bit." But I don't go back to camp. Instead I go back to the skinny dippers to show my face. They're wading out of the water, shivering from head to toe.

"Where'd you go, River?" Jermania asks. "You missed me knocking Randy on his lily-white ass."

"I like to think of my ass as porcelain white," Randy says. He walks without shame, gathering his clothes and racing back to camp. The sound of his chattering teeth leads the way.

"Can't a girl pee in peace?" I ask.

"You could've just gone in the water," Randy shouts.

"Remind me never to get in a pool with you."

• • •

Back at camp, Julie, Pete, and Hutch have a roaring fire going. I try my best to avoid looking in Hutch's direction. As much fun as sneaking around is, I'm scared we were seen.

Julie's prodding the fire with a long stick. Pete looks at Randy and makes a face. The skinny dippers giggle and share a good laugh at Randy's expense. I decide he's not so bad after all, even if we would never be friends outside of this place. I turn in before everyone else, and after the lights have all gone out, Hutch climbs into my sleeping bag. He wraps those big, muscular arms around me, and suddenly I feel like I've been thrown into the water and he's my lifeline back. His touch is so tender, so soft, and I can't remember being without it. That alone is a scary thought. It's the safest I've ever felt. Maybe coming here was the best decision I've made in a long, long time.

• • •

I sleep better when Hutch is holding me, which presents a problem for the rest of my stay at the facility. Being out in the woods for five days has been an exercise in first times. It's my first time fishing, and I manage to catch five trout. I pull my weight carrying firewood, and when we go back out kayaking, it's smooth sailing. Simmons claps me on the back for being such a good sport, despite being the biggest city slicker who ever slicked.

No one is more surprised than I am that I love this life. I look forward to waking up in a tangle of limbs with Hutch, the soreness in my arms that comes with hard work, and the delicious ache that lingers when Hutch makes love to me.

Make love.

I've never called it that before. Mostly because it sounds lame, and a little ridiculous. As I watch Hutch walk back and forth in the camp, getting ready to head back to HCRC, I feel my heart flutter and I want to shout at him, "I love you!"

Instead, I keep it to myself, filing it away where our kind of romance must be kept—in secret.

CHAPTER 29

The day after we return from camping, I decide to take Ransom up on his offer to join his kickboxing class. It's tough, because the guys in it are so much bigger than I am, but I've got loads of bottled up anger and resentment to throw into a punch. I alternate between picturing my mother, Kiernan, past managers who tried to feel me up, teachers who called me stupid, and, of course, Taylor. Even though Ransom insists that violence isn't the way to fix problems, grunting and shouting at a big leather sack is pretty therapeutic in its violence.

"No violence toward *others*," Ransom reminds me.

I know the difference between a person and punching bag. I do. I wonder how many times I'll have to punch inanimate objects before all my anger is gone.

"Anger doesn't fully go away," Ransom says. "We live with our emotions. It's the way we channel those emotions that makes us the people we are."

"I think that's the speech Uncle Ben gave Peter Parker."

He chuckles, and the nerdy boy holding the punching bag for me looks at me with puppy dog eyes. Ransom shakes his head and laughs even harder.

"If anger doesn't fully go away, then why do people always tell you to 'let go' and all that hippie mumbo jumbo? What's the point?"

"Because," Ransom says, correcting my stance before I do a high kick, "you're letting go of specific situations. For instance, I had a lot of anger at my wife for cheating on me with one of the guys on my team. After my accident, I was angrier. It was a downward spiral, and instead of taking responsibility for the things that pushed her away, the things that led me to the darkest time of my life, I blamed it on her. It wasn't 'til a few years ago that I took any of the blame myself. I was angry. It was like I was stuck in a room and water was filling it up, and I kept floating to the top to try to get some air."

I wipe sweat from my forehead. The other guys gather around and remove their gloves, focusing their attention on Ransom.

"How did you stop it?" Nick, my puppy-eyed nerdy boy, asks.

Ransom presses his lips together. I wonder if he even knows. He looks a little unsure. "Well, when the drugs and drinking almost killed me, I decided I didn't want to die. I didn't want to be controlled by my hatred. It was like punching a hole through the wall, and the water—the anger—started flooding away. I could breathe again. I wanted to breathe. I wanted to live. But, like all things, you have to work on making sure that anger doesn't come back. You have to sweat it out in a way that doesn't harm someone else in the process."

Ransom looks at me when he says that. Instead of saying something sarcastic, I simply nod. I recognize that suffocating feeling he was talking about. On some level, I've carried it with me my whole life.

• • •

After my muscles turn to jelly and I've given myself half an hour in the sauna, I hide in the library. I pick up *The Mists of Avalon* and try to get lost in a magical world. The library here is a small room, but the bookshelves go from floor to ceiling. There's the girl walking around sniffing the book pages. When she sees me, she looks embarrassed, and takes her book outside.

The door opens again, and Taylor comes in. He surveys the room, and when he realizes it's otherwise empty, comes over on the couch and sits next to me.

"What?" I ask.

"Heard you almost drowned," he says. "You sure are accident-prone."

"If you call a faulty life vest accident-prone, then sure."

He chuckles. "I think we got off on the wrong foot. I wanted to extend my services to you. I'm sure it's been lonely here for you. If you ever need a friend."

"Pass," is all I say.

"Why don't you like me River? I never did anything to you."

"You want the truth?"

"Hit me." He slouches, like those guys on the subway who manspread.

I wish I could hit him, but Ransom's anger-speech is fresh in my mind. I set my book down and look him dead in the face. "I don't like being threatened. I don't like when people spook my horse. I don't like the way you leer at the girls here, and frankly, I don't like that you take advantage of the people you're supposed to be caring for."

Something dark crosses his face. "I'm not caring for anyone. I get paid to mop the floors and shovel some hay. I'm not some fancy head doctor or counselor that gets bank for listening to how sad your life has been. As for the other stuff, you've got a wild imagination, girly. Horses are like women; anything scares them."

I feel a flash of rage fill my chest. I clench my fists, like I'm ready to defend myself, but I know Taylor would never hit me. Not here, at least. He wouldn't risk losing his barn operation over me. He's all talk, like most guys I've come across. He just gets off on scaring people, and because I'm not going to back down, it just makes him all the angrier.

I level my gaze at him. *You can't scare me.*

"I find your attempts at intimidation hilarious. You don't want to fuck with me."

"That's my line," Taylor says. "Well, you got me figured out. I guess I'll leave you to it."

He starts to head out the door. Pine-Sol fumes and smoke cling to his clothes. When he turns around, he smiles widely. There's a knowing glint in his eye, like a predator who's cornered his prey. Like he knows there's nowhere for me to run.

"I'm glad you had a great camping trip, River. I'm sure

Hutch enjoyed himself, too."

I throw the book across the room after he leaves. Taylor knows. Either he knows, or he's trying to trick me into revealing something. I shelve the book and pass by Hutch's office. He isn't there. He's not in the media room, the cafeteria, or the backyard. I'm ready to break into a sweat when Hutch passes me in the hallway by my room. He's got a great big smile and a little bounce in his step.

"Been looking for you," he says. "Want to ride?"

"You or a horse?" I ask. I just can't help it.

His grin is sly, and turns my brain into fluff as I follow him out into the stables. Jillian is saddling some horses, and has a couple of new people ready to ride. Group activities are great alibis, but a big part of me just wants to have Hutch all to myself, away from all of this. I want to be back in the woods.

Hutch demonstrates how to saddle the horse. Apollo nudges my arm, and I pet his face.

"Nervous?" Hutch asks.

"I wasn't 'til just now. I really don't want to fall again." I put on my gloves and secure the helmet strap under my chin. I'd much rather wear a cowboy hat like him, but that's out of the question. "I have to talk to you."

Worry scrunches his features. He nods. "When we rest in the field. I'll stay close by."

We ride as a group across the deep, golden grass. It's amazing how suddenly the seasons change when you're not looking. It's a little bit like my feelings for Hutch. As I dig my heels into Apollo's flanks, I feel this uncontrollable feeling surge in my heart, swelling like the mountains before me. I lean forward into the hard, cold wind, but I don't slow down now that I've got a good pace going.

After a solid half hour, we stop in a beautiful field, where the grass is tall and there's a trickle of water nearby. The new kids don't want to dismount, so Jillian tells us we can wait here while they ride a little further. I don't miss the wink she gives me.

Out here it feels like we're the only two people on earth. Hutch helps me down from the horse. I wrap my arms around his neck, and lose myself in the magnetic attraction I have for him. He hasn't shaved since the trip, and I love the way his beard tickles my face. We're rolling around on the grass. I land on top, straddling him like my horse.

I rest my hands on his chest to feel his heartbeat. It gets faster the more I rub my hands across his chest. I look over my shoulder, my hair going all over the place.

"Hutch."

"River."

"We have to talk."

"You're not breaking up with me, are you?" He sits up on his elbows. He's a miraculous sight, in his corduroy jacket with its wool lining. He takes a bit of straw and munches on it like a cigar.

"No, dummy. You'd have to be my boyfriend in order for me to break up with you."

"Ouch." His eyebrows rise high on his forehead. "I think I feel like your boyfriend."

"We don't go out on dates. We just hook up."

"I knew you were tough, Riv. But damn."

"I'm stating facts." *Stop stating facts, River. Stop ruining the moment.*

He doesn't seem to like that. I regret saying that because I can see it makes him sad.

"Yeah," he says.

"I'm sorry. I can't help being a dick sometimes. I'm not—I'm not good at this part of things. I'm only good at the sex part."

"You're good at all the parts, River." He squeezes my waist. "Every single part. You're just afraid to let yourself go."

I'd roll my eyes. Here's another counselor telling me to "let go" like I'm some Disney fucking princess. Still, I ignore that because his words, his other words, make me so hot. I wonder how long we have before the others comes back.

No, focus. I tell him about what Taylor said to me. He's pulling me up in seconds, grabbing Elphaba's reins.

"I'm going to kill that—"

"Easy, *counselor*." I grab his arm, but it's like trying to move a tree. "Don't you get it? He knows. Someone saw us, and I'm willing to bet it was Julie. I told you, it's not just a harmless crush. That girl is seriously crazy about you. Do you know she cornered me and all but told me she rigged her own life vest to get her mouth on you?"

He looks at me like I just kneed him in the gut. "Why didn't you say anything?"

"Because! You're too important. I want to protect you. You have more to lose than I do. Everyone expects me to mess up, but you—"

"Don't make decisions like that for me." He turns around, facing the mountains. He takes his hat off, runs his fingers through his curls, then sets it back on his head. When he turns toward me, the sight of him makes my heart squeeze. "I'm going to talk to him. Man to man."

"That's the stupidest thing you've ever said."

"He can't talk to you like that."

"What are you going to say? Don't threaten my girlfriend? You'd be fired in a second. I think—I think I can get him to mess up. We can't go to Helen without proof. Otherwise your career is over. Why are you smiling?"

He closes the distance between us. It is so hard to be objective when he looks at me like that. He takes his hat off and sets it atop my head. It's too big, but he tilts it back so he can see my face. He bends down to kiss me. My lips give way to his too easily, too eagerly. There's no stopping the pitter-patter of my heart. When he pulls away, I can hear the thunderous sound of hooves approaching. He steps back, a victorious smirk on his face.

"Because, you just called yourself my girlfriend."

CHAPTER 30

I make Hutch promise to leave the Taylor thing alone. To trust in my plan.

After my session with Ransom, I find Hutch in the game room. Sometimes he tries to teach me to play chess, but I don't like it, so we change to Candyland, which is more my speed. I tell him about Sky and Leti and how amazing they are. He tells me about the pranks he helped his brother pull back in high school. He tells me about visiting his brother in prison, and how they don't talk much anymore. I tell him Sky and I used to pretend to be fraternal twins just to fuck with people, and in the fifth grade got away with it for three whole days.

I want Hutch to get me a deck of cards, but he doesn't think it would be a good idea. I still miss shuffling them. Sometimes I get nostalgic. We retreat into my room. I lie on his lap while he reads the local paper. In the halls we keep the most distance. We dance around touching each other—a hand grazes here; our feet touch there. Being away from him is like water torture. He doesn't see me for three whole nights and I feel wrecked. I remember times sitting with Sky being all heartbroken because a guy hadn't called her, and I'd tell her, "Get over it. There are plenty of boys in the sea, each one slicker than the last." Now I feel like the same lovesick puppy I used to make fun of.

When he mentions the girlfriend thing, I tell him he's crazy and to forget it. I've never been anyone's girlfriend, really, and I can't start now. I'm my own worst enemy. I'm my own Benedict Arnold. I'm fucking Lando Calrissian. I'm Roose Bolton, stabbing my future in the gut. Hutch drops the subject, but does little to hide his disappointment.

As part of our stay-away-from-each-other plan, I sit at

every lunch table where he isn't. During breakfast, there isn't enough decaf in the planet to keep me awake while Randy tells me about each girl in a long list of conquests and how we should give it another shot.

At lunch, Nick and I rank the best superhero movies. I have a special place in my heart for campy superheroes, while he loves the super serious takes on them. Nick has cute dimples and shaggy hair. If his glasses were round, he'd be my rehab Harry Potter. I can tell by the way he leans in to me when he speaks and blushes when I make penis jokes that he likes me. In another time, I'd have ruined him.

Then I realize I'm not doing much better with Hutch. Just because he hasn't lost his job doesn't mean everything is going to end up well with us. I start to wonder: am I actually becoming a better person?

No, River. You're still the same. Only sober.

...

I keep an eye on Maddie for days. She's been retreating and hanging out less and less with others. Her time here is going to be over on November 1st. I wonder if she's counting the days 'til freedom. I wonder if the first thing she's going to do is go and get high as a kite. I wonder if she'll be right back here the week after.

One thing's for sure: I have to find a way to guarantee Hutch's safety. I didn't want to admit how much Taylor freaked me out. If we were in New York I'd have my bouncers put the fear of God into him. But we're not in New York. We're here, and as much as I hate it, he has a higher hand.

I do have one choice, though. Maddie.

My favorite part of Maddie is that she's predictable. She always takes the same path to the barn. I wait for her to walk past the media room and toward the cafeteria. She has a stack of books in her arms. She doesn't even look over her shoulder. I wait ten minutes before I follow her. My heart is a knot in my throat as I stand outside the barn. What if Taylor is so pissed to see me there that he has someone hurt me? No, he'll be surprised. I bet he'll be too busy trying to figure out who tipped me off or invited me without his permission. I'm playing a dangerous game, I know. But I think this is the only option I have where Hutch and I win. Bringing Taylor down is our only shot. I need something to hold over Taylor's head. I need proof. Concrete, undeniable proof that Taylor is crooked. Hutch can't get that proof, but I can.

I duck through the door and someone gasps.

I smirk and walk the length of the barn. It's cold as hell, but there's enough drugs and booze that no one seems to mind. The table of poker players gets distracted. I feel a little tug in my chest as I walk past them. They have chips piled high—there's even a gold watch and a wallet in there. The old me would have salivated at this and taken a seat between Hairy Guy #1 and Hairy Guy #2. One of them makes my heart stop. In the dim light, his blue eyes shine. His mustache is salt and pepper, and his thick white hair is combed back. There's a cigar at the corner of his mouth. In the dim light, he looks like my daddy before the chemo, before the sickness, before the worst year of our lives. In the dim light, I feel like I've been shaken and stirred and spilled out on the ground.

Then I hear my name barked. Taylor waltzes over and slings an arm around my shoulder.

"What are you doing here, girly?" He squeezes too hard, seconds away from putting me in a headlock.

"What do you think?" I look up at him and then let my eyes linger on the poker table and the keg.

Maddie's seen me, too. In a room this intimate, I'm sort of hard to miss. My heart breaks a little when I see some familiar faces. There's Fran, passed out on the ground with another girl. Nick, oh Nick. He's doing a line off a girl who isn't from HCRC. His lips pull back over his teeth when he laughs. Then he sees me and jumps. He wipes his nose with the back of his hand.

I am not one to judge them. I am not one to be feeling like I've been let down. But I am. I'm even more disappointed because this was me a couple of months ago. Is this what Sky and Leti felt when they saw me come out of that bar? When they had to get help because I made myself sick? I apologized, but I didn't exactly feel sorry. I was too numb to feel sorry. Now I wish I could hug my friends. I want to take back all the stupid things I've ever done. But I'm here for a reason, and I have to play the part of a girl falling off the wagon. I glance at the poker table. There's an open spot with my name on it. I take a deep breath and shake that feeling. I wave a little at Nick, and he bends his head down to do another line.

Maddie's big eyes look frightened as Taylor and I reach her. "River... How?"

"'How' is right," Taylor says, finally letting me go. He takes out his pack of cigarettes and taps them against his hand. He takes one out with just his lips and tongue. His lighter is blue, with a pinup girl painted on the side. He takes a long drag, then offers me one.

I take it. He lights it. It's been so long since I've smoked that it burns going down. "Fuck, I forgot how good this feels."

"You're allowed to smoke," Maddie says.

"I know. I was just trying the whole *super clean* thing." That's a lie. I stopped smoking because I didn't want Hutch to think of cigarettes when he remembered our kisses. The tobacco goes right to my head. A pleasant buzz passes across my skin.

Maddie nods. Taylor's got his arm around her waist now, squeezing hard.

"I saw you on my run," I tell him.

He makes a face, like he's resigned to me being here. Then his face changes, turning his frown into a smile. He softens his grip around Maddie. "What's your poison, Thomas? First one's on the house."

"Yeah?" I smile. It's hard to smile when I feel like running out of the barn and hiding under my covers. "I'm still pissed they took my percs. Do you know how painful it is to have a neck injury without super-strength drugs? Just shoot me."

We sit on top of prickly bales of hay. A girl tries to get Taylor's attention. He shoves a little plastic bag of pills into her hand and tells her to leave him alone. Either she's too high to feel insulted, or she really doesn't care.

"River, River, River," Taylor says my name. I can tell he doesn't know what to do about me being here. "Why the change of heart?"

I shrug, and try my best to look disinterested. I tilt my head and let my face relax. This is more for Hutch than me, so I smile and come up with a lie that straddles the truth. "Helen threatened me with psych again. She's worried I tried to drown myself. I'm so over her motherly shit."

"I can't stand that bitch." He laughs and slaps me on the back. "We cool?"

"If you hook me up we will be."

I guess I am better at being fake than I thought. It concerns me. But I tell myself this is for Hutch. It seems impossible now, but maybe one day, when we're past this, we can have a future together.

He seems to like that response, because he goes off into a corner, takes out a key, and opens a metal box. Maddie jumps on me and whispers. "I don't think you should be here. You don't know him."

I'm grinning so much it hurts. I hate the panic in her voice. "Why are *you* here?" I ask her through a cheesy smile.

"I can't help it. You can. You have friends that love you."

"What about your boyfriends?" I try to give her a friendly nudge.

She shakes her head. "There's no one. I lied. Taylor makes me feel… good."

If I hated Taylor before, I loathe him now. I want to tell her that it isn't real affection, but when I was like her, I wouldn't have listened to reason either. What did it take for me to realize? The scar on my thigh? Nearly burning down a family wedding? Owing the wrong people money? These dark thoughts flood my mind as Taylor comes back. He whispers something in Maddie's ear, and she leaves. She pumps the keg and refills the empty beer pitchers around the poker table. If anything, Taylor is a really good host.

He sits beside me, much like he did in the library a few days ago. This time his arm is over my head, and all his attention is on me. He's wearing cologne better suited for a seventeen-year-old boy who wears polo shirts. He takes a drag from his cigarette and blows the smoke away from me.

"You know," he says, "for such an icy bitch, you're really hot."

I fake-giggle, and busy myself with my cigarette. I look him dead in the eyes. Most people don't like steady eye contact because it makes them uncomfortable. Not Taylor, though. He stares at me right back, and I see the challenge there… and the lust.

"Here." He holds out a little blue pill for me to take.

I smile, and pocket it. "You're not so bad after all."

"No, no, no. Nothing leaves this barn."

Shit. My insides are on fire. This wasn't part of my plan. I can't *eat* the evidence. Will Hutch forgive me if I do this to get on Taylor's good side? Can I forgive myself after working this hard? My mouth feels dry. I fish the pill back out and hold it in the center of my palm. If I look at it long enough, it looks like the eye at the center of a Hamsa.

"Water," I tell him.

He doesn't take his eyes off me as he gets up and gets me a water bottle. His phone rings and he digs it out of his pocket as he walks back to me. In that moment, I throw my head back and clap my hand over my mouth. He looks away, and I tuck the pill into my pocket. I twist open the water bottle and drink. He turns away so no one can watch his mouth as he speaks. All I hear is, "I can't talk right now. Hang on."

He points a finger in my direction, smiles, and mimes firing a gun. When Taylor's gone, I tell Maddie I feel drowsy and that I'm going to bed. She won't look at me, but she nods.

"You can talk to me," I tell her.

She shakes her head.

I leave her.

. . .

When I get back to my room, I feel like the pill will burn a hole through my hand. I drop it in a sock with stars on it, and leave that sock in my drawer. I start to get into bed and freeze. There's a note beneath my covers. My heart seizes, and I run through the possibilities. It's a short list. Kiernan or Taylor; Kiernan or Taylor. I grab the note by one folded corner and hold it at arm's length. I sigh in relief when I recognize the handwriting. I unfold it eagerly, my eyes scanning the words faster than my mind can register them.

"Going up to Missoula for the day. Go to the far woods before dinner. Love."

Love. Is he calling me love, or himself? Does it even matter? It doesn't. I feel even worse for keeping this from him. I reread the note a hundred times, and my mind creates lots of different scenarios. The last time we were in the middle of the woods, it ended abruptly. If two people have sex in the woods and no one's around to see them, do they make a sound?

This time, we will.

CHAPTER 31

I go through the motions of the day and turn in early with the pretext of having menstrual cramps.

But instead of going to my room, I make a loop around the entire facility and end up at the woods. I feel more nervous than I ever have going to meet a guy. The downside to living here for so long is that I can't shave. So far, Hutch hasn't seemed to mind, which just goes to show he's more mature than anyone I've ever been with before. I scrubbed myself down until my skin was red afterwards. I smell like soap and my hair dried in long curly waves that make me look deceptively sweet.

I pull up my hoodie, covering my hair. I nicked a flashlight from the front desk while Greta wasn't looking, and shine it ahead of me. Every step I take makes me forget my worries about Taylor, and Maddie, and my past. Despite being drug free, I feel kind of high and drunk on the possibilities of Chris Hutcherson. God, I want to eat that boy alive. In a non-cannibalistic way.

When there's no sign of him, my excited nerves become ill nerves. Maybe he got held up in Missoula. Maybe he got a flat tire. Ugh, stop making excuses for him.

"Psst," it comes, making me jump out of my skin.

"Psst yourself," I say in a hushed voice.

Not seeing him for a whole day was painful. I twist and turn as he pulls me into his embrace. He pulls my hoodie back. I dive for his lips, but he kisses my forehead, buries his nose in my hair.

"You smell good."

"Sometimes I shower."

"I like you a little dirty."

"You have no idea how dirty I can be."

He picks me up and I squeal. Then I cover my mouth.

"It's okay," he says. "No one but the bears can hear us."

"Stop with the bears!"

He picks me up, and I wrap my legs around his waist. He starts walking me deeper into the woods. The sun has just set, and the sky is still backlit with sunlight.

"Where are we going?" I ask. "What was in Missoula?"

"It's a secret. And I was in Missoula picking up some things for the Halloween party."

We approach a campground, where a small fire crackles. There's a plaid blanket, a lantern, and a pizza box. He sets me down and I just stand there, unable to take a step forward or backward. He watches me, resting his fists on his hips.

"Welcome to our first date," he tells me.

"Is that champagne?" I ask.

He rolls his eyes. "It's non-alcoholic sparkling apple cider."

I walk around the picnic the way someone walks around a museum piece. I admire it from all angles. I admire *him* from all angles. He starts to laugh.

"You should see your face," he tells me. "You look so freaked out."

I hold my arms above my head. "Well! This is… It's amazing. Hutch…"

I go to him. I wrap my arms around him and tilt my head back so he can kiss me. But he doesn't.

"Look, River. I want you. I need you to know that I don't want anyone else. Whatever comes next, after you finish your program, I'll be there for you. Whatever you need."

"I know that."

"I wish I could do more. Take you to a nice restaurant, the movies. I want to give you everything you deserve."

I don't deserve this. I really don't. But I want it. I've always been a little selfish.

"I don't need all that stuff. This is perfect." I take his hand and we sit across from each other.

"When you pointed out that we don't go on dates, I felt like such a jackass."

"That wasn't my intention. You know me. I just say stuff, and half the time it's pretty offensive."

"Well, baby. Enjoy your pizza feast. It's cold by now, but you told me you like your pizza cold and your coffee black."

I stare at him. "I told you that when we were drunk."

He breaks off a slice and folds it in half. "I have a really good memory when it comes to River-related things."

"Good."

We eat the pizza. I have the brilliant idea to hold it over the fire to let the cheese melt a little bit. To his surprise—or dismay?—I eat four whole slices. We drink the apple cider and then we lie on the blanket. He's so beautiful it hurts to look at him. I lie back and stretch under the night sky. I feel full and happy. So much so that it should be illegal to be this happy with someone.

I wonder: is this how my dad and mom felt before everything fell apart? When does love, inevitably, fall apart?

He doesn't give me a chance to think about it more because he upzips his jacket, folds it, and gives it to me as a pillow. He climbs on top of me, kissing me in a way that tells me he's missed me just as much as I missed him. If it's possible, maybe even more.

"Thank you for this," I tell him.

"You don't have to thank me. I want to give you everything I can."

"That's a lot of stuff, Mr. Hutcherson."

He kisses the chill from my lips. "Everything."

Our teeth click because we kiss while smiling. I wrap my hands around his neck and draw him closer. How can we be touching and still not have it be enough?

"Is it too cold?" he asks.

"I think you can find ways to warm me up."

There's a deep rumble in his throat. I feel his cock harden against my leg. I unsnap his belt buckle, and undo his pants in a frenzy. I hold him in my hands, and guide him inside me. I gasp at the shock of him. He takes his time, pushing himself inch by inch.

"God, River..." he moans in my ear. His tongue licks delicious, undulating lines down my neck.

I push myself up, forcing him to fill me all the way. When I cry out, night birds take flight, and animals scurry away. I push him away and onto his back. I grab his hard shaft and drag my tongue from stem to tip, licking circles all around the head. He runs his fingers through my hair and tugs. I shiver, and take him into my mouth. I can taste the salty bubbles of excitement as he gets harder and harder. He moans. Maybe it's my name. Maybe he's telling me he loves me. Maybe he's shouting for help from God himself. I take great pleasure in making him feel like this.

"River, I'm close."

I just look up at him. His dark eyes are dazed, and he leans his head back, thrusting himself up. He fills my mouth. I grab his shaft and move my hand up and down until he's given me all he's got. I sit up and run a hand across my hard, pert nipples. He reaches for me, and I climb on top of him willingly. His eyes go wide when I swallow and lick my lips.

"You are so fucking perfect."

I laugh and rest my head on his shoulder. He grabs my ass with one hand, and uses the other one to play with my hair. "I know."

"River," he says. It sounds cautionary. I look at him with a little bit of worry. Was that too dirty for him? I feel like he should know what he's getting into. Not that he seemed to mind a moment ago. "Will you let me be your boyfriend?"

I sigh. It's a happy sigh, a dreamy sigh.

Yes.

No.

Yes.

It's a no-brainer really. The bad thoughts come back. The last boyfriend I had hurt me. Not just because we didn't love each other, but because he wasn't good. Even people that do claim to love each other end up in ruins. My dad was never the same after my mom. But that doesn't mean that I'm my parents. I'm River Thomas, and I'm in love with this man. I don't know what I'm doing, but isn't that part of what makes me me? Diving into the world with open arms. Maybe he can be my parachute. My anchor. Maybe…

I find his mouth and answer him with a long, deep kiss.

After a little while of listening to the sounds of the night, I say, "That was a yes, by the way."

He just holds me close, and chuckles. "I know."

CHAPTER 32

River Anne Thomas has a boyfriend.

As I walk down the halls of HCRC, I repeat this over and over again. My kickboxing class is excellent, though Nerd Boy Nick isn't there. Ransom tells me I look different. And, because he's a man, he stutters, "Uh, good different. Not bad different."

"Just. Stop," I tell him, and smile.

I actually punctuate everything with a smile.

"Hey Helen (smile). Good morning (smile)."

She shakes her head and busies herself with a stack of paperwork. A couple of people are stringing glittery bats all over the walls. I helped draw a face on a giant pumpkin (we aren't allowed to carve), but it looks more smiling than sinister. I even smile at Debbie as Taylor walks her out of the building with her bags.

"Don't come back, Debbie (smile). I mean that in the best way (smile)!"

"If you ever see me 'round here again, do me a favor," she says, walking backwards into the crisp, fall air. "Shoot me."

"Will do (smile)."

"Are you that excited about family day?" Vilma asks me during breakfast. She's done up. Her hair is in a bun and she's wearing makeup. She's wearing clothes that are not pajamas for the first time since I met her. Before, I couldn't really picture her as a mom, but now I can. She drums her fingers nervously on the table.

That puts the brakes on my smile punctuation marks. "Family day?"

"Why do you think everyone's dressing up?"

I blink a few times, and realize Julie is wearing a dress. Her hair is combed away from her face. She gives me a tight-lipped smile that I can't return. Pete and Randy are in something better suited for Sunday Mass, or the country club. They sit down at our table.

Vilma points a thumb at me. "This one didn't know it was family day."

Pete looks at me with sympathy. "You can still change. No one gets here until around eleven."

"It's not that," I say. "I don't have anyone coming. I forgot about it. My friends travel a lot."

"You can have an awkward time with me and my folks," Randy says. "I might've told them I have a serious girlfriend while I was here. And she might fit your description."

Girlfriend. That's right! I, River Anne Thomas, am someone's girlfriend!

"Sorry, Randy," I tell him. "I think your mom would have a heart attack if you brought a girl like me home."

"That's the point," he says.

Vilma slaps the back of his head, and Pete asks him to behave for once. There's something different between the two of them. I would bet anything that there was something there, except I'm not really taking bets right now. The last couple I've taken have been way, way off. It's probably for the best.

"You can sit at the loser table," Randy tells me. "Apparently that's where everyone who doesn't have a visitor sits."

"You're a dick (smile)."

He shrugs, and bites down on an apple like he's taking a bite out of the center of the earth.

• • •

Relegated to the "loser table," I decide to put on the only dress that I own. It's long-sleeved and heather gray, and I might've stolen it from Sky's closet last fall. I top it off with my chunky black boots, trade Greta at the front door a pack of cigarettes for a lipstick the color of a bloody heart, and I'm done. I walk down the hall, the parents and family members looking at me with disapproving stares.

Randy barks in my direction. His mother, an ivory-sweater-and-pearls kind of lady, purses her lips at both of us. I wink at him, then keep walking. Nerd Boy Nick drops his paper cup of water. His older brother leers at my ass.

Then there are the families that are too happy being reunited to pay attention to me. My heart squeezes at the sight of Vilma's two little daughters racing down the hall. Vilma looks frozen, like she might not be able to get through the day. Then she opens her arms and lifts both of them into a hug.

I take a deep breath and head for the loser table. It feels weird, sitting with others and intruding on what should be private moments. Pete is in a somber conversation with an older lady. She's holding a handkerchief to her nose and crying.

"You too?" Jermania asks me. She holds her head up with her fists.

Maddie is scribbling in a notebook with her head on the table. I go to take the seat next to her, but there's a bowl of Jell-O there.

"She doesn't want anyone sitting next to her," Jermania says.

"Okay." I take the seat on the other side of the circle table. There are a few people here that I've never spoken to before. They don't seem as pissed as Maddie.

"Maddie," I say. She won't look up at me. "Maddie."

She slams her head down into her arms. Her whole body shudders as she tries to sob quietly. Jermania puts a hand on my arm and shakes her head.

"We tried. She's not responding. I got Scrabble. Maybe she can make words instead of speak them."

"Highest word score buys a round," a big redhead says.

"A round of what?" I ask.

"I don't know. Chocolate?"

"I'm game."

I'm getting ready to settle in when I hear someone shout, "River Thomas, I've been looking for that dress for a *year*!"

I jump out of my seat. Heads swivel toward the entrance of the cafeteria, where Sky Lopez and Leti Delgado stand. I don't even realize I'm crying until I start running toward them with wide-open arms. We fall into a giant, screaming girl-hug. I don't even care that people in Eastern Montana can probably hear us.

"Aww, *nena*," Leti says. "Don't cry."

"I'm not crying. I woke up with dry eyes." I lead them out of the cafeteria and into the courtyard where the fire pit is lit. We pull three chairs as close to the fire as we can without getting burned. I sit in the middle and squeeze both of their hands.

"Why didn't you tell me you were coming?" I ask.

Sky brushes my hair away from my face. She's always been the most motherly out of the three of us. Her long dark hair is pulled into a sleek ponytail. She's decked out like it's the middle of winter in New York. She hates the cold.

"We wanted it to be a surprise, duh," Leti says. Her cheeks are rosy. The star on her tooth twinkles in the firelight. Her hair's gotten long, and there are streaks of blond at the end. Then she leans in. "Where is he?"

"Soon, my pretties," I say, drumming my fingers together conspiratorially. "Tell me. Tell me all the news and all the things. I don't even go on the computer anymore."

"I'm sorry I've been shitty about getting back to you. I didn't get a SIM card in Prague. And then I dropped my phone off the side of a boat in Ireland."

I make a face and hold a finger in her face. "Do you hear yourself right now?"

"I know, right? She's traveling the world with her sexy man, and we're supposed to feel sorry for her?"

"What happened to your guy?" I ask Leti.

"We had fun. It kind of fizzled when we were in Italy."

"I hate both of you."

Sky smirks. "Though I'm sure you've been keeping yourself pretty busy. I got your letter in the mail and got nervous when you told me what was happening. Spill. You've been keeping something from us for far too long."

I lean back, staring at the fire. Here are the two people I have to be honest with, even if I can't be honest with myself. I never told them about Kiernan and how bad it got. But now I do. I watch their faces go from disapproving to angry, to shocked, to horrified, then back to disapproving.

"I was embarrassed," I tell them. "I'd never let someone treat me like that before. I didn't even realize it was happening because I was so messed up over my dad. After he threw me through that glass, and I cut his face… I knew he'd come after me. My godfather told me not to worry, that he'd take care of it. But when Kiernan started coming up again, I didn't know what to do. I feel pretty safe here."

"Despite the barn action," Sky mutters.

"I'll get to that later," I tell them. "I'm clean. I'm the cleanest I've been since I was twelve."

"Damn, we were bad," Leti says. "Remember when we would take your dad's vodka, drink all of it, then replace it with water?"

I laugh so hard it hurts. "I forgot about that. He never said anything. Just replaced the bottles because he thought he'd drunk them and forgotten."

"Remember that Halloween we cut school and stayed in my family's new house?" Sky says. "Only we hadn't moved in yet, so the heat wasn't on, and we froze our asses off for hours?"

"How come I turned out bad and you guys did okay?" I ask them.

"Don't say that."

I shrug. "I'm sorry. I've just been doing a lot of thinking about it lately. That's all I do, talk and think and then talk to other people."

"You do more stuff," Leti says with a naughty wink.

"I almost drowned while camping. I fell of my horse. I've gotten better though. Look at my guns, bro." I fold my arm so they can feel my baby bicep.

"Damn," Leti says. "Are there any other hot guys here? I might just commit myself."

"It's not a *psych* ward," Sky says, giving her cousin a long look that says, *behave*.

"You have no idea how much I missed you guys." I squeeze their hands tighter. They're like my lifelines in this great big, crazy world. "I wanted to tell you both that I'm really sorry for everything I've put you through."

"Oh, River, you don't have to," Sky says.

I shake my head. "I do. You guys have always been there for me. You always put up with my messiness, even though it's gotten worse in the last year."

Leti runs a hand over my head. "We're sisters. No matter what you do. No matter *what*."

"In the beginning, I didn't think I belonged here. I thought that I wasn't like the rest of the people here. But I think we have one thing in common. We're all lost. Some in more ways than others. I lost my way and then I stopped recognizing myself. Even if I don't have a hardcore heroin dependency, I was still harming myself. Being the least addicted of all the addicts doesn't make me less of an addict."

"You are being careful," Sky says. "Aren't you?"

"Like with sex or—"

"Both!" Sky says. "Do I have to lecture you about safe sex the way I do to pregnant teenagers?"

I shush her, but can't help but laugh. "Chill, Sky."

"Yeah, chill Sky," Leti says.

"I mean the other thing. I don't want you to get involved in something that might be out of your league. You're not back home. You don't have your godfather there to send a bunch of goons after someone who messes with you. You don't have an army of bouncers to scare off some lowlife not playing by the rules."

"This is like the Wild West," Leti says, more excited than she should be.

"I know I'm not back in New York." I don't know why I don't call it home. Home is Leti and Sky. Home is my dad. Home is Hutch. How can my home be so scattered and still feel so tangible? "But I can't just turn my back on what I've seen."

I tell them about Taylor and his threat to Hutch and me. How I went to the barn. How I hid the pill in my things.

"I think if I have enough evidence against him," I say, "I can go to Helen and tell her everything and she'll have to believe me."

"Why wouldn't she believe you now?"

"Who would you believe? An addict with a penchant for getting herself in trouble, or the hand who's been working beside you for years? Besides, this is Hutch's life. I can't just go in River-style and wreck everything the way I always do. I think this is the only way we can come up winners."

Sky takes in the mountains, the trees, and the facility behind us. Then she looks at me with concern. "What if you do everything right. What if you get your evidence and expose this creep. What's to stop him from ratting *you* guys out?"

"We'll deny it. There's no proof."

"River, think this through."

"I'd personally like to see the person that's got our River Thomas so spun."

"I'm not spun."

"You're *totally* spun." Leti grins and pokes my ribs. "Speak of the devil," I say.

Hutch steps into the courtyard, followed by Helen and a few parents. I can't hide the smile that Hutch brings to my lips, and neither can he. Helen stops by first. She shakes hands with Leti and Sky.

"So you complete the trio I've heard about."

"You have no idea," Leti tells her.

Helen makes her way further down and does her shaking hands and kissing babies thing. Meanwhile, my heart flutters when Hutch approaches us. Leti and Sky giggle, and make fun of me.

"Would you look at her face," Leti says. "I don't think I've ever seen her smile at a guy like that."

"I don't think she's smiled at anyone before."

"I take great umbrage to that."

"How big is his penis?" Leti asks.

We collapse into a fit of laughter the second Hutch reaches us.

"Are the New Yorkers causing trouble already?" he asks.

I love his voice. I love the rich, deep brown of his eyes. I love the way he smiles at my friends. The way he looks at me.

"Why does everyone think we're trouble?" Leti asks. "We've been here for an hour. Not even."

Hutch shakes Leti and Sky's hands. I don't know where to put my hands, so I alternate between smoothing the material of my dress and picking at the dirt under my nails.

"I can usually spot trouble when it walks through my door," he says, and I have the feeling he's talking about me.

"Thank you for all you're doing for our girl," Sky tells him. "I hear she's been in good hands. Though I'm concerned about her doing all this outdoors stuff. What's the score now? River: 0, Nature: 3?"

"Funny," I mumble, but really I do love them joking at my expense. Just this once.

"She's getting better," Hutch says. "You should've seen her the first week she was here. She wouldn't even come out of her room. Now she's volunteering to go on nature trails."

"Are we talking about the same River Thomas?" Sky asks.

"The one and only." He says that so adamantly, so matter-of-factly, that even Leti gasps a little.

"So, hey," Leti says. "What are you?"

Hutch looks startled, but laughs.

"I'm just saying," Leti says. "I get asked that question all the time and I'm like, I'm a queen, baby. Really I'm Ecuadorian. But I feel like I need to know the mix that created all of this. Because I might have to go try to replicate that. Also, do you have any hot brothers who like curvy girls?"

"*Leti*," Sky and I hiss at the same time.

Hutch takes a seat on the lawn chair beside me. I can feel his warmth instantly. He looks at me with those coffee brown eyes. *Mmm, way better than caffeine*. Never thought I'd say that.

"It's a little complicated," he says.

Leti bats her long black lashes, that star on her tooth winking with feigned innocence. "We *love* complicated."

"You don't have to answer her, Mr. Hutcherson."

"It's just Hutch. I'm a mutt, I guess," Hutch says. "My dad's side is British, Irish, and I have a Blackfoot great-grandmother. My mom's side is Polish-Italian, and I have one Mexican grandfather. If an ethnic group tried to settle in the Northwestern Territories, they're probably in my blood. But when people ask me what I am, I usually just tell them 'I'm dysfunctional.' Which isn't entirely untrue."

"Wow," Leti says, gazing at him dreamily.

I pinch her arm.

"So let me get this straight," I tell him. "The entire facility has been hounding you about this for, like, ever. Now these crazies ask you, and you answer them in a heartbeat?"

"Yep." He sets those eyes and that wicked grin on me. "Well, ladies. It's been a pleasure. Are you staying in Missoula?"

"We got an airbnb across from the mountain with the M. It's so lovely."

"How long are you staying for?" I ask.

"Just the weekend. I have to get back to work before my manager stops liking me after all the time I've taken off."

"I'll leave you guys to it." This time he hugs them, and he jumps a little because I'm pretty sure Leti pinched his ass.

"Wow," Leti says.

"I love him for you," Sky says. "He's the perfect balance."

All I can do is grin like fool. I take them to the stables, where they pet Apollo and the others. They meet Jillian, and Jillian is so happy to have someone to speak Spanish with that I think she might cry. They meet Ransom and Simmons. Nurse Jean and Sky talk shop. We're probably the loudest people in the entire place, but I don't care. I haven't felt this unflinchingly happy in so long. They stay the longest of any family. We play Candyland with Vilma's girls in the game room. Jermania is fascinated with Leti's life of traveling and freedom. Julie is in love with Sky's outfit. They're exotic in a New York kind of way, in a world where everyone dresses for comfort. I try to get Maddie to come hang out with us, but she banishes herself to her room.

"Are you going to come tomorrow?" I ask them, seeing them off to their car.

"Of course," Sky tells me.

LIFE ON THE LEVEL

We hug so hard and long that I'm afraid we're going to need a crowbar to pull ourselves apart. I stand in the driveway until their car is a tiny dot on the road. I'm sad to see them go, but at least they get to see that I'm okay. Better than okay, I think. I'm happy.

Walking back into HCRC, I feel like I'm on clouds. I'm so sure I'm on the right path, and now Leti and Sky have seen it. I change into pajamas. Everyone is going to gather in the media room for a movie, though there's some contention about whether we'll be watching Men in Black or Pitch Perfect. On my way to the media room, I decide to go check on Maddie.

I know we aren't the best of friends. I never go out of my way to befriend someone, and maybe that's been one of my problems in getting close to people in the past. She's just as lost as I am, and needs to know she has more options than Taylor. Taylor, who made himself scarce from all the family activities.

When I go to knock on Maddie's door, it's already cracked open, but the shower is running.

I take one step into the bathroom. The floor is wet, and I slip. I hit my head so hard the room rattles.

"Maddie, what the hell? Use a floor mat."

But the wet stuff isn't water. It's a pool of blood, with Maddie unconscious in the center of it.

CHAPTER 33

"Even in my darkest moment, I never tried to hurt myself. That doesn't make me better than the people who do. That just makes me a different kind of lucky. I remember days where I would lie in my bed and think about it, but I'd chicken out because I don't like pain, or I was afraid I might go too far. I remember the sadness, but even in that sadness I never wanted to die."

Ransom looks at me with sad eyes. We've all been forced into special counseling sessions. Especially me, because I'm the one who found Maddie. I'm afraid of my own weakness.

I close my eyes and picture Maddie. Her eyes were half open and she was still crying. Her tears mixed into her blood, steam settling around her.

"River—I'm sorry," she said.

"I don't get why she apologized to me," I say. "I mean, why was she sorry that she cut open her veins and let herself lie there? If anything we're the ones who should be sorry. I didn't try hard enough. I was too busy being happy. But that's when things go to shit, right? The *second* you get a little too happy is when God or the universe or whatever six-headed monster is driving this thing—that's when it decides to shit on you or the people around you."

I stand and pace the room. I pick up the football on his desk and throw it from hand to hand. I see blood and tears and Maddie's sad eyes. They took her away and she barely had a pulse. It was like she was empty, the life all but tapped out of her.

"Helen says Maddie's alive," Ransom says, "but her parents came to take her back to Seattle."

"Where were her parents when she was sitting in the

cafeteria waiting for them?"

He doesn't have an answer.

"I get it," I say. "It's not other people's jobs to fix us. We have to want to save ourselves. But what if you think that you're alone? What's the difference between this dark and dying? I just don't know."

"River, I don't want you to think that you are in any way responsible."

"Why? Because I was nasty to her the first day I met her? I mean, I knew she was sad. I saw it."

"You said you tried to get her to join you yesterday."

"Yeah, but was it enough? You can't baby people, but then you can't leave them alone, either. It's too hard, you know? Is it my fault that I didn't try hard enough? Maybe."

"River, we all have monsters in our closets. No matter how much help we get, it's still up to the individual to want to battle that monster."

"We're just battling ourselves," I tell him. "This place, outside of here. No matter where we go, we're the monsters and the thing fighting the monster at the same time. What do we say when things are bad? *It's meant to be.* What do we say when we're seconds away from making a change? *You can't change the past.* What do we say when things get worse? *Life isn't fair.* What do you say when someone is struggling? *You have to want to help yourself first.*

"I mean, what's the point if the answers aren't really answers, just things meant to make us feel better?"

After that we're quiet for a long, long time.

・・・

I spend the rest of the day with Leti and Sky. I didn't want them to see that side of this place, but they don't complain. We walk across the hills. We watch the horses gallop freely and the cows graze. They cheer me up by talking about New York. About Uncle Pepe, Tony, and the family.

"You're out of here at the end of November," Leti says.

"Have you thought about what you're going to do after that?"

A strangled laugh leaves my lips. "Do I ever know what I'm doing?"

Sky brushes my hair away from my face. It's cold out, and we huddle together around the courtyard fire pit. I breathe in the cold mountain air.

"Where do you want to be?" Sky asks me.

"I wish I could be in two places at once. I mean, I miss the city. I miss the lights, and the Lower East Side. I miss my queen-sized bed, and lattes as big as my face. I miss you and Leti. I miss the smell of the beach. One of my favorite sights is the New York skyline after being away, and you're flying in or driving and it's just there—bright and epic and unforgettable.

"But I wonder if I'm strong enough to stay clean if I'm back there. But if I don't at least *try*, I might regret it. What if I can't do it?"

"You know you'll always have Leti and me no matter where you are."

"I know. Then there's... *him*. Sometimes I wonder if the reason this thing is so strong is because it's forbidden. Like we're just getting off on the idea that we're doing something wrong. And when it's over, what happens then? We're just a normal couple?"

"Don't go there, River," Sky tells me. "You can lose yourself in trying to figure out what it means. You're going to make yourself crazy. Remember when I was trying to justify my attraction to Hayden? I have never seen you look at someone the way you look at Hutch. And I don't know him, but I think I'm a pretty good judge of character. That man loves you."

"You're a *terrible* judge of character," Leti tells her. "But I agree. I'm surprised you've been able to keep it quiet for so long."

The three of us knock on wood.

"Do you want to stay here?" Leti asks.

"In Montana?" I look into the faces of the two people I can't lie to, even when I lie to myself. "I've never felt as free as I have since I've been here. Don't get me wrong, I've had my fun. But while I'm here, while I'm with him, I feel like I can have more."

"And if it doesn't work out, you can always come home," Leti tells me. "We'll be there with open arms."

CHAPTER 34

FIFTY-FIVE DAYS SOBER

The rest of October flies by without incident. Maddie's absence is sad, but like many things, it fades. I start to notice that people leave the facility every day. So far, only two have come back after falling immediately off the wagon. What'll it be like when I leave here in a month? Will anyone miss me? Is it like high school, where everyone promises to keep in touch, but after a long summer we're just fading memories? I know that I for one will want to remember the time I've spent here.

Helen says the Halloween party is still on. The staff hopes to bring back much-needed joy to the patients. Candy and dressing up like someone you're not is apparently a cure for all ills.

Hutch and I spend more time apart, which is a good thing I guess. He's busy with trauma counseling, and more new patients than I've ever seen before. When he visits me at night, he looks tired, like his soul is weary. So I just kiss him, and try to take his pain into myself. My least favorite time of day is morning, because he's always gone back across the hall. It gets worse every time. It's like waking up with a part of me missing.

• • •

Two days before the Halloween party, Julie decides she wants to be friends again.

"Hey River," she says.

I'm trying to carve pumpkins with safety scissors, which proves a challenge. At this rate, I should hire a local kindergarten class to decorate—they'd probably do a better job than us.

"What's up?" I say. I don't mean to be cold, but ever since the camping trip I've been keeping my distance.

She pulls strands of hair out of her messy bun and twirls them around her finger. "I just—I just wanted to see if you needed help."

"I think we've got it under control," I say. She looks disappointed. I push away my pride. Maybe it's because of what happened to Maddie, but I say, "But if you want, I think Nick could use some help hanging the ghosts."

That makes her smile, and I realize I was being petty.

By the end of the day, the room has improved to looking like a fourth-grade class's Halloween party, which is fine with me. There's enough glitter and papier-mâché to give the illusion we're not in a rehab center. Everyone leaves for dinner except Julie, who begs me for help with her Halloween costume again. I don't know when I turned into a bleeding heart, but I concede, and she runs off to get the thrift store bin.

While she's gone, Taylor comes in to give the room a final mop, even though he's just going to have to do it again tomorrow. He makes his way over to me, and leans on the wooden staff.

"How you holding up, Empire State?"

I can't help but look horrified. Maddie called me that, and he knows it.

"Fine," I say, unable to restrain my anger.

He chuckles, which doubles my anger. "I just wanted to let you know that I have some new stuff. You haven't visited in a real long time. I'm starting to miss you."

He doesn't go as far as to touch my hair, but his hand makes the motion.

"Do you miss Maddie, too?" I level my eyes at his. He makes a face, but stays quiet. "Who's your assistant now that she's gone?"

"What makes you think Maddie was the only one?"

"Did you even care about her?"

"You of all people should know that everyone is means to an end."

I want to puke on his face. I want to beat him with his own mop. Just then, Julie walks in. She drops the box of clothes and gasps.

"Oh, sorry. I was just—"

"Hey Julie," Taylor says to her in that slick voice of his. "Can't wait to see your costume."

She turns a bright red, and then he's gone.

I'm stewing in my rage when Julie speaks. "Have you decided?"

Have I decided what? How I'm going to take down Taylor? Where I'm going to be in a month? What I'm supposed to do with my life after this is all over? This place was supposed to be my getaway from my troubles, but now I feel more buried than ever.

"Hm?" I ask, when I realize she's holding up a few garments for me.

"Have you decided what you're going as?"

I try to smile. "Not yet. Let's just work on you first, okay?"

"Okay. I want to be something pretty, but not childish. The problem is that everything for the girls has these frilly things. Who even wears this?"

"I think this is all from the '80s." I hold the lacey gold dress up to examine it. "I don't know how much safety scissors are going to help. I wish I had my sewing machine."

"You can sew?" she asks, as if I just confessed I could travel in time.

"Just basic things. My dad taught me. His mother was a seamstress, and he had to help her when she worked." When I was little, and my dad was down and we had no money, he would make me clothes. Frilly dresses that made me look as if I was a human cupcake. I never bought a Halloween costume because he'd always put something together for me. I was never allowed to tell anyone that my big, tall, manly father was the one making my costumes, but I was happy just to have something no one else was wearing. Something my daddy made just for me. I think of him sitting by our beat-up sewing machine, his mustached face stern as he cuts up fabric for his little girl's dresses.

I feel like there's something caught in my chest as I cut fabric away from this dress. I don't care what anyone tries to tell me. My daddy loved me.

Julie decides she wants to be a space princess, and we put together something out of the gold and silver pieces in the bin. God bless '80s fashion. I make something for myself, which I think is pretty funny. When my eyes are red and my body is tired, I head to my room and lock the door, only to find Hutch already asleep on my bed. He's only wearing boxers. His arms are over his head and his lips are parted. He makes a cute whistling sound when he sleeps. I lean against the wall and admire the glorious sculpture of his muscles. His leg twitches, and he mutters something that sounds like my name. He could be saying "Woof!" and I'd mistake it for my name, because that's what I want to hear coming from his lips.

I feel gritty after spending all day decorating. I barely let anyone help me, which Helen told me was the opposite of teamwork. But I needed to keep my hands busy. I turn on the shower, drop my clothes, and then jump right in. The water is always cold at first, but it steadily warms. I turn up the heat, the steam rising and clouding around me. I turn my back to the stream of water and relax into the water pressure. The one thing I do miss is having a proper bathtub, not just a shower.

I slather foamy body wash on, and breathe in the sea-scented chemicals.

Hands, strong but gentle, wrap around my waist. I collapse into Hutch's hold, resting my head against his chest. He runs his hands over my breasts, my belly, and down between my legs.

"I've missed you," he says.

"I saw you this morning."

He chuckles into my ear. "Still. It's not enough."

I sigh as he rubs me down until I'm shuddering in his hold. I press my ass against his hardness, loving the way his husky voice vibrates against my skin. The shower stall is tiny, and there's not enough room for the both of us to be in here at the same time. I press myself against the cool tiles, and he follows. We're both slippery and wet and holding on to something bigger than the both of us. I gasp as he finds my center from the back and thrusts into me.

"God you feel amazing," he whispers, burying his head in my back.

I get lost in the pleasure of his rhythm and the way he embraces me. He's hard and soft, strong but sweet, and I love the dichotomy of everything he is. A few seconds with Hutch make my worries fall like petals in the wind. He's stirred my heart in ways I didn't think possible. I tighten my muscles, and he pants deeper and faster. When he pulls out, I spin around and grab his shaft. The shower washes away his release.

He grabs me by the shoulders, like he's trying to get me to focus. He looks deep into my eyes, and he opens his mouth like he wants to tell me something, but then he changes his mind and comes down for a kiss. We stand under the water, touching and caressing until our fingers start to prune.

When we're dry and back in bed, he presses me against his chest.

"River," he says.

"Hutch."

"You feel distant."

I turn around to face him, throw my leg over his hip and bat my eyes. I think I know what he means. I've got a lot on my mind. The past, the present, and the future are creating a soupy serving of confusion. But I'm me, and I'm going to deny it.

"You were literally just inside of me."

"Don't be smart."

"Can't help it."

He licks my nose. "You know what I mean. I want you to be able to talk to me. I'm more than just my body."

I bite his chin and he hisses, then smirks. I reach down and grab the hard curve of his ass.

"I just keep thinking about things I can't really solve right now. Are you worried Ransom knows more about me than you do?"

He caresses my face. "Maybe. I want you to be able to talk to me. That's kind of part of the boyfriend thing."

It's still so weird to call him that. Despite that, I can't help but smile. He presses the softest kiss to my lips.

"I don't think you know just how much you mean to me," he says.

"How much?"

"As much as the state of Montana."

"Texas is bigger."

"From here to Texas, then. From Texas to New York to Australia. More than all the lands here or anywhere. I don't think my love for you can be contained on this earth, quite frankly."

I stiffen.

My heart gives a powerful squeeze.

He said the L word. Granted he didn't tell me he L-words me, but still. All of my muscles seem to petrify, and I'm pretty sure I'm holding my breath. He lifts up my chin. I'm unable to break away from the fierceness in his dark eyes.

"I love you, River Thomas. I love all the things that make you you, the broken parts and the good. I just wanted you to know."

I love you, too! I can feel the words lodged in my throat.

It's like we're in a silent staring contest all of a sudden. No guy has ever spoken to me like this before. It's usually a tangle of sheets and passion that burns out faster than it started. That's how I like it: no-strings-attached fun. With Hutch, it's more than just strings. We're sewn together.

The silence goes on for a dreadfully long time, and he's still looking at me, waiting for me to speak. I'm an idiot. I'm a fool of a girl who fucks up, and I'm just going to fuck him up too.

I love you, Chris Hutcherson. I love you from here to New York and as far out into the galaxies as anyone has ever traveled and beyond. I love you in the secrecy of the stars and under the blinding sun.

And yet, I can't bring myself to say it.

I close my eyes and rest my head on my pillow, still facing him. He traces my arm until he falls asleep.

"Goodnight, Hutch."

When I wake, he's gone, and I taste regret on my tongue. I feel shitty about not being able to respond to him last night. I search for him throughout the day, but the staff and patients are dispersed, buzzing about their costumes and the food and the music. Eventually, I give up looking for him.

If he wants to avoid me, fine.

I just want to explain that I do love him. It's just that I don't know how to say it.

The girls decide to get dressed together in Vilma and Jermania's double room. Vilma paints herself a unibrow to look like Frida Khalo. I part Jermania's hair and give her two Princess Leia Buns. Julie spins in her reused prom dress, smiling like I've never seen before.

"What are you supposed to be?" she asks me.

I stand up and hold my arms out. I spin, and my pink skirt billows around me. I've covered my skin in glitter and confetti, and brushed my hair into a high bun at the top of my head. Vilma decided to do my makeup with things from our pooled supply.

"I'm a cupcake!" I say.

She makes a face, like she doesn't see it.

We head down early. I've never gotten somewhere early for *anything*. Look at me! I'm responsible.

Helen comes over and puts her hand on my shoulder. "Great job, River."

I dip into a little curtsy and go to the food table to stuff my face with sugar, while keeping an eye out for Hutch. Ransom declares himself DJ for the night, which is fine because, if it were anyone else, I'm sure all we'd be listening to is Hank Williams.

Randy is dressed in the same clothes he wore on family day.

"What are you supposed to be?"

He leans into me and smirks. "I'm my father when he was younger."

"You don't need therapy at all."

He pulls me onto the dance floor and spins me around to a Michael Jackson song. He keeps glancing over my shoulder.

"What do you keep looking at?" I ask.

He tries to hold me in place to keep me from turning around, but I know who he's watching. And Pete's watching us back. He looks pissed off, and his eyes are on me. Randy and I are not dancing sensually at all, but by the look in Pete's eyes we might as well be naked.

I spin back around and grin at Randy. "Oh my God."

Randy rolls his eyes. "Shut up."

I grab him by the shoulders. "Relax, I'm not going to say anything. But it totally makes sense."

He deflates and shakes his head. "I guess. Pete's really cute and sweet. He's the person I wish I could be if I wasn't so fucked up."

I grab his face and make him look at me. "Listen to me, I'm not going to give you any life advice because I'm pretty terrible at life myself. But you shouldn't hide who you are."

"You know, the first time my dad caught me with a guy was in junior high. I thought he was going to beat the life out of me. Almost did. So I told him it was a mistake, and then I just figured out a way to start having sex with girls."

"Viagra?"

"For the past ten years."

"That's the most horrific thing I've ever heard, and I watched a guy get tortured for owing twenty grand to the Italian mob. How has your heart not given out?"

"You don't get it. You're from New York, where anything goes. My dad won't give me my trust fund unless I get clean and find a wife."

I stop laughing. "It was ten years ago. Don't you think… he might be ready to listen again? I watched my uncle get married to another man surrounded by his Catholic Latin family. Don't be an idiot."

"Drop it, River."

"No. This is your life. I'm just saying. Don't hurt someone just because you're afraid to be who you are. Straight people don't 'come out.' So why should you?"

The music changes to something slower. He grabs my waist

and puts our hands into waltzing positions. I look at the terribly handsome, terribly arrogant guy in front of me. His whole life is a front for someone he doesn't know how to be.

"You know, my dad wasn't perfect," I say, "but I know he loved me. That's the only unconditional love we can count on."

"My dad's not like your dad."

"I could also say there's more to life than money."

He rolls his eyes. "That's what poor people say."

I try to stop convincing him that he's making a terrible mistake. I know better than anyone that you can't make someone change their mind.

"What about you?" Randy says. "You and Nick seem pretty close."

I must look confused, because he doubles over laughing. I stumble on the steps of the waltz, never having waltzed in my life.

"I'm just kidding. Mostly he just walks around drooling over you. You're too busy looking at someone else."

My heart seizes. "You're crazy."

"I might act like a fool, but I see things. Besides, Nick is so high most of the time, the drool just comes naturally."

"Wait, you know?"

Randy nods. "Yeah. Julie tried to get me to go to the barn the other night. Like I said, I need to be clean. Now I just have to work on the bride. Want to be my beard? I'd totally take care of you. You wouldn't even have to sleep with me. My father only had kids for his legacy. If you really think about it, why should I be any different?"

I slap his chest. I can't tell if he's serious or not. Right now I'm still thinking about what he said about Julie. I've never seen Julie at the barn. I feel like I did the time I tried to hotwire my dad's car after he hid the keys from me. I failed.

As the waltz comes to a crescendo, Randy dips me. He must've taken lessons, while I don't like to be led, and I look so awkward trying not to fall onto the floor.

"Don't look, but someone's pretty jealous." He spins me in a circle and then walks away. I'm facing Hutch, who's leaning against the wall with a cup of punch in his hand. He's the Indiana Jones of my dreams in his hat and vest, and, oh my God, he's even got a whip hooked onto his belt. I feel caught, standing in the middle of the crowded dance floor with patients of all ages dancing to pop from 2001. I want to run to him. I want to say the words he wanted to hear when it mattered. I was just afraid.

One of the front desk clerks, a pretty girl wearing glittery devil horns, stands in front of him. She twists her hair around her fingernail. Her smile is sweet, and the laughter that cuts across the room is flirtatious. She's asking him to dance. He shakes his head, but she's not as shy as I would have pegged her as being. Despite there being no alcohol in the room, there's a drunk energy filling the air. People are dancing, not caring if they look silly. The staff is deep in conversation. It's like a reprieve from the usual seriousness.

I'm unable to move, despite Vilma and the other girls dancing in a circle around me to a Pitbull song I regrettably know all the words to. All I can focus on is Hutch and the girl now pulling him onto the dance floor. His strong brow crinkles, like he's still saying "no." But the rest of his face is smiling.

Don't be stupid, I tell myself. You're not allowed to feel jealous.

Yet, I am.

I want to dance with Hutch in the middle of the floor. I want to be able to look at him any way I want and not be afraid of others suspecting. I want to kiss him and hold him and tell him that I'm in love with him. Maybe I loved him the moment I set eyes on him and decided he'd be mine.

The devil clerk puts her hands on his hips. He shakes his head and says something to her. She's trying to make him move.

Would it be so terrible if I danced with a counselor?

I know it would be terrible if I went up to that girl and shoved her out of the way for touching my man.

Who are you right now? I ask myself.

I take a step in their direction and find I have a new obstacle. Nerd Boy Nick. He's either doing the robot or the electric slide and maybe even some moves from kickboxing. He grabs me by my waist and throws me into the air. He catches me, like we're something out of Step Up 2.

"You're so pretty, River. You're like the prettiest thing I've ever seen. You're mysterious and funny and I love the way you laugh, because you only laugh when something is really funny. You don't give people pity laughs, and that's what I like about you, you know?"

Nick stumbles into me, and I catch him.

"Hey, are you okay?"

He brushes me off with a wave of his hand. "Pfft. Yeah. Did you know that my graduating class only had thirty people in it?"

"Mine had 1000."

His eyes are wide. In the florescent light, I can see how wide his pupils are, too. He grabs me around the waist, just in time for the music to slow down. Right, because Boys II Men is something I want to dance with Nick to. I can feel how hard he's holding onto me, and I realize it's not because he's making a move on me. It's because he's got no balance.

Fuck.

"Easy now," Vilma says.

"Get a room," Fran whistles.

Hutch has stopped swaying, though Devil Clerk is awkwardly trying to make the shift from party dancing to sexy dancing. He glances at me, and the look I see there is full of disappointment. He shakes his head, turns around, and leaves.

Great.

"Nick," I say. "We have to get you to bed, okay?"

"Nope, nope, nope." He shakes his head, and his wide smile makes his face looked old and wrinkled. "Nick wants to dance. Nick is feeling brave. Nick has you and that's all there is. Can't you feel it?" He pulls back and starts dancing crazily. At first, people hoot and whistle. Sure, it's all good fun when a Midwestern boy tries to breakdance. But slowly, he changes. He stomps his feet harder and louder than anyone. He rubs his hands all over his body. He rips his Captain America T-shirt.

The dancing comes to a halt around him. Helen and Nurse Jean set their cups down and turn toward us.

LIFE ON THE LEVEL

Nick starts to yell. He grabs my wrists and pulls me against him. "Can't you feel it, River? Can't you feel that music? It's like a prism of lights and stars! It's—oh damn—"

He falls.

Someone screams.

He starts to seize. Chairs slam to the ground as Hutch and Nurse Jean run to steady him. He's foaming at the mouth. Hutch holds him down, and Nurse Jean shoves something into his mouth.

"Call 911!"

Screaming.

Crying.

I look around the room for Taylor, but I can't find him. I know where he is. I know he did this. I run out of the room and race towards the barn. The cold wind licks at my bare shoulders. I rip the elastic out of my hair. The sun is only just starting to set.

At first I think it's strange that the clouds are so black. Then I realize it isn't the clouds. It's a fire in the distance.

CHAPTER 35

I get halfway there before I hear hooves pounding the ground. When I turn around, Hutch is riding Elphaba as fast as he can. He reaches me and pulls on the reins.

"What are you doing?" He swings a leg over and jumps down to the ground. He looks from me to the fire.

In a panic, I tell him everything I know. I tell him about the drugs, and Taylor, and the things I've seen and heard.

"I just wanted to have some proof that wouldn't get you in trouble."

His face is hard and unforgiving. I know I've fucked up even before he says anything.

"You lied to me."

"Hutch, I'm sorry." I run my hands through my hair. Despite the cold, my adrenaline has me burning up. "I was trying to fix things."

"Well, you didn't! If you had said something, Nick wouldn't be getting toted off to the hospital for overdosing right under our noses. Why wouldn't you trust me enough to tell me?"

"It's not that!"

"You have more faith in some bizarre code of honor for criminals than in me."

"How can you say that? Everything I've done has been to protect you."

"Why am I supposed to let you do that when you won't even let me in?"

I shake my head. My head is spinning. "Because! That's not how I'm built, okay? Don't you understand? If I care too much—if I love too much—it's like setting us both up for a world of pain. I can't do that."

"I would never hurt you."

"I know."

"No, you don't. You think you know, but the only person you're trying to protect is yourself. This ends tonight."

He turns to get his foot in the stirrup. I grab his arm and pull him back towards me.

"What do you mean it ends tonight?"

"I mean I'm going to tell Helen everything."

"No. Taylor knows about us!"

"Then let them find out, River! I don't care if the whole world knows it because clearly they would be more ready to believe that I love you than you are."

• • •

It takes half an hour for the fire department to get there. By then the barn is burned to a crisp and so is the patch of woods behind it.

While Hutch and Simmons talk to the firefighters, Taylor drives up to the barn.

"What's going on?" He slams the door and runs up like he's out of breath. Yeah, it must be real taxing to start a fire.

Hutch turns to him like he's ready to pounce. I've never seen him this angry.

"What's going on is someone setting property on fire," Hutch tells him. "You know anything about that?"

Taylor's serious. He's got the best poker face I've ever seen. Perhaps better than my own. "Nope. I was in the kitchen getting more food when I heard the commotion. Was anyone hurt?"

"No," the fireman says. "The place was empty. I smelled an oil-based accelerant, but there's nothing much in there but splinters now."

Taylor stares at the barn for a moment. Hutch puffs up his chest and gets in his face. Simmons looks confused. I manage to get in between them. No matter what, Hutch isn't thinking straight.

"Easy, counselor," Taylor says, flicking his eyes to me. "I

was coming to get you because Ransom needs you back at the main building."

"Tell him I'm a little busy," Hutch says through gritted teeth, then low, so only the three of us can hear, "cleaning up after your mess."

Taylor smirks. "I'd be careful about throwing accusations around. That's how people get hurt."

"You threatening me?"

"Not just you," he says, looking at me. "Anyway, Ransom needs you. The sheriff's here. They've made an arrest."

"Arrest?" I feel the ground falling out from under my feet.

"They found drugs in someone's room. What a shame."

Hutch grabs Elphaba's reins. He gets me up first, and shouts to Simmons to hurry back when he's done. He rides close to Taylor, who's as cool as the late fall breeze.

"This isn't over," Hutch tells him.

"You might want to sleep on it, before you do something you'll regret."

Hutch shouts at his horse, and we race through the dusk back to the main building. Jillian takes Elphaba back to the stables, and we run into the ranch. Ransom looks grave as he tries to usher people back to their rooms, but no one listens.

"Those aren't mine!" Randy screams at the top of his lungs. Two officers have him by the arms and a third is carrying a large plastic bag of something.

Randy catches my eye. "River! You know those aren't mine! Tell them! Tell them! Get your filthy hands off me, you pig!"

Pete and some of the others run out of the building to watch him get taken away. I can't bring myself to move.

Ransom is shouting, "I said get back in your rooms!"

"Go," Hutch tells me.

"But—"

"River, please." He looks exhausted and hurt. "I have to talk to Steve."

I swallow my words and worry, and go to my room. There's nothing I can do for anyone right now. I pace until I think I've worn two inches into the ground. I go stand in the hall and press myself into a corner where I can't be seen. There is crying coming from different hallways. I hit my head against the wall.

I see someone slinking in the shadows into the library. Julie. She's no longer in her costume, and she pulls her hoodie over her head. I follow her in and close the door behind us.

"River." She places a hand over her heart. "You scared me."

"I'm a little on edge." The smell of smoke and hay and disappointment cling to me like smog. My hair is wild and my makeup runs down my cheeks.

"Are you okay?"

I push her against the wall, pressing the side of my arm into her neck. She whimpers. Shuts her eyes. How many times have I seen people do this? I walked in on my old man a couple of times. Bouncers I've worked with. Bad men I was unfortunate enough to know. I wonder if I look as crazed as they did.

"Who put the drugs in Randy's room?" I know the answer, but I need her to say it.

"I don't know!"

"He told me you invited him to the barn. Why?"

She shakes her head. Her panicked eyes search for an escape. I press my arm harder. "You're hurting me."

"How many people have been hurt because of you and Taylor?" I could've stopped it though, couldn't I? If I had trusted Hutch. If I hadn't been too scared. If I had stopped thinking like a con artist for just one second. A terrible grumble escapes my throat. I give her one last push and then let go. She falls to the floor in hysterics.

"I'm sorry! He told me I had to keep an eye on you. After Maddie stole from him I was the one who found the pills in your room and returned them to him. You don't know what it's like to be me, River. Everybody wants you. I can't even get someone to look in my direction. But Taylor, he's not always bad. Nick wasn't supposed to take too much."

I can't look at her. I breathe deep and hard. A hard pulse settles in my temples.

"You walk around like you own everything. I have nothing except for Taylor."

"Taylor is using you."

She shakes her head in denial.

"You want to know what it's like to be me?" I ask. "Imagine waking up one morning and finding out that the woman who gave birth to you can't stand the sight of you. Imagine spending nights and days clinging to the only person who wanted you, and then having him just wither away and die. There is nothing in the world that can get him back, and sometimes it feels like being asleep is the closest thing. Better, even, because no one will be capable of loving you unconditionally ever again.

"You don't *know* me. You don't want to. You have to ask yourself right now: how many people are going to have to get hurt because of Taylor?"

She wipes the mascara tears from her eyes. "He'll hurt me."

"No, he won't. We won't let him."

"You can't promise that."

Julie's just another lost girl, like Maddie. Like me. The world is full of lost girls like us. There isn't always someone there for us. But I can be there for Julie, the way I wasn't for Maddie. I can still make this right. Then I realize not all the evidence is gone. I still have the pill he gave me in my sock drawer. It's not much, but at least I can take the brunt of the heat away from Hutch.

"Don't worry. I still have a few tricks up my sleeves." I hold my hand out, and she stares at it for a little while. "Come on. There's still a room full of cake and I'm not about to let it get stale."

That brings a small smile to her face. We sneak into the rec room. The place is deserted. Lots of our decorations aren't holding up very well. We each eat a slice, and I let her vent about Taylor. How he would bring her presents and flowers. How he knew just what junk food she liked best. How he always knew the right thing to say to her. Sure, she talks about having had a giant crush on Hutch. But when she realized that wasn't going anywhere, Taylor was there.

"I dated a guy like that once," I tell her. "He would treat me like crap. I was usually too drunk to care. Most of the time he was nice enough that I thought it made up for it."

"Until your accident," she says.

I watch her curiously. "At least you pay attention during group."

She shrugs. "That's what you're supposed to do."

"There will be someone out there for you that'll know your worth. Someone who would never hurt you."

"How can you be so sure?"

Because if I can find Hutch, there must be a little bit of hope for everyone else, too. "I just am."

. . .

As I walk into my room, I feel a hand grab me. I panic and strike out with my closed fist. It collides with something hard.

"It's me," Hutch whispers. "Sorry."

He cranes his neck down the hall, then we rush into my room and lock the door. "Why didn't you just wait for me in here?" I ask him, a little more annoyed than I intended.

He shakes his head. "It didn't feel right after—"

"Telling me I have a criminal's code."

He sighs. "I'm sorry. I wish I could take that back, but I can't. I'm supposed be good at keeping calm and setting things right. You just turn me upside down."

"I told you. I break everything in my path."

"That's not true."

He sits on my bed and holds out his hand for me to take. I sit on his lap. It's so easy to sink into the feel of him. He brushes my hair back and rubs my arms for a long time.

"What happened with Ransom?"

"I told him that I wanted to have a meeting with the whole staff and Helen. She's staying overnight in Missoula with Nick."

"God, Nick. In all of this I forgot about him. I'm terrible."

He rubs my back. "I'm going to tell Helen that Taylor is behind all of this."

"We still have no proof. They can't search his belongings without reasonable cause," I say. "He burned all the evidence after Nick OD'd."

"How do you know?"

"Because," I say. "I know a lot of criminals. I know guys like Taylor. He's a narcissist and a sociopath. He'll throw anyone under the bus. I think we need more people to come forward."

"Who else was in the barn?"

I shake my head. I don't think I can tell him that. "I can't get them in trouble. They've worked so hard. Not everyone who went took stuff. I didn't."

"This isn't a position I thought I'd ever be in."

"I can think of a few positions I want you in." I kiss his mouth, pushing him back on the bed. We both smell like smoke. We're both weary. And I'd even go as far as to say we're both scared about what tomorrow will mean for us.

"River," he says in that deep voice of his. "God, I can't even think now. All I want to do is get you naked."

"I need to shower."

"I like you this way."

"A burned cupcake?"

"My burned cupcake." He pulls down the straps of my tank to have full access to my shoulders. A thrilling sensation starts at my core and twists all the way to my heart.

That reminds me.

My heart.

By the way he takes my nipples into his mouth, he must not be so mad that I didn't tell him I loved him back. He kicks off his boots while licking his way around my clavicle. I undo the button on his pants. I didn't think he was serious about not showering, but when he flips me onto the bed I forget about everything except for his face, his body, his everything, pressing against me.

It's different than the other times we've been together. It's like we both need this comfort for more than just each other. Like we're both searching for an answer that the other holds.

"River…" He gets lost in my hair, and I get lost in the feel of his cock inside me. He holds my face in his hands. My small window lets in a hazy bit of moonlight. Every time he looks at me, I feel like he's looking for something that I don't know how to give.

But in this moment, I realize I gave it to him a long time ago. I gave it him with every look, every kiss. I gave this man my heart, and I was too slow to realize it.

My daddy used to say that the last thing you should gamble with is your heart. But he was wrong. He spoke after having lost everything to my mother. With Hutch, I have a royal flush.

Hutch slows down, taking his time. With every thrust he explores my deepest depths. Chris Hutcherson is making love to me. Acknowledging it startles me. I gasp, and catch his mouth with mine as I come.

As my breathing slows back down, he stays inside me. I give him a little squeeze that makes him close his eyes and growl into my neck. I thread my fingers through his hair.

"What?" he asks.

"I just—" I take a deep breath. "I love you, is all."

I want to memorize his moonlit smile. "Caught on, have you?"

I roll my eyes. "You're ruining a perfectly good moment."

"I could never have a bad moment with you, River Thomas. I love you."

"I'm only going to say it the one time," I say playfully.

He nips at my neck. He pumps into me again, holding me like he'll never let go. He gasps, pulling out just as he finishes.

We switch. He takes up most of my bed anyway. We clean up a little, then he pulls me into a tight embrace.

"What was that thing you said before?" he asks.

"I love you."

"See, you can say it."

"You're impossible."

"And you're perfect."

I laugh, too loud, then bury my face into his shoulder.

"Everything's going to change tomorrow, isn't it?" I ask.

"I'll take care of everything."

"That's the same thing that I told Julie."

"We got a little bit derailed." He squeezes me a bit.

"I hope she helps us. If you're there, she will. Vilma might help. Are you sure the others won't get in trouble?"

"I'll talk to Ransom. As soon as Taylor throws us under the bus, I don't think my word will count for anything."

I bite my lip, almost too nervous to tell him what I'm about to. "Not all our evidence is destroyed. I—I have a pill."

"What?"

"I have a perc. In my sock drawer. I was going to stockpile evidence against him, but then things got a little messed up."

He traces my face with his sure, strong fingers. "I'm proud of you, River."

"Why?" That's the last thing I expected him to say.

"Most people I've met here would've swallowed that pill a long time ago."

I lean forward and bite his bottom lip. "If you want to give me something else to swallow, I wouldn't say no."

He squeezes me, and growls against my skin. "God, what are you doing to me?"

"I'm pretty sure I've ruined you for other women."

"I'm pretty sure there will never be another woman. You're it for me, River."

We're both so tired from the day, and from rolling around in bed, that I don't even remember falling asleep. I dream of riding a horse across a grassy hillside. I dream of Hutch telling me he loves me. Then my dream shifts, and the color drains from it. I'm at a poker table with my dad, only he's not my dad. He's the man from the barn. When I look down at my cards, they're all blank. Someone's shouting my name. I fold. Someone flips the table over. There's glass and more shouting.

I open my eyes, groggy. "What time is it?"

"River," Hutch says, scrambling to his feet just as someone else clears their throat.

"It's time for you to go," Helen says.

I feel like I've been kicked in the gut. My body flushes with shame. She's not alone.

CHAPTER 36

Ransom and Nurse Jean stand behind a sleep-deprived and pissed-off Helen. The worst part is the disappointment on all of their faces. They look down at the ground as Hutch and I scramble to get dressed. Our clothes are scattered all over the floor, and the room most definitely still smells like sex.

There is nothing we can say or do at this point that will come off in a positive light. Hutch walks past them and across the hall, where I can hear drawers opening and closing. Even though he was prepared to lose his job, this isn't the way he wanted it to go down.

"My office," Helen says, then storms out.

"Ransom—"

He holds up his hand. "What were you two thinking? After everything that's been happening here…"

"We met before," I tell him. "Before I came here. I didn't know he worked here and he didn't know I was going to be a patient. We didn't know."

Something dawns on him. "You're the mystery girl that left him high and dry two months ago."

I smile weakly. "That's me. I love him, Ransom. I don't think he should get fired. I'll leave. I'll go somewhere else."

"It's not that simple," he says. "There's been an accusation."

I furrow my brow. "What do you mean?"

"Julie Bellows has come forward to say that she and Hutch have been having a relationship."

"Julie." I clench my teeth. "She's lying. Taylor's making her lie!"

"Calm down, River."

"You tell me some little bitch accuses my boyfriend—"

"Boyfriend?" Ransom asks. "I didn't think it was possible for me to be more disappointed in Hutch. He knows that you shouldn't be involving yourself this way. Addiction isn't just something you forget about after sleeping together. It's a sickness."

I run my hands through my hair and pull. This isn't happening.

"If you're going to lecture someone," Hutch says, now standing at the door, "then go ahead and lecture me all you want." He's got a large knapsack and his winter coat. "You're right, I knew better. I'm the one who should've exercised more control."

"Don't talk to about me like I'm some textbook case, both of you."

"Let's go," Hutch says. All the emotion and life has gone out of his voice. "Helen's waiting for us."

• • •

Helen watches us from her desk. Ransom takes a seat off to the side, twiddling his thumbs. Simmons cracks his knuckles, and for a long time that's the only sound we hear. That and the squeak of sneakers outside in the hall, where dozens of patients are waiting. News of Hutch and me has spread faster than wildfire.

"Helen—" I start.

She puts her finger up to silence me. Instead of looking at me, she turns to Hutch.

"What were you thinking?"

Hutch looks down at his lap. I wonder what it feels like, having his whole life unravel at the seams.

"I wasn't. I love her."

I cut him off. "You don't understand, Helen. We met before here." I explain our circumstances, as if that's going to restore our credibility in any way.

"Not only is that irrelevant," Helen says, "even if I believed you, Julie Bellows claims Hutch has been having relations with her as well. That he comes to visit her in the night. That he brings her gifts. She even said another camper caught the two of them in the woods. When he was questioned, he described you in the act after *skinny dipping*."

"Wait a minute," Hutch starts. "River is my only— my only instance. I have never, *ever*, so much as flirted with another patient."

"You have to understand why it's hard to believe you now," Ransom says.

Hutch nods.

"Hutch wasn't with Julie during the camping trip," Simmons says. "I knew about their relationship. I'm at fault as well. I'm positive Julie was back at the camp with us after everyone… after the… skinny dipping incident. She never left. I can vouch that, at the very least, that part of Julie's story is a lie."

Helen sighs. She massages the bridge of her nose. When she looks back up, her steel eyes settle on Simmons. "You knew about this?"

Simmons nods.

"I'll deal with you later."

I don't know if I'll ever be able to thank Simmons enough. Hutch reaches out and squeezes my hand. Then he realizes the whole room is watching, and withdraws it.

"Look," I say. "I know the circumstances are wrong, and I'm not saying that I should be the exception. What we've been doing is wrong on many levels. I came here to deal with my addiction, and we tried to stay away from each other. I just couldn't. I found a man who makes me feel like I matter."

I stop to think. Isn't that what Julie said Taylor made her feel? Maddie said the same. But Hutch isn't Taylor, and I'm not like them.

"I love him. We had a consensual relationship before I checked into this place, and no one can take it away from us."

"Hutch?" Helen asks.

I feel like we're in court giving our closing arguments.

"I'm prepared to face the consequences. I was going to resign today, and tell you everything." He brings out a letter from his duffle bag. "Let River stay and finish her program. I know

I shouldn't ask for favors, but you know how important it is."

Helen takes the envelope from Hutch's hands and sets it on her desk. "Anything else?"

I stand. "Yes. Taylor's the reason Nick overdosed. Taylor set fire to the barn. He's been running his own private black market there."

Helen looks as if she just might have a heart attack. "That's a serious accusation."

"I was there. So were Nick, Maddie, and Fran. Julie's been there, too, though I didn't see her the one time I was there."

Hutch shakes his head at me. "Taylor's your guy for everything that's been happening here. Come on Helen, you know me. You know I don't just do things like this."

"I have proof," I say.

"River—let them investigate."

Helen stands, her chair scraping against the wooden floor. "Chris, you need to leave. I'll take into consideration everything you've said, but right now, the best thing you can do is go."

"No," I say.

"River, it's fine."

It's not *fine*. I grab his hand, but he pulls himself free from me. I feel ready to break down. I hate the way he's giving up so easily. I hate that I don't know when the next time I'll see him will be. He's just gone, out of her office and away.

"You have to get rid of Taylor," I tell Helen. I slam my fist on her desk, which I know doesn't help my case.

Ransom walks over to me and makes me focus. "What did we talk about?"

I concentrate on breathing. "Hippie anger things."

He shakes his head and tries not to smile.

"Please," I beg her. "He gave me a pill. At the barn. I put it in my sock drawer to save for when I collected more evidence."

"Ransom," Helen says. "Go look."

We're quiet for a long time. I slump down on my seat.

"It's really not fair that I'm here getting the third degree for sleeping with my boyfriend while Taylor, who framed Randy and gave drugs to this whole stupid county, is just walking around freely."

"You haven't exactly made this situation easy for me," Helen says. She opens Hutch's resignation letter and a deep frown forms on her face.

"What?" I look at the clock. What's taking Ransom so long to find a stupid sock?

She puts it in a drawer. "I understand the reasons you kept it quiet. I do. I was young once, even if you don't want to believe it. I guess I expected better from him, and from you."

"You're a shrink, right?"

She smiles begrudgingly. "Why?"

"So shrink this. When I came here, I hated everything, right?"

"Right."

"Hutch switched me to Ransom because we both agreed we needed to be professional. Only it couldn't stay that way. When I met Hutch, I didn't even know his name. I saw this big sexy man, and I had to have him. It was more than a drunken impulse. It was a need. It was like everything in the universe was pushing me toward him. When I left, I still thought about him, but I resigned myself to the fact that I'd never see him again. Except, I did. And then I was with Ransom as my counselor. You gave us the opportunity to go back and we didn't. Helen, I love that man. And if that's wrong, then that means I've been doing the right thing my whole life, and we both know that's not true."

"What are you asking from me, River?" Helen asks.

"I want you to properly investigate Taylor. I was at that barn, and so were others. I know he's using Julie. She's just a mark." Something dawns on me. She was empty-handed when she was going into the library, and she left with me. She was also the one who took the book from me the first time. Where's a better place to hide drugs than the room people hardly ever use? "Taylor's been fooling everyone here. He's the best con artist I've met outside New York. Check the library. You'll find a bunch of books with holes in the center. That's how he delivers. Helen, please, believe me."

Helen spins in her chair. "I'll speak to Nick when he wakes. I'll go to the library myself. This isn't going to be an overnight thing, River. It'll take time."

"What happens to me?" I don't want to leave. I want to finish my program, and then explore the rest of my life.

Ransom runs into the room. He's empty-handed. At first I think that Julie moved my things. He looks at me with tears in his eyes.

"Ransom?" I can barely get his name out.

"I'm sorry, River." He looks from me to Simmons. "I had to do the right thing."

Moments later, the cops from yesterday are standing at the door. One's got cuffs in his hands, another steps forward with a clear plastic bag of pills.

"Those aren't mine," I say.

"Hutch told me you smuggled pills in," Helen says.

I shake my head. "He didn't."

"Yes, River. He did. Is it one pill or a dozen? Why should I believe anything you say?"

"It was just the one pill! I got it from Taylor at the barn—"

"The barn that's burned to a crisp?" Her brow creases into a thousand lines. She looks angry. Worse, she looks disappointed.

The patients that have gathered outside in the hall have multiplied. I even catch Julie's face in the crowd, a small, triumphant smile playing on her lips. Vilma and Jermania are there too. They can't look me in the eye. They don't step forward to say that I was right. It's just like with Randy, except I'm too weary to resist.

"River Thomas, you're under arrest."

CHAPTER 37

"Sky," I say. "I've been arrested. I need bail money. Please call me back."

I'm too exhausted to do the math on the time difference. I'm too exhausted to remember if Sky is in the middle of her shift or not.

That was my one call, and it ended with me talking to an answering machine. I slam the phone down.

"Easy, now, lady," the cop tells me. "What'd that phone ever do to you?"

I all but hiss in his direction. I haven't said anything since they arrested me. We pass a cell full of guys passed out in disheveled costumes. Was Halloween just yesterday? A hairy old man whistles in my direction, and I curse a slew of vitriol at him.

They lead me to a cell where there's a woman sleeping on a rectangular bench. There's a single toilet that looks filthy, but still cleaner than the worst dive in the East Village. I take the bench on the other side of the cell. I hate the way this place sounds, hollow and cold. Every metal surface rattles; every heavy boot echoes.

At least my daddy never had to see me like this. Getting my prints taken. Getting my mug shot filed. The light from the flash still dances in my vision.

That was my one call.

Why didn't I call Hutch?

"*What?*" I ask the officer still standing at the cell.

"Never booked anyone from New York City," he says.

He chews gum like a cow, and watches me like I'm something out of the Coney Island Freakshow.

"Here's a little something from the Big Apple," I say,

flipping him the bird. He just chuckles and walks away.

That's good, real good. Now I'll never get out of here.

I try shutting my eyes. They didn't tell me when I'd be able to go. Honestly, I wasn't really paying attention. I kept seeing the eyes that followed me down the hall into the police car. Two patients arrested with drugs, arson, and an employee sleeping with a patient—Helen's going to have to face an internal investigation from the state, and soon.

I've been the girl who stumbles out of a bar, and I've been the girl who slinks away in the middle of the night. I don't embarrass or humiliate easily, but this… this stings.

I've utterly fucked up. Not only that, but I was actually trying my hardest. I wanted to make things work. I wanted to get better. How many lives have I messed up with my actions? I feel everything inside me churning like gooey primordial soup. I run to the toilet. It's metal and smells like old urine. I clutch the sides and puke. I taste bile and chocolate cake.

When I'm done, I wipe the back of my hand. I stay on the ground. Regret gives way to anger.

The anger stays.

The misery stays.

The loneliness clings to me like a cloak.

"Oh, goodie," the woman on the bench says. "I've got company."

I make a *hmph* noise and nod at her. Her hair is mussed up and her lipstick is smeared on her face. All things considered, she looks like she might've been beautiful once, before her life took her for a spin.

"Not a talker?" she asks. "That's alright. I can talk enough for the both of us."

I get up and go to my bench. I lie down and look at the ceiling, feeling worse by the second.

I actually tried, and this is where it got me.

"Let me guess," she says. "Solicitation?"

"Why the fuck does everyone think I'm a hooker?"

That makes her laugh. It sounds like a motor revving. "I don't. I just wanted you to talk."

"Thanks," I mutter.

"I'm in here because I took a bat to my dirtbag husband's head. He's alive, unfortunately. I was told I was 'angry.' Wouldn't you be angry if you came home to find him getting a blow job from some little troll of a cunt from the trailer park?"

I picture an actual troll woman and laugh. "I'm sorry. That's not funny."

"I hope she gives him herpes."

"That's a little vicious."

"Life's a little vicious, darlin'. You gotta grow fangs if you don't got any."

I sit up and lean back against the cold metal bars. "Where's he now?"

She shrugs. "Home. I spend every night bartending and he spends it pretending he's out getting a job."

"Well, technically he was."

She smiles. "I like you. What're you in for?"

"I was the fall guy," I say softly. "And I was too stupid to see it coming."

"You got a name?"

"River."

"I'm Clara. Nice to meet'cha. Since we're going to be in here a while, want to tell me about it?"

I groan. I'm tired of telling people my feelings. I'm tired of spilling my guts out only to be treated like a social experiment.

"No," I say. "What I want is a cigarette."

"I hear that." She bangs on the bars. "Hey Sam! Sam! Get over here!"

A young guy, not one of the ones who arrested me, drags his feet. His uniform is too big for him, like he's wearing a costume.

"What now?" he asks, looking over his shoulder.

"Think you could spare two cigs for me and my friend River over here? I'll get you a drink on the house next time you stop by." She lifts her eyebrow in a way that brightens her whole face. Sam smiles at her, and fishes two cigarettes from his pack.

"Two drinks," he says, holding them just out of her reach.

"Fine. But you better let me out here soon, 'cause I want to shower before my shift starts."

He lights them for us, not trusting us with a lighter, and walks away.

"You were always going to give him two drinks, weren't you?" I inhale deeply, the smoke numbing my skin quite nicely.

"Yep. Can't start high, though. Now, tell me. Nothing exciting ever happens here and I'm tired of thinking of my shitbag husband."

"Not much to tell. I left New York before I could do more damage to myself. Came here and wound up in jail."

"Ah," she says. "One of those HCRC kids?"

"Yep. Except I'm not a kid."

Her brow wrinkles. "Of course you are. You've still got a whole life ahead of you. You ain't even gotten started, honey."

I watch the smoke billow from my lips. It coils, like the anger in my heart. "I actually fucking tried!"

"You gotta try more than once, honey."

I shake my head. I tell her about everything, even about Hutch. What do I care at this point?

"And now I'm here." I take the last drag of my cigarette like it's made of gold. "Isn't that fucking hilarious? I should've stayed in New York."

"By the sounds of that fella, you don't really mean that."

I don't, but it feels good to make empty threats, the same way it feels good to make a wish. "Maybe it would've been better for him. I don't want to drag him down with me. I'm like a rock sinking into the ocean."

"Didn't he already lose his job?"

"Yeah, but he's not going to *jail* with me on some trumped up drug charges. I just—I just want to get my hands around that rat bastard Taylor."

"You'd best leave it alone, honey. Trust me. Pretty little thing like you might end up dead, or worse."

I scoff. "What's worse than being dead?"

"Growing up so broken and crooked you don't even recognize yourself."

"Thanks, Clara. But I've been taking care of myself for

a long time."

She flicks her cigarette butt into the toilet. "Seems like it's about time you start asking for some help. Though you look as stubborn as the mules in my backyard."

"Do you really have mules in your backyard?"

"I might, but now I'm not inviting you to visit them on account of your sassy mouth."

We laugh for a little bit, and settle into our shared misery. Sam returns and lets Clara go free.

"Nice to meet you, River. If you get out of here, stop by and see me at the Golden Rose."

I should tell her no. I should tell her that's the last place a girl like me needs to be.

"I will."

• • •

At some point, I fall asleep. I wake up with all of my muscles aching, and disoriented. I reach—I actually *reach* for Hutch's body beside me. The reality of yesterday crashes around me like broken glass. I go to the sink and rinse out my mouth.

Sam walks back, a look of pity in his eyes. "River Thomas, you've made bail."

My heart leaps to my throat when I see Hutch. I stop short of jumping into his arms. Before we leave, they explain to us that I have to appear before a judge in a week, and not leave town.

"Wouldn't dream of it," I tell Sam.

"Tell Clara I said hi," he tells me.

"Tell her yourself."

Hutch looks at me with confusion and a little bit of awe. "How did you manage to make friends in jail?"

"I just used what Ransom taught me."

We get in his car. This isn't the reunion that I wanted.

"I wanted to come sooner," he says. "You should've called me, River."

"Where'd you get the money to bail me out?"

"I put up my land as a property bond."

"Hutch!"

"It's fine. Just, don't leave town, okay?" he tries to smile. "Simmons called me after they took you in. They wouldn't let me see you at first."

He's here. Even though he wasn't my one call.

"Helen called me. She said you were right, but by the time they went to get Taylor he was gone."

"That's my fault."

"It's my fault, River."

"So Taylor is gone. You're fired. I'm guessing I can't go back."

He makes a right onto a dark street. "Not right now. But we can find you another treatment center. You were so close to finishing. There are twenty-eight-day programs we could look into in Seattle."

"Can you just—stop for a second?" I stare at the darkening road.

We don't talk until we get to his house. His house that he put up as a bond for me. We head inside, and I decide to take a bath. I fill up the tub until I can fully submerge myself. I use his body wash to make bubbles. I hold my breath until it burns. I clean my skin until it's red all over, but when I'm done and dry, I still feel dirty.

I put on the clothes he brought and find him sitting on his bed. This is the bed where everything started. I need to get up. I feel like a lion trapped in a cage as I walk around his house.

"River, please sit down. We have to talk."

I sit beside him. I can only function in short bursts. "I need to get my stuff from HCRC."

"Do you want to eat first?"

"No, I don't want to eat first. I want my car. I want my things."

He nods, an angry wrinkle forming between his eyebrows. We get in his truck and he goes ninety in a sixty-five zone. We're there in no time. He hesitates to go in, but I tell him I need him with me, and he follows.

We're like pariahs. We're lepers. Everyone whispers about

us. They've already trumped up rumors that I'm carrying twins, one from Randy and one from Hutch. I'm their new boogieman. I'm what happens when you break the rules. And maybe that's a good thing. Maybe it'll help others do better.

While Helen goes to the locker to get my things, Vilma and Jermania run up and hug me.

"We've got your back, River," Vilma says. "I told Helen I was at the barn."

"I told her Taylor tried to give me drugs in exchange for a blowjob," Jermania says.

"Why didn't you tell before?" I ask her.

She shrugs. "I didn't think anyone would believe me."

Isn't that the same reason I gave? When did we learn to be so silent?

"Don't you ladies have group?" Helen asks them. They make themselves scarce. Helen sets my box of things on the table. "River, I hope you understand why I can't let you back in."

I can feel myself starting to cry, so I scrunch up my face and bite my tongue to have a different feeling to concentrate on.

"The facility can't afford that kind of—"

"Reputation," I say, when she can't find the word. Is that really all we're worth? Our reputations?

I rummage through the box. There's my flask. It sloshes when I give it a shake. My pain pills rattle in their orange containers. "Finally. I missed my eyelash curler. Where's my phone?"

Helen looks confused. She goes over the list of things that were taken from me on arrival. "It was there…"

"Taylor," I hiss. I grab my box and turn around. I wouldn't have put it past Taylor to go through my contacts. Maybe even respond to the anonymous messages I was receiving. I had also texted Sky and Leti my new private e-mail and information.

"River," Helen says. "They're going to find him."

"He's probably in Canada right now."

"Well, when the dust settles, there are programs I can recommend. I know things haven't been what you expected, but you've worked too hard to throw it all away. I should have trusted you."

I look at Helen, someone with all her awards and diplomas. Someone who's so adult she gets to run things and make decisions. No matter how much I try, I don't think I'll ever get there.

"Don't worry about me, Helen."

• • •

Hutch follows me out into the parking lot. I throw my things onto the passenger seat.

"River—"

"No, listen to me. I will never be able to thank you enough for doing what you did. I'll pay you back. All of it. I have some money from my dad's health insurance. It felt like blood money, and that's coming from someone who's actually had blood on her money."

"River—"

"I just need space, okay? I just need to think and be alone."

He grabs my elbow. It takes everything in me to stay standing. It takes all of my strength not to collapse into his arms and let him take me home. But I pull away, and I wish I could look away from the hurt on his face.

"The entire time I was here, I was trying to be a better person. Someone who rode horses and went camping and roasted marshmallows. But that's just a dream. I'm a mess. I'm the thing that you get when a train and a semitruck collide. I am who I am, and, you know what? Maybe that's not so bad."

"I love who you are." He takes a step closer, and bends his head down.

"Who do you think I can be? What kind of job am I supposed to get with my prints on file? Or with my references? I think you aren't seeing the reality of this. You aren't seeing who I really am."

I unlock my car. I feel the pull that's always there between us.

"You think I don't know that my career is over? I know."

I shake my head. "You're just lost in the fairy tale of us."

"Believe me, River—from the minute you set foot in my office, I knew it was over. For me it was never a choice between you or my career. You were always more important. You will *always* be the most important person to me."

I rake my fingers through my hair and tug. I can't breathe. I see him and only him. I don't want to. Then again, I don't really know what I want.

I will never be done with you.

"It's done," I say. "Everything I tried to keep together has unraveled. That's all I know how to do."

I open my door and get in the driver's seat. He tells me I shouldn't drive. He tells me to stay here for a little while. But I need to move.

"If you don't let go, I will run you over."

"I'll be damned if I let you walk away from me."

He looks like he's ready to pick me up and take me away. Maybe there's a little part of me that wants that too. But the rest of me wants to keep running until I figure out what I need. I peel out of the parking lot, bumping into his hip. I glance in the rearview mirror. He gets up. I hit the gas.

"Don't worry," I say. "I've already damned myself enough for the both of us."

CHAPTER 38

ZERO DAYS SOBER

I white-knuckle grip the wheel and hit the gas. I'm not even sure which direction I took when I left Hutch standing in the HCRC driveway. Everything looks the same. When I see a sign for Missoula, I know I'm heading back north.

I head to an ATM and take out so much cash that the person in line behind me watches me with wide eyes. I check myself into a motel downtown at fifty dollars a night. I throw my things on my bed and go through the inventory again.

Eyelash curler.

Clothes.

Pills.

Flask.

Money.

I find a slightly crushed cigarette in the pocket of one of my shirts. I push everything into a pile, then lie next to it. The bed is too soft, and smells like chemicals and stale cigarette smoke. I hurt from my heart to the tips of my toes. I keep seeing the way Hutch's face looked when I told him I'd damned us. He was the person who broke through my walls. One thing went wrong (well, lots of things all at once), and I rebuilt those walls in a *second*. If I close my eyes, I think of his kisses. If I open my eyes, I think of the warmth of him against me. I wish my mind was cloudy. I wish I could push away all the hurt and worry and the strangled feeling in my chest.

I really tried.

"Fuck it." I uncap my bottle of pills and take one out. When

I pop it into my mouth, there's a minty taste on my tongue. That fucking bastard. Taylor tried to sell me back my own pills!

I growl to myself, then twist off the top of my flask. I breathe in the sweet smell of Irish whiskey, my daddy's favorite. At least Taylor didn't take this.

"Bottoms up, Dad."

I bring the cold metal to my lips and drink deep.

• • •

When I get to the Golden Rose, the whiskey has burned its way through my veins. I'm lightheaded and pleasantly buzzed. There's even a smile on my face.

God, I'm such a lightweight. There was a time I could put away half a bottle and still be standing. Now, I smile at the bouncer and flash him my ID.

"Clara!" I say, holding my hands up in the air.

The bartender looks so much better after a shower and fresh makeup. Her hair is high, and her lips are pinup-girl red. "River Thomas. Of all the dives, you had to walk into mine."

I drum my fingers on the bar top. The crowd is a mix of college kids and old timers. There are two pool tables and a jukebox blasting classic rock, and the lighting is so dim you have to squint to see your hand in front of you.

The guy next to me has a pornstache, and smokes an unfiltered cigarette. "Can I buy you a drink?"

"Nope."

Clara turns her head back and cackles in that way of hers. "What's your poison?"

"What do you think?"

She looks me up and down. Grabs a bottle of amber liquid and pours me a glass, with a soda on the side.

Before I drink it, she sets her hand on mine. "You sure?"

"I'm sure my poison is whiskey. I'm sure I'm probably poison, too."

She smiles, but only shakes her head a little, before returning to cleaning a glass. I shiver a little bit as I drink it. It's been a long time. Why did I even like this stuff in the first place? It burns all the way down. Then I start to feel the pleasant warmth that comes after, and I remember. *That's why.*

I look around at the people here. Mustachio beside me keeps looking at me. He drinks a Budweiser and nods his head to Johnny Cash.

"What's your story?" he asks me.

Ugh. You'd think guys get better lines the older they get.

"Don't have one," I say, drinking my soda. I really should've eaten today. "Hey, Clara. I heard from a little taxi bird that this is the place for a card game."

Her red lips curl, but there's sadness in her eyes. I know she doesn't really want to serve me, but I know where she's coming from. People make their own choices, and you just have to let them. Besides, she's not my mother. She's not going to stop me.

"If you've got the buy-in. Tonight's a bit of a new crowd, so you'll fit right in."

"Sounds good to me."

She cocks her head to the side and leaves the bar in the hands of a young guy who has a faster pour than anyone I've ever seen. Clara leads me to the women's bathroom, then past another door.

"Don't usually get girls here," she says. "You sure you want to do this? The guys who play, they play to win big. If anything goes wrong, well, we can't exactly call the cops, because this room doesn't exist."

"Never been afraid before," I say. "I know how this works. Besides, everything I learned, I learned from my daddy."

"Yeah, well, so did I, and look how I turned out."

I'm not sure what she means, but she unlocks the door. She sticks her head in the room and gives the bouncer a thumbs-up.

"Dealer," the brute of a man at the door shouts.

I scan the room before I sit down. There are at least six games going on at the same time. A withered old man serves as the bartender. A bison head is tacked up on one wall, and a buck deer on the other. My eyes burn a little from the haze of cigars, but I inhale it deeply. This is where I belong.

LIFE ON THE LEVEL

This one's for you, daddy.

There's an old man with a long white mustache and a leather cowboy hat. He glances at me with his pale blue eyes, and I can see him smirk, like he's thinking I'm an easy mark. I'm blonde and a girl, and I've gotten that my whole life. When I come to places like this, I never smile. I keep my eyes hard and steely, just like my daddy used to.

There's a guy in his thirties, with days of scruff. You can tell he hasn't left in at least twenty-four hours. He glances up at me, scratches the back of his hand, then looks at the pot. He's got a handful of chips, maybe a couple hundred bucks.

"Fold."

The only other woman at the table, and maybe in the room, is decked out in some Dolly Parton outfit. She looks pretty boss with her big hair and fat, glossy lips. She's doing pretty well. She smiles a lot, though, which is the opposite of my tactic. She takes a stack of chips and adds them to the pile. I love the sound of them clinking against each other.

"Raise."

The mustached man flicks his cards onto the table. "Fold."

Another dude, this one in an old band T-shirt and Montana Grizzlies baseball cap, folds. He gets up and goes to the bar.

I keep walking around the table to get a look at the other players. My heart stops when I see him.

Taylor looks up from his cards with a cringe-worthy smirk. "Hey, River Thomas."

I breathe deep to steady my nerves. I want to jump across this table and pummel his face.

"You call, or what?" the dealer asks. He's a sturdy old man with slicked-back hair. I remember him from the barn. He was the one that reminded me of my father. I like him all the more for not having any of Taylor's stalling.

Taylor pushes in an even bigger stack of chips. "Call and raise."

Someone whistles.

He's bullshitting. He's buying the pot. They go around the room one more time, and everyone folds. Because he doesn't have to show his cards, he just scoops up the chips and starts stacking them away. From the side glares and short mumbles, I can tell he's not exactly a favorite.

"You in, Blondie?" the dealer asks me.

I hand him a wad of bills and wait for him to count them. I take a seat, making me the seventh player. The whole time, Taylor watches me.

"Have a good night?" Taylor asks me.

"You two know each other?" the woman who looks like Dolly Parton asks me. She's to my right, and a guy who looks like Willie Nelson is to my left.

"Unfortunately," I say.

"Empire State over here's just cross that a small town hick outsmarted her."

I lean back in my seat and tilt my head to the side, zero bullshit. I want to tell him that I know a few cops that would be happy to know where he is right now. But mentioning cops would make *me* the one no one likes. I thank Clara for forcing me to drink that tall glass of soda after my shot. My head starts to clear, which isn't always the best feeling. I start to feel like Hutch is everywhere. The old painting of horses on the walls reminds me of riding. The deep brown wooden walls remind me of his dark stare. Every remotely young guy with a full head of thick, black hair makes my heart jump.

Regret, you are my least favorite friend.

Still, I shake it off and take the second deck of cards the dealer hands me. I break and shuffle while keeping my eyes level with Taylor's acid green ones. I *missed* this sound. Hell, if I ever really get clean I'll probably take up being a magician just to have a deck of cards.

When Grizzly Hat comes back, we play. I fold my first two hands because I have zero possibilities. My daddy was, for the most part, a tight player. He stayed in if he had strong hands. But the thing that made him great was that he knew how to read people. Not just at poker tables, but in everyday life. He was a small-town conman in a big city.

"Call or fold, Blondie?" the dealer asks.

I'm caught off guard. I can't sink into reminiscing about my dad. I have to keep my head in the game. I pick up the corner of my cards. Dolly and Blue Eyes are out, and Willie and Taylor are in.

I knock my knuckles on the green, signaling I call.

"Not much of a talker," Grizzly Hat tells me.

"Oh, she talks," Taylor says. "She's just had a rough time lately."

The dealer makes a face. "I hate when we get couples."

I glance around the table to make sure all eyes are on me. I scoff, holding my cards close to my chest. This time, I let a grin creep on my face. "Couple? He wishes."

This makes everyone snort and laugh at Taylor's expense, which he most definitely doesn't like. The dealer burns a card, then there's the turn. I know Taylor's full of shit because I have two kings and an ace kicker. He should've folded a long time ago. I add four hundred to the pot.

"You sure you want to do this?" I ask him.

He calls and adds another hundred, which I know is just for show. He's trying to scare me off.

Burn, and then there's the river. Another king. I have four pair with an ace kicker. He'd have to have a flush to beat me, and considering everyone's already folded, I'm sure he doesn't. If I don't smile at all, then he smiles too much.

I check, deciding not to bet. I want to see his cards. He raises, expecting me to fold.

Everyone sits back, eyes flicking from me to Taylor like pendulums. I exhale deeply. I drum my fingertips on the table, just like my daddy used to when he wanted to run out the clock. At the very last second, the dealer warns me.

"Call." I add a handful of chips into the pot. "Show me what you've got, Taylor."

His face falls. He doesn't move.

"Come on, son," Willie Nelson says.

"You afraid of losing to a girl?" Dolly smirks.

Taylor grimaces and flips over his cards. He's got the shittiest hand of all. A single high card. I don't smile. I am steel.

I am stone. I am ice. There's a small cheer that goes up around me. Dealer pats me on the back.

"I knew you were buying the pots," Dolly mutters in her high-pitched little voice.

"Not against the rules," Taylor says, a smirk returning to him.

The dealer button moves to me. Someone sets a shot of whiskey beside me, like a congratulatory prize.

I let Dolly shuffle the second deck, and look at Taylor. "You're not going to get away with it."

I should keep my mouth shut. I deal. My own cards are crap, but I want to see how far I can go. I like playing big, but straight up, which is hard to do when you're surrounded by strangers. Cards start to fall all around the table, and there's that tension that comes with playing with people who visibly hate each other.

Just on the flop I have two pair of tens, with an ace kicker. Not bad, but not amazing. Maybe this time Taylor does have something to beat me with, but my pulse races, and I find myself adding another five hundred. I know I have Taylor when he splashes the pot. Willie Nelson doesn't like it. He gets up abruptly.

"I counted these," he says before heading over to the bar.

There's the turn, and I raise. Taylor calls. On the river I get three pair with an ace kicker. I keep my eyes on him and wait. I'm raising, pushing him to show his hand. He doesn't go for it. He folds, and I buy the pot.

Taylor bites his thumb. Before I realize it, I'm up, and it's midnight. My eyes burn, I'm so tired. There aren't breaks in places like this. The dealer button gets passed along. I fold the next hand to give myself a break. Taylor follows me to the bar. I grab a beer just to have something in my hands and to wet my tongue.

"And here I thought you'd be halfway to Canada by now."

"I was hoping to find you. I know what makes you tick, River." He sets something on top of the bar. My phone. It's charged halfway. There are some missed calls from Sky and Leti. Then from that unknown number.

But I'm not afraid anymore. What do I have to lose? I've always thrown away the person I loved the most. Why? Pride? Because I don't know another way to be?

That's not true, is it?

What did Clara tell me when I told her I tried, and still failed? *You gotta try more than once, honey.*

"Now you just owe me a bottle of Percocet and we're even," I tell him.

"Oh, we're way past that. Just you wait."

I return to my seat to find Grizzly Hat gone and a new player at the table. He's stiff. Uncomfortable. He sits back and watches each and every person at the table. His sure, strong fingers count the chips in front of him.

"Hutch," I whisper.

CHAPTER 39

"Are you her boyfriend, too?" Dolly asks him.

She lifts the corners of her cards, then grins across the table at Hutch. Out of everyone here, he looks like he belongs the least. Even the professor with his sensible sweater and big glasses fits in better than Hutch.

"Sure you want to do this?" I ask, though I know it's too late.

The cards are on the table. I've never seen Hutch play, but I don't have to. He doesn't know what he's gotten himself into. I have trip aces on the flop, and a full house on the turn. Hutch is betting sloppy, throwing his money in against me and Taylor. Hell, everyone sees him as an easy mark so the pot keeps growing. I want to tell him to get out. I know what he's trying to do, and he shouldn't.

I try to catch Hutch's eyes. He's like an open book, the way he catches the back of his head, the way he looks at me like he has a thousand things to say. The way he looks at Taylor like he might just kill him when this is all over.

He takes out a wad of money. "I need to buy more chips."

"Stop it," I say, hard.

He doesn't listen to me. How many times have I been down to my last hand and my last dollar, then borrowed from the house? I don't have any right to lecture him. Except, this is my world. I know what's going to happen.

"Taylor just brought *all* his friends here," Blue Eyes mutters.

"We're not friends," is all Hutch says.

"Whatever you are," Dolly says, "I fold like a hooker over a politician's knees."

That makes me laugh. It's the first time I've laughed all day and it feels good. There's the turn, and I've got four of a kind, queen high. Taylor's still in the game, but he's only checking. He's more interested in the showdown between Hutch and me.

"Why did you come here?" I ask, relenting to the aching questions running through my mind. With all the effort I'd put into not thinking of him, I made him materialize out of thin air.

"Figured this was the only way to get through to you."

All eyes are on me on the turn. I drum my finger on the green. I turn the chip in my hands. Hutch doesn't belong in this world, and I've got to get him out. That's what I've been trying to do from the start.

I win the hand. A couple of people bow out, muttering that this is getting too personal for them. Some people even go to other tables. The buy-in is too high for Taylor at this point, and he does a shitty job at keeping his feelings to himself.

It's just Hutch and me. Dolly shuffles my cards, and I'm dealer. It's either the luckiest night of my life, or the game is rigged.

"How'd you find me?"

He raises the pot by five hundred. A few tongues click, and instigators holler. "Small town."

"Not that small."

He smiles. It's heartbreaking. "What else do I have, River, if you're gone? I told you, I'll be damned if I let you walk away from me again."

I take a sip of my beer. I feel heavy, and the room spins a little, but I've got a killer hand. At least, I think I do. When did I start to doubt myself like this? The last two months has thrown me off my game.

"You like to gamble, don't you?" Hutch asks me.

I deal the turn, but I don't even look at it. "That's obvious."

"How about this. If I win, you walk out of here with me. I know that you love me, and I know it's been the worst couple of days. But I'm not giving up on us."

"What if you lose?" someone asks.

When Hutch sets those dark eyes on me, I think I might just break apart. "Then I'll walk away, no questions asked."

Dolly looks from me to Hutch. "Don't be stupid, girl."

I know the cards that I have. I know that for all my life I thought I was broken. There has to be something wrong with you if your own mother can't find it in her heart to love you, right? But what about Leti, and Sky, and the rest of the family that took me in when I was at my worst? What about my dad, who, for all his faults and vices, was the one who stood by me? What about Hutch?

I've been loved my whole life and I've been too stubborn and stupid to see it.

I burn a card, and deal the river. He doesn't even look at it; he just pushes his cards in. He's baiting me. If I ask to see his cards he might lose, and then he'll walk away. I keep asking him to, but he's just as stubborn as I am.

"I'm all in, River," he tells me. "I've been all in since the moment I met you."

The room is quiet. Even the other tables have turned around to watch us. I'm trying not to break. I'm trying to keep myself together, because that's what I'm supposed to do. My daddy didn't raise me to fold when I have such a good hand. My daddy raised me better than that.

But he also raised me to be loyal and to love unconditionally.

I look at my cards to give myself some time to think. What is there even to think about? The man who loves me, the man that I love, has laid everything out for me.

I'm afraid to be weak. I'm afraid to be foolish. I'm afraid to let someone hurt me so much that I'll never be the same again.

I throw my cards onto the table. "You got me."

The entire back room of the Golden Rose claps as Hutch makes his way around the table and scoops me up into his arms.

We cash out. At the end of it, we walk away with twenty grand. We leave together, emerging out of the men's bathroom, which has a few local drunks pissing on themselves when they see us. I hold his hand tighter than ever because I don't want to let him go. When we reach the parking lot, he pulls me into a kiss.

"Don't do that to me again."

"Let you win, or nearly walk out on you?"

He pulls back. "Let me win?"

I push him against his truck and kiss him over and over again.

I don't hear the footsteps. I don't hear the cock of the gun until it's already pointed at me. Hutch pushes me away, and reaches for the gun at his hip, aiming it at the man in front of us. I don't recognize his face until the motion-sensor lights in the parking lot light up his scars.

"Hey Riv," Kiernan says. "Did you miss me?"

CHAPTER 40

I've always hated guns. I know that it's Montana and that everyone here grows up with them. But so did I. I've seen way too many injuries and deaths. I start to shake, and my heart thunders against my ribs.

"Kiernan." I say his name like I've seen a ghost.

"You know, I've been looking for you." He moves a little further back, and aims his gun at me.

"If you so much as take another step," Hutch says, "it'll be the last thing you ever do."

Kiernan laughs. His cool, green eyes sparkle in the dark. His ash blond hair is longer than I remember, and swept across his face to cover the marks where I cut up his face. The scar on my thigh burns at the sight of him.

"Look at you, Riv. Gone and found yourself a John Wayne. You know, when I got a call from you, I wasn't expecting to hear some guy's voice. Then he told me where you were, and I thought—wow. Little River Thomas, trying to clean herself up. I never thought I'd see the day."

"You're a lot of things," I tell him, standing between Hutch and Kiernan. "But you're not a killer."

"I've had to become a lot of things since your godfather got me banned from every table in the city. Do you know I have to go all the way to fucking Jersey to sit at a table?"

"Cry me a river," I tell him.

He takes a step forward and raises the gun over my head to point it at Hutch. "I've always hated when you said that."

I know he's going to shoot. I can feel it like a deep freeze in my bones. I charge at him.

"River!"

I go for the gun, pushing his hands up over our heads. We fall to the ground. The gun shot rattles my insides, and I hear the gun fall on the ground. Kiernan grabs me around the throat, flips me over, and pins me to the ground.

"Drop it!" someone shouts.

Another gun hits the floor.

The barrel of a gun appears at Kiernan's temple. "I said drop it!"

It's a woman's voice. High-pitched and shrill. Dolly?

Kiernan lets go of me and raises his hands over his head. A crowd has gathered around the parking lot. There are police sirens in the distance, and for a moment it feels like I'm back home. Hutch comes to my side and pulls me into a bone-crushing hug. I tap him to signal that I can't breathe, and he releases me.

Kiernan is arrested, and a few moments later, Taylor is brought out in cuffs by the same mustached man that tried to buy me a drink at the bar. The undercover cops look so different here than they do back home.

"Are you okay?" Hutch asks. He brushes my hair back and holds my face in his hands. I pull him close to me and push myself up on my tiptoes so I can kiss him. It's the adrenaline. It's the dark of the night. It's knowing that Hutch is alive and unhurt, and here for me.

It's just us.

Dolly clears her throat behind us. "If you don't mind, I need you to come down to the station and give a statement."

We drive down behind them. The station here is bigger than the little jail cell I was in a few days ago. Taylor spits at me as a cop pushes him past us and into a cell. Under the florescent light, I can get a better look at Kiernan. It's strange, looking at him after so much time has passed—I feel like I'm looking through a mirror leading into the past. I can't believe the girl who let herself be with him is the same person I am now.

Dolly pulls the wig off her head.

"Holy shit," I say.

"This thing is too hot to be comfortable," she says in her

high-pitched voice. Then she looks at me, and smiles. "For someone from the big city, you sure do shock easy."

"I don't know why people keep telling me that," I say.

Hutch squeezes my hand to let me know that he's still there. I haven't forgotten.

"New York is pretty boring compared to Montana."

One of the desk clerks laughs, and a look from Dolly—Detective Rosado—silences him.

"We've been following Taylor Patrick for a while," she says. "There's never been enough evidence to hold him, and he's changed aliases several times in the past ten years. I have to say, River, when you sat down at that table I couldn't have asked for a better stroke of luck."

I smile. "My daddy used to say there's no such thing as luck in poker."

She shakes my hand, and after a paramedic takes a look at us we're free to go. All of the previous charges against me are dropped. I remind them that Randy is also innocent. I decide to press charges against Kiernan. I might not have been able to get him arrested back home, but him pointing a gun at me changed that. Too bad that's what it took.

A cop car drops us off at my motel. I gather my stuff and we walk to Hutch's car from there. This town is so small that I can walk from the poker room to the precinct, then to my motel and back to the poker room, in the span of twenty minutes.

Hutch drives like we're in the Indy 500, and I cling to his side the whole time. He decides to carry me into his house, and I let him.

"I told you," he says.

"You told me a lot of things."

"I told you I wasn't done with you."

It's like that first night again. We're fumbling in the dark of his house. Money falls out of our pockets and scatters all over the floor, but I'm too busy stripping the clothes off him.

This time I know just where the bedroom is. I press my hands on his chest and lead him through the door and onto the bed. He takes my hand and kisses me from my wrist to the inside of my elbow and back down again. I run my hands through his hair and pull.

"I need you, Hutch."

He answers by ripping my shirt right down the middle, and before I can blink, my underwear is somewhere across the room. I gasp at his speed, his urgency, and his recklessness.

He pushes me down onto the bed and goes down on me. He licks me up and down, dragging circles around my clit that make me shout. For the first time since *the first time*, we don't have to be quiet. I dig my nails into his shoulder to bring him back up. He comes willingly, sliding me up the bed. He pins my hands over my head and parts my legs with his knees.

"You didn't actually let me win, did you?"

I answer with a mischievous smile, and a bite on his lower lip. I start to answer, but his dick finds its way inside of me. I wriggle against him. I shout his name. I tell him I love him, and I'm pretty sure his distant neighbors now know it, too.

When we're finished, he rolls off me, panting and sweaty.

I find my way back into his arms. *Try harder*, I tell myself. I rest my hand on top of his chest, feel the way it rises and falls with every word and thundering heartbeat.

Try harder.

"I love you."

He kisses me. "Are you going to show me your cards?"

"Isn't it enough that I folded?"

"You never fold."

I sink into the blissful feeling of his warmth. "For a long time, I had nothing left to lose. It was just money. Then suddenly, it was you. It's like you said. I'll be damned before I walk away from you again, Chris Hutcherson."

CHAPTER 41

TWENTY-EIGHT DAYS SOBER

Starting over is harder the third time around. Mostly because I'm afraid of change. But also because I've never lived with a boyfriend before.

After all the charges were dropped against Randy and me, Hutch's house belonged to him again. We donated some money from our gambling night to HCRC. Helen and Ransom sent us a beautiful letter and apology. Though I don't think I deserved it. The rest of the money went to my twenty-eight days at a rehab clinic in Seattle. It was the worst and best possible way to spend those days without Hutch, without anyone else.

In some ways I loved HCRC better. My Seattle counselor was nothing like Ransom. She wanted to talk too much about my mother, which is fine. Not everything can be fixed with pretty words, and I accept that. But the food was better at HCRC too, and the people were friendlier, and as much as I hate to admit it, I missed being in the outdoors. Nothing compares to Montana.

It's strange how a place, and people, can change you. I know I'm still me at the core. But I feel different. More open. Free.

Though Helen offered Hutch a reference, he declined. He's getting a degree in child psychology while tending bar in Zoo Town. We both have a lot of making up to do. I'm not sure what I want to do with my life, but I'm happy figuring it out with Hutch at my side.

But first, he needs to see where I come from.

...

We take a trip to New York. I love the way Hutch walks too slowly against Midtown traffic. I love his face when he sees a man walking around with a cat perched on his head. I love his smile when he meets Pepe and Tony, and the rest of my adopted family. We leave flowers at my dad's grave, and I dig a hole in the ground and leave a poker chip from my last game.

"You don't like it here," I tell him, as we're walking around Central Park.

I've got on more clothes than an Eskimo, but he's okay in just his wool coat. "It's different," he says. "The snow's black."

"That's because of car exhaust, and people peeing and walking on it all day."

He rolls his eyes and pulls me against him. "It's loud."

"There are literally millions of people living here."

"The food's good."

"I know!"

New York makes me happy, but Hutch makes me happier. I was afraid that my feelings for him were replacing my need to gamble, but I was wrong. My feelings for Hutch are just love. It's a strange and funny thing to be really, truly in love for the first time. Sometimes I want to deny it. Other times I want to revel in the certainty of us.

I've never believed in luck or destiny, but walking into that bar and meeting Hutch was just that.

• • •

We pack up my storage unit, and he's surprised by how much black clothing I own.

"When we get back to Montana, I'm going to get you a proper pair of riding boots. And a cowboy hat."

"Cowgirl hat," I correct him.

We make love, and kiss, and make love some more. It takes a week to pack and load things into the U-Haul attached to his truck. Leti and Sky come to see us off. You'd think I was moving to Australia, the way they cry.

When we get across the bridge and into New Jersey, I

make him stop.

"Changing your mind?" he asks, holding my hand for moral support.

I watch the skyline a little longer. The buildings reach unapologetically to the sky, like the trees in Montana. The sky does seem a lot smaller over here. I tell myself that I'll always be the little girl from Queens with the best poker face this side of the Hudson. I tell myself to stop running away from who I was, because there was nothing wrong with her. She was different, but still the same. She is me, and I am her. We can't run from the past, the same way we can't pretend to be someone we're not. That's how you remain broken.

I breathe in cold New York air as if it's the last dregs of the last cigarette I'll ever smoke. In a few days we'll be back in Montana. I was wrong. It's not the middle of nowhere. It's exactly where I need to be.

"This is just a place." I shake my head. He lowers himself for a kiss. "You're my home."

ACKNOWLEDGMENTS

As always, a huge thanks to Adrienne Rosado, agent extraordinaire. To Sarah Younger, my equine instructor and wonderful friend.

To the excellent team at Diversion Books: Laura Duane, Mary Cummings, Sarah Masterson Hally, and Trent Hart. Thanks for giving my trio of misfit girls a great home.

Horse Creek Recovery is completely fictional, but the people who struggle with addiction are not. Thanks to everyone who was willing to speak to me about their recovery journeys.

An enormous thanks to Candice Montgomery and Erica Cameron for answering my emails on the technical aspects of recovery centers. To Elizabeth Briggs for being a thoughtful beta reader. To the badass ladies of NA Hideaway. Your stories and support mean the world to me. To Brodi and our French poker crew. You guys are Ace.

To my friends and family for being the world's greatest cheerleaders.

For anyone who wants to do more research on rehab and recovery, some of the books I read were *All Bets Are Off: Losers, Liars, and Recovery from Gambling Addiction* by Arnie Wexler, and *Sex, Drugs, Gambling & Chocolate: A Workbook for Overcoming Addictions* by Dr. A. Thomas Horvath.

For everyone starting over, struggling, or just trying to get through this funny thing called life. And finally, for the angry, broken, lost girls. You are not alone.

 ZORAIDA CÓRDOVA was born in Guayaquil, Ecuador and raised in Queens, NY. She studied English Literature at Hunter College and The University of Montana. She is the author of the Vicious Deep trilogy, *Labyrinth Lost*, and the On the Verge series. She lives in New York City. Send her a tweet @zlikeinzorro.

MORE FROM ZORAIDA CÓRDOVA

LUCK ON THE LINE

Despite her name, Lucky Pierce has always felt a little cursed. Refusing to settle for less or settle down, she changes jobs as often as she changes boyfriends. When her celebrity chef mother challenges her to finish something, Lucky agrees to help her launch Boston's next hot restaurant, The Star. Even if it means working with the infuriating, egotistical, and undeniably sexy head chef.

James loves being known as Boston's hottest bad boy in the kitchen, but if he wants to build a reputation as a serious chef, he has to make this restaurant work and keep his scandalous past out of the headlines. Getting involved with his boss's spoiled, sharp-tongued daughter is definitely not on the menu.

As the launch of The Star looms and the tension and chemistry heat up in the kitchen, they're going to need more than a little luck to keep everything from boiling over.

LOVE ON THE LEDGE

Sky Lopez thought she had it all—the perfect job, the perfect relationship, the perfect life...until she discovers her not-so-perfect boyfriend has been cheating on her. So when her uncle asks her to help plan his Hamptons wedding, Sky jumps at the chance, leaving all of her "perfect" future plans in the rearview mirror.

The wedding doesn't prove as good a distraction as she'd hoped, because when her relatives and friends find out she's single, they put Sky in their match-making sights. Never mind that she's only twenty four. Never mind that she doesn't want to settle for anyone other than Mr. Right. Seemingly everyone in Sky's life wants her to get married and have babies. Like, yesterday.

So when Hayden—a sweet, sexy roofer—plummets through the ceiling and practically falls into her lap, she can't help but think that maybe nice guys do just fall from the sky.

Soon Sky finds herself juggling crumbling wedding plans, the cheating ex who's trying to win her back, the cute plastic surgeon her family thinks is perfect for her, and the hot roofer she can't seem to get off her mind.

As the wedding date draws closer, Sky will need to choose one—or none—to keep herself from falling off the ledge, and maybe into love.